NOTHING SPECIAL

NOTHING SPECIAL

NICOLE FLATTERY

BLOOMSBURY PUBLISHING

NEW YORK · LONDON · OXFORD · NEW DELHI · SYDNEY

BLOOMSBURY PUBLISHING
Bloomsbury Publishing Plc
50 Bedford Square, London, WCIB 3DP, UK
29 Earlsfort Terrace, Dublin 2, Ireland

BLOOMSBURY, BLOOMSBURY PUBLISHING and the Diana logo are
trademarks of Bloomsbury Publishing Plc

First published in Great Britain 2023

A catalogue record for this book is available from the British Library

ISBN: HB: 978-1-5266-1212-0; TPB: 978-1-5266-1213-7;
KENNY'S EDITION: 978-1-5266-6500-3;
EBOOK: 978-1-5266-1210-6; EPDF: 978-1-5266-6254-5

2 4 6 8 10 9 7 5 3 1

Typeset by Integra Software Services Pvt. Ltd.

Printed and bound in Great Britain by CPI Group (UK) Ltd, Croydon CRO 4YY

MIX
Paper | Supporting
responsible forestry
FSC® C171272

To find out more about our authors and books visit www.bloomsbury.com
and sign up for our newsletters

For my mother and father, with gratitude

'You may think I'm not searching and He – Drella –
may think I'm not searching, but I'm searching.
Which one of us, who isn't searching, for God?'
                    Ondine in Andy Warhol, *a: A novel.*

beautiful town.
2010

My mother had a book she liked to read to me as a child. She must have discovered somewhere that it's good to educate your child. She must have encountered that fact amongst a haze of other facts at the time. She might have even once seen a mother and daughter on a bench working their way through the pages of a book, the mother pausing only to kiss the daughter on the forehead. They probably looked like they were having the best time of anyone on the planet. This was the type of image that would have obsessed and overwhelmed her.

I think that she got it in a gift shop. It had that sort of sheen, the invariable pleasantness of the gift shop. In the book there were different types of farm animals with various attributes listed alongside them. I guess my mother felt sort of bad about raising me in a city amid the noise and crime. The graffiti scrawled everywhere, signalling mass discontent.

The farm arrived late. I was much too old for the book. I understood that even then. I was at the age where I was starting to become aware of the many unconventionalities of our lives – our family arrangement, our dreary, rattling apartment, the aura that seemed to engulf us as a trio, the diner, our dirty and sombre street. My father wasn't around, and even if he had been my mother insisted he wouldn't have had any interest in reading. He wasn't smart. She wasn't embarrassed by this, why did the men she slept with have to be smart? That's vanity, my mother declared. She believed many things to be vanity. Like you need to be smart to point at a page. So I never got to know my father, and he never got to know the book in which sheep took on existential qualities. They appeared sinister to me whenever my mother and I sat on the floor together. There was something happening under their dry, calm frolicking.

If it was late, if my mother had been drinking, a lot of what she said was unpredictable. She often pointed at a cow and said, 'That's a sheep.'

'A sheep,' I repeated.

I knew it was dangerous to correct her. I knew, in my heart, that it wasn't a sheep. A sheep would have had a halo of fuzz encasing its cartoon body. The accused animal stared out of the pages as if to say: I've done nothing wrong. It was one of my happiest memories. My mother's presence and undivided attention was special, irresistible. I think that everyone felt that way around her. I liked being close to her soft face, watching her gentle frown lines, her breath sweet in my ear as she whispered lies. Silence, nothing – my mother's trembling hands turning the pages. Then she would point at another animal, a donkey maybe, and say, 'That's a sheep.'

'A sheep,' I repeated.

I went along with all of it. I did until the end. Whenever I was in my mother's retirement village – they sometimes called it a village as if they were all careening down country lanes on bicycles – and a nurse enquired what my mother

and I had been talking about, I simply said, 'Sheep.' This
is the type of tepid, pointless humour I bring to my daily
life now. Where I've lived for the last three decades, it's not
about wit. We don't have those sorts of desires. It's more a
matter of corresponding. I'm having as ordinary a day as
you, my thoughts are as standardised as yours. The laughs
are chaste here.

In the mid-1990s, when my mother and I still weren't
speaking, I became fixated on the farm book. I was having
some personal problems which, like all difficult people, I
believed could be traced directly back to my relationship
with my mother. Was I caring enough? Was I responsible?
The answer to both of these questions was no and it was
probably because my mother hadn't read to me enough as
a child. Then I remembered the farm book. The internet
was newly available to me, and I searched for information.
Eventually, I emailed the publishing company responsible. I considered this a highly productive act. A spiritual
mission. And I thought I owed it to her. People were still
getting to grips with email then. There were articles in
magazines I subscribed to – how to send an email, how to
receive an email, etiquette, helping us to learn a language
we didn't yet understand. Say hello, kiss somebody's ass,
say goodbye. All best. Computers still sat, fat and white,
in front rooms where the owners could keep an eye on
them. I knew the keyboard instinctively. I like to think we
recognised each other at once.

I think, at first, the publishing company were alarmed
by the amount of emails I sent – every five minutes or so
a new email burst out of me, like a shrieking mechanical
bird from a cuckoo clock. A new email, a new idea, a new
vision. I could only picture the recipient of my emails

as a girl in her early twenties, no older. I imagined her with a neat desk, combed hair, more sophisticated than I was at that age, a healthy, freckled complexion from an educational trip to Europe, all of this effort belying an internal disorder, a gloomy impatience. I told her that my mother had adored the farm book. I never knew where she acquired it. I deliberately used the word 'acquired' to set the tone. Acquired. This new language made everything sound hollow. In my second email, I asked what year the farm book had been published, and who had been involved. In my third email, I argued that it wasn't strange for a person to love a book. The makers of the farm book – were they still alive? – couldn't have known the spell they were going to cast on my proud mother's heart when they grouped the animals together in this particular formation, when they dreamt those warm-faced sheep and set them down.

In those days, the days of my emailing, I felt the emptiness of my apartment like a punch. I'd had a number of worthwhile relationships in my life, but now I couldn't fall in love like I used to. What was there to do instead, what to do with all that energy and focus? Collecting, shopping. There seemed to be a lot of rooms in my home and I had a desire to fill them all. My possessions would smile at me with a new camaraderie. While I waited for a reply to my emails, I visited websites that were designed to appeal to me, an easily seduced woman in her mid-forties. I guess I didn't know what to do with my time. I'd lost control of that. I needed furniture that I could manoeuvre around the room for hours. I needed appropriate trousers and blouses to sit and type in. It was essential that I look like a typist: grey, unforgiving and forgettable. A role I'd once played so effectively.

I kept at this project for a number of weeks. I estimated that I sent over 200 emails, most of them containing unasked for information. I explained that my mother had worked in a diner down the street from our apartment. Her life had been limited in that respect – not that her work made her some receptacle for sympathy. I outlined, in one particularly garrulous email, a day in my mother's life. I was highly detailed. I told them about her insatiable taste for coffee. She always bought some in the store downstairs to drink on her way to work. She made another pot in the diner, a perk of her job, and drank that throughout the day. She smoked constantly. One evening, I told them, a thief in the diner had cut my mother's face with a pocket knife. She was hysterical about it. I walked in on Mikey, the man we lived with, cleaning the wound with a dirty dishcloth. Like a lot of people, she didn't love her job and complained often. Unsavoury types wheezing all over her, touching her. Men used to jump the counter, wring her little neck, and the following week she'd serve the exact same people, as if nothing had happened. She could only do this because, as she told me and Mikey, she had a greater understanding of human frailty than the average person. She called the customers 'her poor souls'. What else? I didn't know because I was no longer sure if what I remembered was my mother's life or the life of a different woman, a woman who worked in a diner in a movie. My mind felt that porous. There were so many images that were familiar. But my mother was tetchy so the number of things she liked was easy to categorise. She liked the unique solitude of the diner after she closed up at night. And she liked the farm book.

I imagined a young woman reading these emails – the emails about my guilt, about how I'd treated my mother,

about the fractures in our relationship – and slipping
on her coat, walking to the subway in the dark, thinking about all the things she had to do, her endless list,
hundreds of things. My correspondence disappearing like
a hallucination. Perhaps she was new to the city and it was
opening up to her like a dream. All that noise, the allure
of strangers, the heat.

Some rude bitch replied. They think you can't see their
personality through formal language but you can. You
know by their clipped and arrogant tone. People want
you to crawl on your hands and knees even through the
computer. They want you to beg. I continued typing. I
imagined the meeting they must have had about me, this
new sort of person they were ill-equipped to deal with.
Of course, they had crank callers in the past, people who
kept them on the line with sad details of their lives, their
voices quivering with regret. It's easy to dismiss a call like
that, roll your eyes at a colleague to communicate that
the caller on the other end is murderously stupid, make
comical faces, hang up and walk away. Nobody wanted to
turn on the computer and read about a deranged person's
life. I was the minority then. Now, I'm the majority.

They sent another email informing me that unless I
ceased they would be forced to take legal action. I imagined a judge reading my emails to a packed courtroom,
a spiralling situation. Where would I even get a lawyer?
I didn't know anybody like that. Well, it seemed like an
overreaction. All I wanted was a copy of the farm book
so I could organise a reconciliation between me and my
conceited, selfish mother. I wasn't embarrassed at any
stage of this. Sometimes, I become embarrassed in short,
unexpected flushes when I see my life clearly as it is now –
the chat shows I keep on rotation, my underwear rising

coarsely over my trousers as I reach for a box of cereal in the supermarket. Blah, blah, blah. The banal things that come out of my mouth. I watch my face from outside myself. It's no longer young or sincere. There is a certain classlessness that I think he would find amusing. Not that I care anymore what he would find amusing.

My mother's nursing home was a short drive away. I went most afternoons, and acted like it was out of duty. It was my duty; I felt a responsibility towards her that was born out of my own superstition and guilt. After we had reconnected, and she got older and more helpless, I moved her closer to me. During my visits, my mother was impulsive and often made nasty comments. The nurses – I envied their skills, patience and professional distance – smiled at me earnestly. I found it funny, the forgiveness they immediately extended to her. They thought she was sharp and depressive because she was elderly. They couldn't have known she had always been that way.

The nursing home wasn't the most expensive, but everything in it looked solid which appealed to me. There was an inexhaustible priest charged with holding everyone's deathbed confessions; some old nuns in the dining room pouring ice cream into their mouths as if it was some last, measly grasp at pleasure. My mother suspected me of cheapness but I was actually spending more than I could afford. I wanted her to have comfort at the end of her life. I listened to all her complaints without argument. I tried to retain a neutral tone. She often went to the recreational room to talk with a group of other residents she called 'the girls', who, without any particular effort on her part, she'd become the leader of. She ascended that ladder so quickly. It was partly because she was from New York, which conferred on her an artistic quality she never possessed, and partly because my mother was always exceptionally good with women, who both admired and were terrified of her.

She spent a lot of her time in her room watching the home movies that Mikey had made of her. She'd requested a VCR for this exact purpose. Her ghost walking down our street to work, her in the diner, her, despite the fabulous show of her early cynicism, still believing something good was going to happen. These movies were made after I left home so there was something unsettling about them, how they imparted new information about lives I believed I knew thoroughly. I tried to discourage her from watching them. There was something terrible and sick about the act. I disliked seeing her lying on the bed, her gummy mouth open, her eyes glued to the screen, doing unknown damage to her brain with large doses of nostalgia. The nurses assured her she'd been very attractive. 'Sexy,' she corrected them. Mikey knew how to film her. Those videos confirmed to me that my mother had her own secrets. I knew she encouraged puppyish devotions in male customers, let them buy her the odd meal or take her out for a drink, turned away quickly when their wedding rings caught the light, smiled forgivingly. I knew my mother got what she wanted. But her secret was inside herself, how she carried herself. It took Mikey to catch it. Mikey, who was always waiting for her, who often drank with her until she was numb, or until she felt like touching him. I don't hate him for this, or consider him bad or evil. It doesn't make me love him any less. Through the decades, and the broad reconfiguring of men's behaviour, I saw him through other people's eyes, staying on our couch, sleeping with my mother when she wasn't sober. I was told I was supposed to be filled with righteous indignation, denounce him publicly. But I knew my mother took from him too, and in ways that were perhaps worse – used his kindness, his naivety, used him as a babysitter for me so she could do whatever she felt like. I don't know how all of this was supposed to get me worked up and thirsting for revenge. It only made me sad that he thought he could translate their drunk fumbling into love as she withheld all real affection.

During the last six months of her life, she started asking questions she wouldn't normally have. I blamed the younger nurses who, demonstrating calm in the face of death, scattered their gossip magazines around the home. The front pages were occupied with celebrities, their obedient, hard smiles, but the back pages were full of stories about women initiating sex on planes, in night-clubs, in offices where they were, would you believe it, the bosses. The descriptions of danger, the lust, the graphic positions. My mother and I had never been close enough to talk about sex. I'd left home at eighteen, so our opportunities for adult conversation had been minimal. That was almost late to leave home then, we followed our friends, we did what our friends did. Now, she was greedy, rapacious: there wasn't much time for her to gather all my secrets. One Sunday morning, after Mass, which we sometimes went to together, my mother asked if I'd ever faked an orgasm. She was sucking on a straw stuck in a supermarket brand of orange juice.

'Why?' I asked. 'What does it matter?'

'Women do it.'

'Yeah.' I wiped away the spit collected at the side of her mouth. 'Sure.'

'Even the well-paid ones?'

'Especially the well-paid ones.'

She sniffed and removed the straw. She fixed me with a cold, determined stare. 'Why?'

'I suppose it's to do with kindness and being pleasant.'

'For goodwill,' she said, with disgust.

'Did you never?'

'No,' she said. 'It's so insulting. I never did.'

She was pleased with herself. I wanted to explain how it was potentially more insulting not to fake it but she had already moved away from the conversation, away from me. Over the course of a few weeks, she enquired about my sexual life in a way I found both horrible and freeing. Had I ever cheated? I had. How did I find giving a blow job? Rewarding but only because you're aware of your own generosity throughout. Had I ever been propositioned for an affair? Several times, but the needling tone of the emails and messages designed to set up the affair disgusted me so much I realised I didn't have the constitution for it. In the town where we lived, my reputation as distant, dreamy, eccentric only made me more popular for propositions because if I said no, the men's egos would barely be damaged. That bitch etc. My mother nodded sagely at this information as if it was centuries old. Had I ever had sex with someone who earned less than me? I didn't know where some of these questions came from. She was, because of the magazines, shallowly concerned with the financial nature of these transactions. I must admit I found these little chats oddly inspiring. Once I woke up in the middle of the night and realised I was trembling with laughter at the idea of my mother's uncooperativeness. I imagined her looking at a parade of men who had tried to pleasure her with total indignation. She didn't have the ability to fake one measly orgasm. Tears

streamed from my eyes. I couldn't believe she'd been that
ill-tempered, so steadfast in her refusal to please people.
Maybe I loved her after all.

A short time after I had been told to stop emailing the
publishing company, and life had resumed in its normal
manner, I received a book in the post. It was, of course,
the farm book. The world seems to know instinctively
when you're about to give up on it. There was no note. I
don't know if it was done to appease me, or out of kindness. I pictured the assistant, a double of my younger
self, smuggling it out of the office, bravely paying for the
postage herself. Either way the gesture touched me. I sent
the book to my mother and she called. We had spoken a
number of times since Mikey had died. Her voice down
the phone, a familiar poison. Neither of us had taken his
death well. Time afterwards, for me, was patchy, impossible. I couldn't conduct normal interactions, watch
movies, pay attention to the news. What on earth was
everyone in the world talking about? We were a comfort
to each other then. It was a way of keeping Mikey alive.
By 1996, when I sent the farm book, she had been sober
for over a decade and was relearning her place in life. The
past had tortured her enough. She was looking forward to
the future. I understood that. I visited her in New York;
we had some good times. We were both more relaxed.
Our tempers had dampened with age. I couldn't work
myself into the furies I used to. Many of her comments
had lost their sting after she had quit drinking: she'd lost
her venomous touch. 'I'm not as catty as I used to be,
now I don't have customers to practise on,' she said. One
day, after she'd moved to the retirement village, I saw the
farm book on her bedside table. She had brought it with

her. When I pointed it out, she said something dismissive. That was just her. My mother was never capable of real cruelty. Everything I'd mistaken for cruelty had been disappointment, heightened emotion with no release, a desire for human contact she wasn't getting. I had no idea what true cruelty was then. But I learnt.

The evening before my mother died, I sat in the recreational room with her and the girls watching television. The opinions of these women were ancient and made me miserable, but I enjoyed the little cakes that were available during allocated television time. The girls mostly liked game shows. We usually had a pot of money to add an edge. We often disagreed on what was the most entertaining show. Dorothy, my mother's favourite companion, didn't like the one presented by a stern woman with huge, electrified hair. She was disturbed by her assertiveness, her rampant ambition. I liked it. I always liked it when people are authentically themselves, even if that self is unbelievably ugly.

'Witch,' Dorothy hissed.

'Absolutely, Dorothy,' I agreed. I tended to agree with everything said in the recreational room. That evening, we watched a show with a male presenter whose entire appearance spoke of sleazy backrooms, who grinned at us all like he was performing tricks. He seemed to vibrate at a level I didn't think was possible, always smiling as if unhappiness was implausible. His guest that night, the man competing for money, was quietly spoken. His eyes communicated that the game show was a novel experience for him. He was on $16,000.

'A good amount of money,' Dorothy said.

'You'd get through that, no problem,' my mother sighed, always pragmatic. 'Especially if you have a family.'

The next question: 'Who shot the artist Andy Warhol?'

I looked straight ahead at the television. I didn't move my face. Three wrong answers bobbed around the right one. I could tell by the competitor's reaction that he didn't know. The problem is nobody knows how to listen anymore. People pretend game shows are games of knowledge, they congratulate themselves on their intelligence, but really they are games of listening. The answer is always in the presenter's question. The competitor made meaningful eye contact with the camera. All his training now seemed remote. The presenter repeated the question. The answer bubbles didn't move. He asked for 50/50. Two answers disappeared.

'He doesn't have any lifelines left,' Dorothy said. 'I'm worried for him.'

'Valerie Solanas,' I said, through a mouthful of cake.

'What, Mae?' my mother said. 'Speak up.'

'That's the answer.' I shrugged. 'Valerie Solanas.'

We continued to watch the man on screen. He hummed. He jiggled his right foot. He looked imploringly at the audience. He covered his face with embarrassment. He got the answer wrong, as he was destined to. I could tell by the presenter's face that he was let down: none of his guests had his ruthlessness. The competitor was ushered out of sight and replaced.

'Solanas,' my mother said. 'I remember her. She was around town. She had some good ideas, like a lot of unattractive women.'

'I'm going home.' I stood up. 'Time to go home.'

'But you won,' Dorothy said, holding out the pot. 'Your money.'

'Keep it Dorothy.' I petted her head fondly.

The name had awakened me. On the way out, I kissed my mother on the cheek. Her focus was still on the television. She had never paid much attention, always dwelling in the basement of her own disappointments, hardly glancing up. I wish I'd done something more memorable, held her hand for a little while, looked into her eyes. But no, a quick peck and I kept walking, heading in the direction of home. She hadn't been a bad mother, not really. The next morning a doctor rang to tell me she'd passed away during the night. Not even her insults were available to me now. When I replied, I didn't recognise my own voice. It sounded like something that had been locked away for years, just taken out of a box. There was no point in lying to me, the doctor said: it hadn't been entirely easy. No, I agreed, it hadn't.

The priest was kind and spiritually content in a way I found annoying. The funeral took place in the church beside the retirement village. Not many people came. Her girlfriends from the home all sat in the front row, as if to announce themselves as the chief mourners, like there would be any competition. Some friends of mine were there, a few nurses who'd shrieked at my mother's dirty jokes. They had liked her. I always forgot about her incredible appeal. It was often hard for me to see her the way other people saw her. I tried to lose myself in prayer, mumbling the odd sacred word I knew. Faces from my mother's life appeared and disappeared before me, and then her own weary face emerged from the mist of a grill, her uniformed back as she walked down a trash-strewn street. My mother had fed a lot of people and she looked refined while she did it. Where were all those people now?

All of them allowed her to shovel food into their wet, unsatisfied mouths and then slipped right past her.

Afterwards, in an attempt to get me to open up, the priest told me I could ask him anything. Anything religious, he added hastily. It was an extension of the game show.

'Do you think she's in Heaven?' I asked.

He cleared his throat. 'Yes.'

I laughed. 'You're a rotten liar, Father.'

I drove back home. I sat in the driveway with my seatbelt on, enjoying the silence. I touched my cold, wet face. The next day, I returned to get my mother's things and found the nurses watching one of Mikey's videos. One of them was crying. Why could I never see her the way other people could? They seemed worried I might be annoyed with them, disturbing my mother's memory. I wasn't. It was so beautiful to be filmed by someone who had loved you. Play it, I said. Play it until the end.

a very elegant young woman.
1966

When I was seventeen, I rode the escalators in the department stores after school. Macy's, Bloomingdale's, places no one would ever find me, or think of looking. My mother was at work and after work there were her private after-work adventures, so I needed something to do. If she was at home, I'd only have fought with her anyway. Screaming, rages. We lived in a small apartment above a laundromat. There wasn't much room for the three of us. I heard some of the girls at school call our street dirty, unsafe. So what? Their lives weren't much better, and I didn't care. I no longer had any interest in being left alone in the apartment with Mikey. I still enjoyed his company, his open eagerness, but I'd grown weary of his attempts to have authority over me. I never did anything especially bad, but I was to be watched: my restless energy, my occasionally lacerating insults. I was embarrassingly close to saying to Mikey, 'You're not my father.' It was true, he wasn't, but I didn't want to be that kind of person – uptight, with ideas about family that I'd picked up from a commercial. We were supposed to be cool with everything now. I had a list of things I wanted to be, a shopping cart of qualities. The problem was Mikey acted the part of a father so badly, always tutting, always scrutinising. I knew these displays were enormously taxing on him too. Why put us both through it? I avoided him and rode the escalators with ritual concentration. I didn't have many friends at the time. Whenever I spoke my classmates stared back at me with taunting eyes. They knew I was pathetic, but the truth was I knew they were pathetic too.

That school year had started badly. I had only one friend, Maud, whom I'd known since childhood. We lived near each other and were bonded by the similarity of our names: Maud and Mae. The alphabet seemed then a good enough foundation for a lasting friendship. After all our time together, it was inconceivable that Maud could be lured away from me even if I didn't particularly like her anymore, felt no fondness or connection to her. School was dull. The boys were distant, unreachable, and the other girls were becoming adult in a way that I found both boring and disgusting. They stood ornamentally in the bathrooms, looking in the mirrors, their faces still and full of make-up stolen from their mothers. We were seventeen. I could see them already making themselves small and stylish, reconfiguring their internal circuitry, reducing their lives. Their new habit of staring at their mirror images with clear, empty expressions seemed like a disease to me. I wasn't known for being a knockout or especially intelligent. I hadn't exchanged one role for the other, bartered in the way women do, feeling a violent hatred at whatever hand I was dealt. I already knew there was something lethal attached to female attention and jealousy.

At the start of every school year there was a dance performance. It was in the spirit of good cheer, as most

of us were from poor, hopeless families. Several of the
girls had the drained pallor of the sleepless, some already
substituting in the family home for mothers who were
long gone. I was alone in my dislike for the dance performance – it was pious, the teachers seemed too pleased
by it, as if they were rewarding us for our terrible home
lives by letting us prance around on stage. The boys
just watched. Maud told me – she still had an interest in rescuing me then – that it was because I didn't
know how to enjoy myself. I said she had no capacity for
original thought. The dance performance was the only
excitement we got. That September, several of the girls
who were talented, whose talents and flexibility were
spoken about with awe and contempt, appeared on the
small wooden stage and moved in sync to the Four Tops,
'Reach Out I'll Be There'. They passed the idea off as religious, seeing God, him returning the love. We watched
their black gym skirts, like our own but transformed, flip
and whirl as they span in circles. The audience moved as
one, a single entity with the music, fully convinced of the
power of redemptive love and care. Two performances
were happening in the same way I sometimes felt there were
two hearts beating within myself. When one of the girls,
a curly redhead I only half-recognised, collapsed, I was
relieved. Her petite frame slammed on the stage and she
shook frenetically, without rhythm. Maybe she foamed
at the mouth. A lot of what happened was lost in the
urgency. I later saw the same girl through the contort-
ing glass of the principal's office, stemming her nosebleed
with a tissue. I told Maud, in secret, that I found the
fit exciting, that I was glad the performance had ended
early. It had been tawdry, unartistic. Maud told the other
girls. We were at the age where we exchanged confidences

in hope of shapeless rewards. It was quick. I was ostra-
cised immediately.

I'd never thought of myself as a weirdo, but now that I'd
been declared one I figured I should embrace it. At first,
I felt agitated by my mistake as if I had, with one throw-
away comment, condemned myself to be alone forever. I
knew there was something wrong with a lot of my desires,
something shocking and pitiful, and it was important
not to voice them aloud, in case what had happened
with Maud happened again. Then I began to see things
differently. This was the freedom I needed to reinvent
myself. Maud knew too much about me: my mother's
drinking, Mikey's eccentricities. With Maud, growth
had been impossible. I went to places where I thought
other weirdoes might be: cafés, movie theatres, art galleries when they were free. I never had much luck. In the
afternoons, families gathered around paintings. I thought
it was impossible to be born into a family like that, but,
no, other girls had been. I saw them every day. I liked
the quiet in these places. I often sat alone on a bench,
swinging my legs, my chin turned up to the art. I could
sit there for some time. I wanted to have a very profound
experience. Instead, I just daydreamed about walking into
a gallery one day and buying an expensive painting. This
was a standard daydream. Perhaps my mother wasn't my
mother, the hospital had made a mistake and I would get
reimbursed by the state of New York. I could be a rich
orphan. I'd heard of that happening, and I needed that
sort of miracle.
    The idea to ride the escalators came out of nowhere.
I wandered into a department store one afternoon and
felt unexpected excitement. They weren't places I often

went, due to my mother's small income and Mikey's
hatred of anything attractive, false or superficial. On my
first trip I felt like an unwanted lump in a civilised land-
scape, but that changed. I noticed how comfortable the
women looked, how they appeared more comfortable
in the department stores than they did on the streets. I
liked the view at the top of the escalator, how it broke
the department store into fragments. I had tender feelings towards the crowd wedged below, spending money,
buying cocktail dresses, exploring their taste, defying
death. Every day that week, I smoothed down my t-shirt
and brushed my hair in the bathroom before I stepped
on the escalators. I felt, as I moved, that I was more available for public consumption than I was at school. The
adult atmosphere suited me. I wanted men to notice me,
and I wanted something to happen, something amazing
and unlikely. My eyes met suited men moving in opposite
directions. We had wordless exchanges. I have dark desires
that will never be satisfied, they said. Me too, I replied,
without saying a word.

I couldn't admit it but I liked having a routine when
my mother had a routine. I knew that at the same time
I was riding the escalators she was determinedly setting
tables, folding napkins, moving as surely and mechan-
ically as me. Both of us humming with a hidden energy.

I tried on gloves. The assistant handed them to me,
without question, when I explained my father would
be arriving shortly. 'Perfect hands,' she said and held
them up to the light. This was the sales assistants' old
routine. I didn't fool myself into thinking my hands
were perfect. The gloves were as soft as kittens. When
my father never arrived, she gave me a faint, but horrible look of sadness.

'Do you want to wait a bit longer?' she asked. 'It hasn't been long.'

'It has,' I said. 'It's been sixteen or so years.'

I stole a lipstick. I was interested in how the store might turn on me if I was caught, how it might bare its teeth. But I wasn't caught.

The escalators in Macy's in Harold Square were cramped, wooden and always felt like they were moments away from a catastrophic event. Over the course of a few weeks in October, they became my favourite. I liked the gradual process of moving forward, the snippets of conversation I overheard as I creaked upwards. It made me feel less alone. Several weeks after I had first started, and a while after I came to understand a large part of the reason I was doing it, I met a man travelling down in the opposite direction. There was nothing troubling, nothing perverse, about his appearance, but as he passed, he pressed his hand over mine. A firm grasp. It was affectionate even though the contact was only brief – his hand over mine under the hot department-store lights, our fingers meeting on the escalator rail.

Several days after the man first touched me, I went back to the Macy's escalators. I spent much longer on my appearance, convincing myself it was important work. The department store had made me vain. It had that power. In the mirror, my face was wide with an off-putting and perpetual look of terror, as if I was permanently in a doctor's waiting room, getting undressed, waiting for bad news. I had a smattering of acne across my cheeks and chin, heavy hips and legs that couldn't be described as shapely. My eyes were my most distinctive feature, brown and huge and demanding. The first morning I dressed up

for him, I put my hair in curlers but I didn't like the effect.
It was too dignified and I wanted to appear relaxed, hip. I
brushed the curls angrily out with my fingers. I examined
my pores and plastered them with powder. I put on the
new lipstick and pouted. I danced around. Every morning, I spent a humiliating amount of time in front of the
mirror for a man that I'd only met for one second. I had to
work on my face, because I didn't have the right clothes. I
wasn't like some of the other girls at school whose outfits
were designed to project adult knowledge. My face was
my only instrument and I had to learn how to use it. I
moved it into different shapes to see what it looked like
animated, if any permutation was risky. I already knew
men expected some version of a fantasy, that attention
had to be paid from every angle. I opened and closed
my mouth, fluttered my eyelashes, stared at myself, the
creation I'd made. I finally understood the girls from
school. Our bathroom smelled like mould and damp, but
it was the only place I could work on my invention. If
Mikey had walked in, he'd have thought I had lost my
mind and maybe I had.

For a full week, I went to Macy's and I didn't see him.
I waited seven days, seven days of moving up and down
the rickety escalator, seven days of waiting by the revolv-
ing entrance door, seven days of standing. It was worth
it. It was the same as the time before – I was moving up,
he was moving down – except when he slipped his hand
over mine, he said, 'Meet me outside.' At that moment,
Maud's puritanical face floated into my mind. I'd kissed
a few boys, let them reach into my underwear. I had to
stop them, because we'd been taught boys couldn't stop
themselves. I often gloated to Maud that boys couldn't
control themselves around me. Whenever I said this,

she pressed her lips together and looked towards the sky. 'That's strange,' she told me once, 'because you've a very goofy personality.' It would be a lie to say that I didn't know what I wanted from this man. I wanted an inner change, knowledge so secret that no external threat could touch me. I'd always been attracted to that. When we exited Macy's together, I expected an alarm to go off, in department stores everywhere, an alarm ringing in the hosiery section, in lingerie, the sales assistants mobilising to save me. An alarm ringing throughout New York City. But every floor remained large and bright, and people kept moving.

'I looked really silly,' I said when we got out onto the street, 'going up and down the escalators all afternoon.'

'Hungry work,' he replied. 'You deserve a free meal.'

I'd taken one of my mother's bras. It was light and covered in stiff, pointy rose petals that I felt could possibly burst out of my shirt. I was mildly shocked my mother wore something so racy and intimate underneath her plain waitressing uniform. The man sat opposite me with his hands clasped on the table. He was younger than I expected, maybe mid-twenties. His shirt was pressed, his shoes were shined, he had a snotty, cramped air about him. There was nothing of the teen idol, the young men girls my age were always embarrassing themselves hope-lessly for, who they talked about constantly as if taking pleasure in saying their names. I didn't understand that behaviour. Why desire someone you'd never meet? The man opposite me looked like someone who brooded. I could see him in an office, sitting at a desk, frozen and remote, trying to gauge the level of his suffering. What else was there to say about him? He wore a tie. He was

there. He seemed surprised by the situation too, or affected
the gestures of surprise to flatter my ego. The restaurant
was a tourist spot near Rockefeller Center. I had sarcastic
thoughts about the plushness of the booths, the old piano
music that was popular amongst these people, people that
Mikey had taught me to treat with disdain. He was well
off but I had something he wanted too. The entire city
was tuned to a different frequency: young, wild, open to
experimentation. Girls that looked like me or, more accur-
ately, girls that I tried to make myself look like were hot
property. Everyone was constantly assessing each other's
usefulness. But this was the first time I'd been alone with
a man and everything, although I was aware of its cheesi-
ness, carried weight: the menus, his creaseless shirt, the
oversized ice in our tap water, our jackets sprawled over
each other in the booth. I ate a single peanut and hid the
shell in my napkin.

'Are you in business, Daniel?' I asked.

'Of sorts,' he replied.

'My uncle Mikey says all businessmen are pigs. Are you
a pig?'

He laughed, and I felt miles away from myself, from
the bathroom where, that morning, I'd pushed my mother's mascara wand around my lashes, rubbed the lipstick
from my teeth. Miles away from school where I sat alone,
looking at the other girls, as if peering through a crack,
seeing something I shouldn't.

'I've come to the same conclusions as your uncle,' he
said.

I looked around the restaurant, it was dark and large,
the clink of glasses, the low murmur of respectability. I
felt hostility towards the rich, but I wanted to be with
them too. The only time I'd been to a restaurant before

was when Mikey had brought my mother and me to a place he'd read about, and become hung up on. The trip was a peace offering to me and my mother, a concession to a conventional lifestyle. This was obviously what he thought fathers did – provided the thrill of dining out. When he paid with coupons, counting them out one by one, it was a tense and strange scene. My mother didn't speak or look at him on the subway home; denying him conversation was her punishment for what she described as a spectacle.

Daniel was obsessed with the arbitrary details of the restaurant, examining the napkins, turning the cutlery over in his hands. I watched him with bemusement. He was young enough to be in his first job and was obviously concerned with how he was seen to be spending his money. Despite this, I was attracted to him. He was more impressive than any of the boys I'd been with. He touched his finger to the rim of his glass.

'Do these look like the right glasses to you?' he asked.

'Nothing bad will happen to you if you drink from the wrong glass once,' I said. 'You won't die. Besides I'm hungry and you brought me here.'

He kept one finger resting on the glass. 'What would you like?'

'A hamburger.'

He ordered for both of us. When the food arrived, neither of us seemed to know how to navigate it. We ate mostly in silence. I took a bite of my burger. I held it towards him and we both watched as the ketchup oozed out.

'The middle is the best part,' I said. 'Take a bite.'

'No, I'm OK.' He smiled helplessly.

'My mother works at a diner so I know hamburgers.'

'I don't doubt you.'

'It's always good to have a taste of the best part.'

'So,' he said, leaning forward, 'what else would your uncle Mikey say about me?'

'He'd say that you're a snob and the city is becoming overrun with cheats like you, they're just abandoning you in high-class restaurants all over the city. Why do you need the right fucking fork? It's so base.' I took a sip of my wine. 'He'd say something like that.'

He pressed his finger into the dimple to the left of my mouth. 'Cute,' he said. He leaned back into the leather and I could feel his leg brushing against mine. 'Families are screwed.' The plates had been cleared. He had lost some of his reserve.

'I wouldn't really know, my dad isn't around. Parents are like dimples.' I pushed my finger into the right side of my mouth. 'It's nicer when you have two.'

He gave me a new smile, one I hadn't seen before. He'd been practising his face in the mirror too. 'You're lucky you don't know your dad. I've only just met you,' he said, 'but I can tell you think for yourself. I can talk to you. When my father was around, my mother said I had to work through my anger towards him. Anger, she said, is very distorting. So she sent me to this doctor, she's obsessed with this quack. That's when I was about your age – what age are you?'

'Seventeen.'

'So I was seventeen and the doctor – you should have seen this fucking guy – put this chair in front of me, and I had to pretend it was my father, tell the chair every-thing I thought of it. It was cathartic or some bullshit. I dreaded these trips. The building where it all went on then was somewhere in Midtown, the doctor was less upscale then. The place where he used to be looked bombed-out. You know, curtains drawn, always smoky, could never find the source of the smoke. The doctor thinks he's a philosopher but he's just stuffing old ladies full of pills. I'd have *loved* to have been pumped full of drugs. Instead, I got the chair. There were other people in the group too. They were loony, insane. They'd all be heaving, sobbing – and don't get me wrong, I was sobbing too. I was sobbing with the best of them. They had bad lives, had made bad decisions. That room was where I realised everyone is nuts, you just have to work out to what degree. A little bit or a lot. Everyone in that room was a lot. I don't know where this doctor finds his patients, honestly. It was impossible for me to imagine their lives, outside of the room, imagine their lives when they weren't screaming at chairs. And then I'd have to go home to my dear old dad in his usual spot. We'd have what he called a mannerly discussion – how are you, how are you, and I'd pretend that I hadn't spent all afternoon screaming at a chair that had his coat on it. My mother thinks this doctor can cure anything, but truthfully I hated my father for how he treated her. He cheated on her constantly. But it was fine because he told her about it. As if that wasn't just about alleviating his guilt.'

I didn't say anything for the duration of this story. I couldn't believe he would dishonour his own family so quickly. I thought it spoke positively of me, how easy I was to talk to, how attractive I was.

He finished his drink. 'Then he died,' he said.

'The doctor?'

'My father.'

'Oh,' I said, reaching for his hand. It seemed like the restaurant lights were illuminating us only. 'I'm sorry.' I rubbed his thumb. 'Have you considered they aren't actually your parents though? There might have been a mistake in the hospital. I've heard of that happening.'

'Do you want to get out of here?' he asked, his hand still in mine.

The street when we stepped outside the restaurant arrived like a dream about adulthood – neon signs flashing on and off, open displays of affection between sophisticated couples, couples fully absorbed by each other. We walked with solemn purpose, talking about school, Maud, his mother who he still lived with. I made no jokes about this. He didn't seem like he would be receptive to them. No, he didn't strike me as a playful person. It was cold, and he slipped his free arm around my waist. I was anointed. I moved forwards as if I was still on the escalator. On the subway stairs, he turned towards me in the dark and kissed my forehead. I liked the intense look on his face, it spoke of real passion. As we descended into the subway, I felt like I was stepping into grey and murky water. We stood on the platform as if partaking in a spectacular view. We were alone in the station.

On the train, everyone in our carriage seemed small and shrank further in comparison to us. I touched the collar of his shirt, which was properly starched. I fiddled with one of the buttons, and he smiled down at me. At first, we spoke. I think he mentioned something about us being only children, the unlikely chance of it. Then he kissed me on the lips. The rest of the journey was a dark and wordless blur.

In the elevator of his building, I pressed the button to appear active, and also to be useful, like a bellhop. It was part of the charade. I live in a place like this, with an elevator, and a doorman, and I'm decisive, useful, you'll want me around. All my tricks, all that work – and for who? Not for myself. Out of a sense of duty, as if I was performing a public service. I felt weak when I stepped into his apartment. Fringed lamps, vases full of flowers, framed paintings, reproductions that looked familiar from my time in the galleries. They were pastoral images, fields – stuff liked and chosen by his mother. I tried to keep a straight face as I touched the trinkets on the mantelpiece. I shouldn't have been allowed in here. I should have been wrestled to the ground before I stepped into the elevator. He invited me to sit on a formal two-seater, which appeared new to me. I couldn't shake the idea of him and his mother moving a worn, older couch out of the apartment; her bossing him, telling him to turn this way and that, ways that were impossible, berating his lack of strength. His mother was likely a shrew. The scenario struck me as a horribly intimate scene between mother, son and couch. I sat perfectly still. He held a single finger up to his lips and pointed at a door to indicate that his mother was sleeping. Then he went into the kitchen to make coffee.

While he was gone, I eased myself into the couch. I pulled at the armrests. This must be where she sat, talking to her son, or writing checks, or whatever. It took a lot of discipline not to think about her when she was in the next room. I leafed through a copy of *National Geographic*. I opened the page to a photo of a tribe, twenty of them gathered together, hunched, unsmiling. I looked at it until he returned.

When he put the tray down, he pointed to the photo and asked, 'Would you like to travel?'

I flinched. This struck me as a pedestrian thing to say. It made him sound like an idiot, and not a person I had a rare connection with. 'No,' I said, correcting him. 'I'd like to have a family that size, a big family, and do useful things for them.'

'What useful things?'

'I don't know. Forage?'

'Where would you forage? Macy's?' he smirked. 'So tell me, Mae, why do you ride the escalators?'

'I like the view. Is it new?'

'Is what new?'

'The couch,' I rubbed my palm across it. 'Your mother pick it?'

'You're such a strange girl,' he said. He offered me his hand and I followed him into his bedroom. For several seconds, I stood in the doorway and made and remade his bedroom in my mind. But there were no postcards, no photographs, nothing I could pull a narrative from. He kissed my neck. Although he hadn't told me much about his work I knew there was another version of him, a version that would be at his desk tomorrow, bantering back and forth with other men in suits, scrunching up paper and lobbing it across desks, talking on the phone with absolute tenacity. All of his vague tenderness would be gone. I was its only witness. His shoes, I noticed, as they lay abandoned on the floor, were clean and polished. I thought this was a good sign – he'd be fastidious in the act. The ideas I had were all from movies: the rumpled sheets, the erotic cigarette afterwards. To relax I thought of the highest point on the Macy's escalator and of the slow, calm descent.

He touched the stiff flowers on the straps of my bra and I realised that they were needy, wrong. He quickly pulled them down. I was self-conscious about the size of my breasts, but it seemed futile to hide them. When I

was naked, he rubbed my small, pudgy stomach in circular motions as if I was a sick animal. His face was ecstatic,
and I thought about how twisted and evil his features
must have been when he screamed at chairs. When he
was on top of me, I felt there was an attempt to understand me. There was a closeness I didn't expect. He said
things that were hard to understand and I responded
with a low moan. He was gentle, but he was trying hard.
It struck me as sweet then. His eyes were glazed with
concentration. I think, in that moment, I'd have let him
do anything. It hurt but the pain was located outside
myself, untraceable.

In the bathroom, the tap was dripping loudly, each drop
landing with a decisive plop. I'd bled and he offered to get
rid of the sheets. I rummaged through all the cosmetics
on the shelves. Moisturisers for wrinkles, calming oint-
ments, body-firming creams. She had everything, and a
whole shelf dedicated to pills, yellow, pink and blue. Every
bottle was half-empty. It was telling what his mother was
susceptible to. By the time I left the bathroom, I felt I
knew her better than I knew him.

I lay with my back to him. 'Are you at work tomorrow?' I asked. 'What do you do?'

'I don't know what I do,' he said, stretching his skinny
arms towards the ceiling. 'I keep trying to fit in there and
I can't.' He leaned over and tickled my elbow. 'If you
figure out what I do in that office, will you let me know?'

I rolled on my back and looked up at the ceiling. 'I will
ask Maud. She knows everything.'

'Thank you.' We lay in silence. Sleepily, he asked me,
'What was the song? What was the name of the song the
girl had a fit to?'

'"Reach Out I'll Be There" by the Four Tops.'

He laughed deeply. His real laugh, the first time I'd heard it all evening. It was as if a suspect had just turned sideways in a police line-up and I could now identify them. 'That's something,' he said. 'That's really something, Mae.'

I didn't respond. Whatever easy confidences we'd shared before no longer seemed possible.

He fell asleep shortly after.

The next morning, I didn't hear him leave. Whether he did it intentionally to hurt me seemed irrelevant. He was gone. My clothes were where I had left them. I stood at the window and watched a young girl cross the street. The city was already awake. She gazed back up at me. Her small, tyrant mouth opened in a little 'o' when she saw I was naked. The traffic lights blinked amber. I got dressed slowly. I was careful with myself as if I was recovering from an operation. It didn't bother me that I was ridiculous and alone. It seemed to be an indignity to be putting the same clothes back on, but the indignity wouldn't be obvious to anyone else. When I sat on the subway, I'd be empty of all expression, totally unremarkable.

The loveliness of the apartment was diminished in the morning light. All of it invoked sadness and pity in me as if I was visiting a formative place from my distant past. In the kitchen, I could hear clattering. A woman's voice called to me, 'Come and have something to eat.' Her voice was authoritative. 'I don't let anyone leave on an empty stomach.'

On the dining table sat two plates with half a grapefruit on each, two cups of coffee. In the kitchen, a woman stood with her back to me. She didn't turn around when I sat down. A brief and uncomfortable conversation with

a sour woman, nothing more. What else was there to
do anyway? Get the subway, go to school, feel humiliated. I broke the skin of the fruit. I spooned it into my
mouth. When she turned around, she was gaunt and her
eyebrows were high and frightening. She looked at me
with cold blue eyes. A woman you expected to see at a
beauty salon chatting about the useless things she did to
heal herself. Gab, gab, gab. That's how she'd spend her
days. I wasn't afraid. She sat down opposite me but didn't
touch her grapefruit. Instead, she reached for her cigarettes and lit up. She surveyed me like you might a car
wreck, with a general interest in disaster, regarding the
likelihood of it happening to you. She flipped a magazine
open on the table. There was a picture of a woman before,
and the same woman after, with different hair-dos. She
licked her thumb, flicking past advertisements.

'Want to do a quiz?' she asked.

'Sure.'

Her eyes focused on the page. She flicked the ash of
her cigarette into the silver bowl at her elbow. I sensed
something in her: a hard, blunted competitiveness that
found its release in her scrubbed floors, in her carefully
assembled trinkets, her ugly comments.

'Are you a pushover?' she asked.

'I don't know. I could be.'

'That's the title of the quiz, dear. These questions will
tell you if you are or not.' She smiled but her lips barely
moved. 'Do you often do things that you don't want to
make others like you?'

'Maybe.'

'That's not an option.' She jabbed her cigarette at the
page. 'The options are: Sometimes, Never, Always.'

'Never,' I said.

'Never?'

'What did I say?' I raised my voice slightly. 'I said never.'

She smiled in a noncommittal way. 'This quiz is lousy,' she said, suddenly, extinguishing her cigarette. 'Usually, they've better, more interesting quizzes. I can't be alone in thinking everything has gone to hell.'

Her hands shook as she turned the pages. I looked at the gold wedding band on her finger. 'You have a nice place,' I said, finally.

'Thank you. I try to keep it clean but my son likes cheap things.'

By the window, I could see the bedclothes from the night before. They rippled in the breeze, brazenly white and clean. She must have gotten up early and washed them. My vision blurred. I spooned another piece of grapefruit into my mouth.

'Your couch,' I swallowed. 'Is it new?'

'Yes.' She closed the magazine and pushed it away. I felt that I was in the presence of someone who wasn't well, and hadn't been well for a long time. 'My son bought it for me because he's going to Vietnam.'

'That must be hard for you as a mother.'

Her mouth puckered. 'Very hard.'

'Well, you can sit on the nice couch and think about him when he's gone. Think about how brave he is. When is he going anyway?' I dropped my spoon with a clatter.

'Soon,' she said. 'Any day now.'

'You must love him very much.'

'I do.'

'I hope he doesn't get killed.'

'There are worse things for a mother.'

'Could he not get out of being enlisted on account of his psychological issues?' I asked. 'That's how my uncle escaped.'

'My son doesn't have any psychological issues. Of course,' she faltered, 'he was troubled when his father left.'

'Left?'

'His father left a few years ago and went to live with a woman in Los Angeles. One of those duplex houses, you know split-level. Tasteless. A live-in maid and everything. Obscene.'

I could feel my face get hot, the onset of tears. There was nothing I could do to stop them. The conversation in the restaurant played back to me. I could hear how stupid I'd been, how trusting. He must have modified himself for every woman he met. I'd been a fool. I wasn't striking, or interesting; it was the recognisable signs of poverty he was searching for. The dirt underneath my fingernails, the thin soles of my unbranded shoes, my skin pockmarked and oily. Not the kind of girl you'd be seeing again. He'd done this before: his eyes like searchlights scanning department stores and subways for a girl that would undress easily. Perhaps even for a girl who would be grateful for a night in his apartment, a glimmer of luxury. I hated him so much then, and I hated his mother, and I hated the city too. 'Your son is a cornball,' I said, sobbing.

She stood up abruptly and disappeared. When she returned she handed me a tissue and two pills. She pulled her chair close to mine and pressed the tissue to my eyes. There was something maternal about the gesture. She rubbed the tears from my cheeks. 'My son is a cornball,' she said. 'Don't think I don't already know that.'

'And he's bad in bed,' I said, wailing now.

'Please,' she said, reaching for her cigarettes, 'unburden yourself.' She lit one and passed it to me. 'Take these with water and they'll relax you. You'll wake up tomorrow and you'll be brand new.'

'Everything's been horrible lately,' I said, swallowing the pills. 'I've been so alone. The dance performance... and I hate Maud.'

She nodded understandingly. She looked out the window. 'I can tell that about you. I can spot loneliness. I hate it here, in this apartment too, if that makes you feel any better. Anywhere can be a prison. If it wasn't for the doctor, I don't know what I'd do. I might throw myself out of that window.' She pointed to the window. 'The first time I met the doctor, I thought here's someone who really cares about me. My husband and son never cared about me. All day, I talk to myself and when my son comes home I don't speak to him, not a word, isn't that funny?' She started laughing. 'I can tell you feel very trapped too, surrounded by people who aren't giving you what you need.'

'Maud,' I hiccupped.

She grabbed her purse and took a card out of it. There was an address embossed in gold letters. She brushed the hair from the front of my face. 'Tell the nurse in the waiting room that Mrs Ritter sent you. That you're an urgent case.'

'Urgent?'

'Urgent.'

She took $10 from her purse and put it in my jacket pocket. It was the same size and shape as the occasional note my mother handed me after work. 'Get the doctor to give you anything you want when you're there. And they are to send me the bill.'

'Why?'

'Because you're the fourth girl I've met this month, but you're my favourite,' she said. When I got to the front door she called to me, cheerfully, 'I'm the pushover by the way. I'm the fucking pushover.'

On the street, I felt still and empty, the pills kicking in. I bought a sugary doughnut from a vendor and tore chunks from it. The sky had darkened and behind the clouds the sun was a dark halo. On the bus, I touched the gold-embossed lettering of the card. The sky opened and the streets were washed clean. The little bus carried me across the plains of the city. I looked out the window as the water poured down. Cars with black-glass windows slid by. You could zip up and down this city all day and not see anything at all.

sallad.

2010

I still liked going to the city. After my mother died it became easier. My weekends were freer. My evenings too, now I no longer had to sit by the phone, hang around the recreational room. I started going to the movies again. A lot of the films were hollow and predictable. Events that I'd once known as real, that I'd lived through, were now available at the multiplex. I kept expecting to see Shelley playing the heroine. Every blonde was her, beamed from the past into the future.

I always booked a hotel room – with its miniature soaps which I carried back in my bag to my normal life – in an unfamiliar part of town. Of course, they were all unfamiliar parts of town now. I didn't resent this, the great flattening, the commercialisation, the large stretches of unexplained ugliness. I felt no compassion for the city I'd grown up in and I wasn't engaged in some nostalgia project. I defended myself against any such corniness by only going to the most generic places – the chain coffee shops, the hotels with the exact same large glass showers, with their lazy gestures towards luxury. In the evenings, after a day of walking, I came back to my room and washed my body carefully with the small, box-shaped soap. Parts

of life seemed closed off to me now: people were stin-
gier with their conversation, I spent less time in front of
the mirror, there were fewer numbers to dial, even fewer
people answering. I still scurried, rat-like, through the
streets as if someone might recognise me. Who would?
I was an older woman and everyone was young and rich.
The young people were fully committed to their own
lives, only in tune with minor shifts in their personalities.
I looked at the university students in the cafés, sitting in
front of laptops, banging on the keys, frowning. It was
wonderful to watch them work. I hadn't gone to college.
I hadn't finished high school. I considered pretending
to choke, getting one of them to rush to my side, but I
knew it was too much. I had no right to make demands
of them. They seemed busy. There were streets I avoided,
out of necessity. They still, despite the enormous changes
they'd gone through, had an ominous quality.

Mostly, on these trips, I went to galleries and scowled
at the art, as if it all disappointed me. Secretly, I wanted
someone to catch these looks of disapproval, understand that I was knowledgeable, to strike up a debate. It
made sense that these were the only encounters I could
imagine – those with a time stamp, a stranger wishing
me good luck and sending me on my way. It had been
several months since my last relationship ended, and I'd
turned, for solace, to a television show where a single
woman dated around New York. It was trash, brainless,
but I enjoyed the repetition of each episode. The woman
always closing her apartment door on men who weren't
nice, or men who were too nice, the abundance of choice.
That apartment door had become a familiar staple in my
life. The show was meant to be aspirational but I found it
weird and terrifying. If their lives were so great, why did

they all look so pinched and miserable? The man I'd been seeing before had treated me badly, but I'd quite liked it, it had made me feel alive. I liked talking to him, despite everything that accompanied the conversation. There can be many private costs to good conversation. I imagined myself telling a girlfriend, like the ones that appeared on the show, that 'love can be very slippery'. My mother hadn't liked this man, not that I ever trusted her taste. She was proud that, like her, I'd never married. She claimed that 'the two of us had never just lain down and taken it', as if our confusion, and general bad luck, was some sort of feminist enterprise. A lot of the art now reminded me of him. Couples wandered through the gallery corridors in blissful, uncomplicated early love, a period I associated with dehydration and tourism.

But art was still something I prided myself on being interested in. I remembered someone telling me that art was what women of a certain class took up when they lost their looks. The scarves, the flattering light of the rooms, the tasteful consumerism. People will say anything, however general, if it allows them to be perceived as witty. Despite my commitment, I still didn't know how to behave in these places, if the works were supposed to bring about unrest or calm. I once caught a young woman's eye when we were standing in front of a painting. Her boyfriend was whispering something in her ear, and her eyes suggested incomprehension touched by boredom. I knew we were alike – undereducated, easily led, desperate to please, desperate to have fun in these places where fun wasn't allowed. Her boyfriend kept his hand on her lower back throughout. I marvelled at the ease of it, how gently corrective the gesture was. I wanted to say to the girl, let's blow this place, go and eat croissants, get high, sit in the park and discuss your predicament. A part of me never grew up, a part of me still couldn't take these places seriously.

What I always liked more than being inside the gallery was the process of getting in. It's similar to an exclusive nightclub, it has the same tension. Standing obediently behind the white cord, hemmed in and controlled, desiring, waiting to see and waiting to be seen. The high point is the energy in the ticket line. Inside, it's so bright that it feels like sunlight has been pumped in to impress the tourists. The atmosphere of a long, summer afternoon. Even now, there is something separating me from the pleasure everyone else is easily enjoying. Behind the glamour and the beauty, I can sense the endless disappointments and dollar signs; the paintings lose all colour, lose all meaning: they become machines. They include a lot more work by women now and pat themselves on the back for it. 'Forgotten Female Artists' and the rest. In the reading material, there's no indication as to why these particular women have gone from forgotten to remembered, from failures to darlings. I once remarked to a girl in the elevator, after a show, that sometimes people are forgotten for good reason. She turned away from me and looked out the expansive glass window as we glided downwards. Most people just work out the items of value in the gallery and discard the rest. It has become big business. In the gift shop, everyone is content. They are glad they made the effort. In every gift shop, there is always the same exhausting amount of tack – the Brillo boxes, the playing cards, the bananas. I don't linger.

One Saturday, at the end of June, I saw Maud standing at the front entrance of the Whitney. There she was, out

of context, wandering into a section of my life where she
didn't belong. It had been the longest time. The day was
sunny, and I had to shield my eyes when she approached.
She had recognised me first. You think you're capable
of change. She touched my arm lightly and I turned
around. She looked good, a few minor tweaks, improve-
ments, a surgeon had done a clean but subtle sweep of her
face. Her husband stood silently beside us and adjusted
the sweater tied around his shoulders. The material
was lovely, soft. I imagined their lives together: dinner
at an early hour, drinking cognac in leather armchairs,
the stupid impulses of their youth forgotten, everything
resolved. She introduced me as her friend with a special
emphasis. Her *best* friend from high school. I got the
impression that I'd interrupted their Saturday afternoon
stroll, the small delight they took in wandering around
the gallery together. Faces streamed past us into the
building. I watched, with minor curiosity, the flickering
impatience of the husband. Later, I knew they would
turn on their matching bedside lamps, in their sedate
bedroom – the lamps casting a faint, cosy glow – as they
discussed me. Maud explaining how I left high school
without warning, never reappeared. Then her emphasising and praising her own instincts, stressing how she,
and she alone, knew something had gone wrong with
me at seventeen. My behaviour was totally erratic. She'd
replay the moment she saw me at the gallery doors again
and again. It was like seeing a ghost, she'd stress to her
husband.

She made me enter my number into her phone. I didn't
put up much of a protest, just stabbed self-consciously at
the screen as if my unfamiliarity with the object revealed
something disappointing about my lifestyle. Maud made

a few polite remarks about how well I looked. I expected
nothing to come of it. Before I left, I reached across to her
husband's sweater and rubbed it between my fingers.

'What is this made of?' I asked.

He recoiled slightly. Both of them said they didn't
know.

Sometimes, over the years, I said things that were alien
to me, alien and old-fashioned, and I thought, or I said
aloud, 'I sound like Maud.' It was mostly when I was
being brattish or desperate. When Maud left a voicemail
on my phone she obviously sounded less juvenile, more
assured. But still, no matter how wooden and formal her
intonation, her younger self slipped through. Your voice
always betrays you – the pained inhales, the exhales,
the hesitations, the momentary wobbles. She wanted to
meet, she'd love to meet. Her girlfriends, these days, were
busy. I wondered when everyone got girlfriends, all those
trusting friendships, and where was I? I thought of the
television show, the sweet way the women collectively
treated catastrophe, their photogenic days out. I'd once
had a friendship that deep, but with none of those beats
or moments. I'd once had a friendship that disarranged
my life. I entertained some new and ridiculous ideas –
Maud and I designer shopping, Maud and I licking icing
off cupcakes in a lush city park. It was her nervousness on
the voicemail that endeared me to her, made me forgive
her, forgive her predilection for the Whitney gift shop,
forgive her new face. I was no longer interested in punishing people anyway. I called her back and agreed. I let her
choose everything. I knew she'd like that. I could see us
in a restaurant window in a 16:9 aspect ratio, just two of

a million women lunching in New York City, taking a
competitive record of each other's lives.

The place was tucked away. If I hadn't spotted Maud in
the window, shyly moving the cutlery back and forth, I
might not have found it. When I entered she stood up and
greeted me with a kiss on each cheek. Her perfume was the
same as the one my mother used to wear. I knew this kind
of greeting, to my mind so awkward and forced, barely
registered with her. Our table was covered with a white
tablecloth. I wanted to take an inventory of everything
– the flowers, the waitstaff, the two sets of hands resting
on the table, one with a wedding ring, one without. I felt
like I was on vacation, entering a foreign country, where, for
my own safety, I had to register new details. The restaurant
was filled with mostly young patrons issuing dispatches
from their lives. It was a Saturday morning, so many were
dishevelled, recovering from the night before. They were all
uniformly attractive, in a forgettable way. I recognised how
they held themselves, as if they were already famous or as
if fame was only one phone call away. From the speaker
came the low, folksy tones of Joni Mitchell.

'Joni,' I said dumbly to Maud as a greeting. 'It's Joni
Mitchell.'

She nodded. 'Reminds me of being a sad woman.'

'I still have all her records,' I said. It was the kind of
embarrassing, teenage admission that I thought might
put us at ease.

'Preparing for hard times? Romantically?'

'Romantically, the hard times never left,' I said. 'You
know my problem Maud, men could never resist me.'

Maud nodded and smiled provisionally like the conversation was moving in an unplanned direction. Her face
was serious in a way I didn't remember it being, almost

religious, as if lunch were an activity she undertook with great gravity. Around us the diners paid no attention to Joni's ramblings about love and self-degradation. The music was only blurry background noise to them – they'd heard it somewhere before, knew a recycled version, distorted through the years. In front of me, Maud moved her hands energetically, talking about her husband William, the latest exhibitions, what hotels I stayed in when I came to New York, the total lack of crime now, the excellent food, the latest good novels, the *relative* lack of crime now, the culinary imagination of a lot of local bistros. Maud talked a lot, that was still one of her traits. She lowered her voice, perhaps not consciously, when she asked about where I lived now, as if I had descended from a mountain, as if I was a fugitive. She signalled to the waiter who, it occurred to me only when she ordered our salads, she knew. They exchanged mild, flirtatious glances. A flush rose on Maud's neck, but the waiter remained professional. The sexual tension was all part of the service. The staff were all chillingly attractive too. Maybe there wasn't a single ugly, clumsy person left in New York. Our salads were given to us in large glass bowls. They were huge and decorative, and looked like a picture of a salad you might show a child to make a point. It was so ceremonial. I didn't know where to start. I plunged haphazardly inside and pulled out a strange sort of radish.

'What's this?' I asked, interrupting Maud's monologue. 'I don't know if I've ever seen one of these before.'

'You were always curious, Mae.' She paused. 'To your detriment.'

'What is it though?' Maud rummaged in her salad and emerged with a similar radish, only longer and more humourously purple. She examined it. 'I don't know,' she said, as if conceding a larger defeat.

'Don't tell them,' I said, gesturing at the door where the waitstaff emerged and disappeared. 'They'll only worry.'

She laughed, covering her mouth. I'd forgotten that Maud, underneath her prudishness, had a good sense of humour. There had once been something that drew us together. We had giggled a lot as girls, leaning on each other's shoulders, weak with hilarity. I reminded myself that whatever habits she'd acquired in adulthood were probably like mine, to stave off loneliness. I reached across and squeezed her hand. 'It's so good to see you,' I said.

She snorted. 'What's left of me.'

Her nose was noticeably thinner, her forehead stretched and taut, her lips plumper. All of these changes had only made her look more fragile. 'You look good,' I said.

'Fact is,' she said, 'every woman like me has a doctor.' She kept looking around, as if expecting the waiter to return so they could resume their relationship. 'William pays. You didn't get married then?'

I shook my head. 'There was someone a little while ago but—'

'But?' she said, expectantly.

'But I guess what I liked about him was how badly he treated me.'

'I get that,' Maud said. 'I totally get that.'

Was this what I'd been missing? Friendship? Having my worst, basest desires confirmed as expensive dogs bounced up and down the sidewalk outside? I was hit, all at once, by a feeling that felt close to happiness. I liked it here. I liked how people talked so openly. I liked the woman sitting opposite me with a forkful of salad. 'Love can be very slippery,' I said.

'Oh for sure. For sure,' she agreed. 'I've been married for thirty-five years, you don't have to tell me that. I know you Mae, I knew you'd never do anything as stupid as marry rich.'

'I couldn't betray Mikey like that.'

Her face lit up. 'Mikey! Oh, Mikey. You know, I think I had a crush on him when I was a girl. I'd hang around your apartment just to see him. He was delightful to be around.'

'He certainly made life back then less intolerable.' I put my fork down. 'Did you really have a crush on him?'

'Yes, yes I did, I remember he had so many convictions. You don't get that anymore.'

'He had a lot of complaints and he aired them often and aggressively. You might be confusing complaints for convictions.'

'And he was cute. I can see why your mother liked him. He knew a lot about the world.'

'What about your husband? Does he not know anything about the world?'

'He does,' Maud said, vaguely. 'He has good taste. But we never had a lot of fun together. You know, growing up, I think I was a little jealous of your family set-up. It had this vital, ramshackle quality.'

I couldn't let this go. '"Vital?"' I said. '"Ramshackle?" What are you talking about, Maud? I'm pretty sure you said Mikey was a lunatic.'

She smiled bashfully. 'He didn't like me anyway.'

It was unbelievable that I was thirteen again, talking to Maud about whether a boy did or didn't like her. 'He was amused by you.'

The mention of Mikey had wrenched me out of my friendship fantasy. I watched the waiter clear away our salad bowls. Then, with a mannered deference that seemed almost comical, he poured coffee into two coffee cups. I touched the edge of my cup. 'He's dead anyway,' I said. 'Mikey. He died back in the eighties. It was sudden.'

'I'm sorry, Mae. But you know death is never really the end.'

'It is,' I said. 'It's conclusively the end.'

She waved her hands as if it was not for her.

'My mother passed away recently too.'

'Oh, your mother, what a woman,' she said, deep in thought. 'She was so unique, she had such great style. She really was marvellously attractive. In truth, I modelled myself after her for a lot of my twenties.'

'She was an alcoholic.'

'That doesn't prohibit you from having great style.'

'She gave up in the eighties,' I said. 'It was hard for her. I was happy she did it.' I smiled. 'I'm sorry I didn't get to see you in your twenties.'

'I was a disaster.'

'I can imagine it easily.'

I caught something uncertain in her gaze, but it slipped quickly beneath the surface again. 'I had all these ideas about myself. I had this dress I used to wear – and I think I had an awful time at these parties. I mean I'm nearly sure I did. I used to come home and cry. The enduring memory of my twenties is me lying on the bathroom floor and crying. I looked like a puddle. I had an alarming attraction to drama. Life was really terrible and disgusting. But I loved it probably because it was terrible and disgusting. Then I met William. I met him on the street. I used to say to my friends – "Him? He's just a man I met on the *street*." It was the seventies,' she added with relish. 'People were really striking on the street then.' She blinked. 'We've been married for thirty-five years.'

'Parties,' I sighed, 'are the problem.'

'Did you go to many when you were young?' she asked. 'I went to a few.'

'My daughter took me to a party not long ago.' She picked her phone up off the table and started moving through a number of images. She held one up to me. Maud's daughter standing in front of several bouquets of flowers. She had a set of veneers so large and imposing they were almost animal-like. She was slouched and her eyes were dead as if she was tranquillised. It was hard to fathom that she must have once been a child that threw herself onto Maud's lap and cried without relenting. 'Gorgeous,' I said.

'Gorgeous,' Maud repeated, without inflection. 'She's in movies.'

'I've kept up. Anything I know?'

Maud's face tightened further. 'Independent films.'

'I will keep looking out for her,' I said. 'I go to the movies a lot. It's always exciting to see new work.'

'Do,' Maud said, wearily. 'Like I said, she brought me to a party recently. It was for a friend of hers, a director.' She laughed. 'He wanted money. Am I supposed to be stupid? By the end of the night, I felt battered by the party. I felt assaulted by it. I stood at the door, waiting for someone to release me from the charade. I felt like doing something crazy – have you ever felt like doing something crazy?'

'Occasionally,' I said.

'Will we order drinks? Goodness, the service here has gotten terrible.'

'I shouldn't,' I said, 'I—'

'—were we like that?' Maud interrupted me.

'Like what?'

'Like my daughter and her friends. Status-obsessed. All that ego. Didn't we have fun?'

'We had fun, Maud,' I said, softly.

'You know, I'm sorry I wasn't a good friend to you.'

'It doesn't matter now, really.'

'Well, it does. I'm glad we did this,' she said. 'I'm glad we caught up in this way.' I noticed, with horror, that she was blinking back tears. 'I didn't think you would come. I missed you. In high school, you were always yourself. I wasn't a true friend to you and I regret that. I'm sorry about everything that happened. You were clearly going through something—'

She waited for me to fill in the blanks. I said nothing.

'I said things to other girls... unfair things that I didn't necessarily mean. But we had good times, didn't we? All that laughing – it amounted to something, right? I thought friendship was going to be like that forever. We would bicker, but we would still love each other and *laugh*. I expected my life to be a lot funnier. Life was supposed to be completely different. I think I've found it hard to find people I can talk to, if I'm being honest. It's something I'm facing up to. I never had a friendship like that again. It was never that good and easy again, Mae.'

I couldn't believe I'd hurt her, and that that hurt had left such a lasting impression. 'I'm sorry,' I said, at a loss. 'My leaving school... it was just a strange time, it was really nothing personal.'

'But,' she said, propping herself up on her elbows, her gaze fixed on mine, as if she was about to finally receive the information she'd long been waiting for, 'where did you go?'

'I got a job, Maud,' I said. 'Secretarial work. My family needed the money so I got a job.'

every pill listed.
1966

I was thoroughly unprepared for the way things began to slip away from me. In the weeks that followed my encounter with Daniel and his mother, my home life began to seem like a snapshot from the past – grey and ugly and flimsy. The apartment and its thin, yellowing walls: I had no privacy. The place had nothing to do with me, the tough, little person who'd faced Daniel's mother. I got lost in school, wandered up one set of stairs, down another, went into rooms where I didn't belong. I was constantly groggy. I couldn't hear anything the teachers said, the words dripping slowly but continuously, like drips from Daniel's bathroom tap. The escalators had lost all of their allure. I occasionally had visions of Daniel in different scenarios – at a crowded apartment where people were touching him eagerly, another girl climbing into his bed, at a child's birthday party where he wore a red party hat without ridicule. I sometimes saw myself standing naked in front of him, and was strengthened and titillated by the image. In school, I just watched the back of Maud's head. I wanted to be her best friend again, and I wanted to hurt her irreparably. I knew her secrets and I tried to categorise them, in case I ever decided to release them. Her blowing chunks after the first time we drank alcohol? Whose life would that ruin? I wanted nothing but the total destruction of Maud. I watched her talking to other girls; her twisted and exaggerated face was hideous to look at.

Dropping out was an option, but I couldn't take the strain, the inevitable meeting about my life. The paperwork, my mother's martyred face, the melodrama. After school, I sat in my mother's diner, sometimes doing schoolwork, sometimes with a book open in front of me. Oftentimes, when I wasn't feeling convincing, I held a pen. I got unlimited free milkshakes, and numbed myself out with the sugar. The bustle and movement of the kitchen, the low, persistent hum of the television, my mother's face moving in and out of my eyeline. I thought about the girls Daniel brought home, girls from broken homes or no-homes, probably. Their easy tones of disappointments suffered, of expectations repeatedly not met, girls who knew their hardness and brashness was what they had to offer. Daniel had taught me something, but not what he intended to.

'Mae,' my mother told me, 'you're a dreamer. You're getting worse. If you don't do some work, I'm going to get you a job here.'

'Be a waitress?' I said, laughing.

My mother looked up. 'Shut your stupid mouth,' she said.

It became easy and comforting to think of myself as a sick person. It was a great solution, I enjoyed the idea of something definable being wrong with me. All these bad thoughts, and then: the doctor, his clean white coat and medical instruments. Once I started diagnosing myself, I couldn't stop. Promiscuity, shoplifting, evil behaviour, all obvious signs I was disturbed. It made me tragic, and tragedy was something I could practise in the mirror. My eyes downcast, explaining my fragile personality to a love-sick boy. When I woke up in the middle of the night, muttering and crazy, he'd rub my back, fetch my various pills, smother me with love. I was searching for a way to be different as if there weren't lots of girls like me here already, and even more pouring in off buses, waiting to be told their families were a mistake, an aberration: they were the special ones. One afternoon, I took the card Daniel's mother gave me. I'd been keeping it in a drawer; the pull was inevitable. As I walked to the gold-embossed address, I was resolved – it was free, after all. I wanted to confirm that the apartment and meeting had been real. It had, since I returned home, taken on the strangeness of a dream. I needed to know what his mother had seen in me. Maybe she was just a crazy old lady but maybe she was a prophet. I often thought that my father might have been wacky, drooling, totally insane, but I couldn't be sure. That would explain it all. It was something that wouldn't even occur to my mother to tell me. Sometimes, when faced with my aggressions, my mother said things like, 'Your father enjoyed making scenes too.' It was all shit. I don't think she knew my father long enough to figure out what he enjoyed.

I expected the building to be different from the story Daniel had told. Broken windows, marks of dereliction. Instead, it was elegant, inconspicuous, in no way different from any of the others on the street. A sign confirmed it as a doctor's office. I stepped inside. I wouldn't be there long, see the doctor, find out what was wrong with me, get some pills, go home, curl up like a baby in bed. The waiting room had a sickly, sweet smell. All decisions were

made by the receptionist. She was middle-aged, and wearing layers of clothing. She exuded calm. It was early and
there was only one other girl waiting, picking her nails,
tapping her hands against her knees. I approached the
desk and told the receptionist I didn't have an appoint-
ment but Mrs Ritter had sent me. I sat down and looked
at the tinsel on the Christmas tree. I hadn't thought about
Christmas at all. The other waiting girl had a wild, unchal-
lenged confidence. She was so thin that her ribs protruded
and her back stippled as she doubled forward in her seat.
She was wearing almost nothing. Her skin, between the
flashes of clothing, was milky and clean, as if made from
an expensive material. I watched her take quick, delicate
sips from a carton of milk. She was maybe three or four
years older than me. She slowly unwrapped a chocolate
bar and leaned over to me. 'Do you want some?' she asked.
    I took a piece out of politeness.
    'Are you here to see the doctor?'
    'Yeah,' I replied, turning away. I put the chocolate in
my mouth. Her arms were marked and her breath smelled
rancid.
    After several minutes, the receptionist called her name
and the girl stood up. She crushed the carton in her hand and
placed it back on the seat, as if to undo the violence of the
previous action. She bent down next to my seat. 'Make
him wait for it,' she said, 'he likes the tease. He gives you
more that way.' She stood up and wiped her mouth. 'Do
I have chocolate on my face?' she asked. I told her she
didn't. Then she skipped behind the door.
    I sat for another hour. Young people came and went.
A woman who I mistook for Daniel's mother appeared,
but when she turned to face me it wasn't her at all. She
was sharp in the same way, masking it under an air of

civility. Everyone seemed to know each other but in a way that required no engagement. They were all wrapped up in their own intentions. They all had one eager eye on the doctor's door. I overheard a girl telling a tall, fashionable boy that she had to lie down for her shot today and that it was so uncomfortable. A nurse moved from person to person, asking what they were there for. When she got to me, I said, 'I just want to see the doctor. A routine exam.'

'You and everyone else,' she replied, in a smart-alec way.

The doctor, when he stood in the doorway and called my name, wasn't handsome or remarkable. Everyone was waiting for him, and he was entirely forgettable. He barked at a man smoking a cigarette, 'Would you mind keeping that shit out of my office please?' He left the door open for me.

When I told him Mrs Ritter had sent me, he shook his head.

'How do you know her?'

I kept smiling in a hazy way, as if to convey mystery.

'Poor thing, Mrs Ritter,' he said. 'There's some things medicine can't fix.' He told me to get undressed and lie down on the bed. I did, and he touched my body without talking. I stared up at the colours on his ceiling – mauve, blue, meditative colours. These touches weren't sexual, but healing, gentle. When he was finished, I sat up and buttoned my shirt. I looked at the painting on the wall nearest me.

'Do you like that?' he asked.

I nodded.

'Does it remind you of anything horrible?'

'Not at all.'

'It can,' he said, pushing himself away on his chair, the wheels spinning, 'it can do that to some people, but I guess you see things in a different light.' He smiled in a kindly way.

'I like to do that. Go to galleries and look at the art and things,' I said. 'I guess I'm frustrated by what they teach in school.'

'Who isn't?' he asked. 'Who isn't?"

He took out his stethoscope and pressed it to my chest. His ears were slightly oversized and his eyes far apart. When he leaned closer to me, I noticed an overwhelming antiseptic smell.

'Am I OK?' I asked, quietly.

'Physically, you're well. But otherwise?'

'I don't know,' I said, 'I could be insane. I keep doing things that are nothing like the way I want to behave.' I tucked my hair behind my ears. 'But then I don't know how I want to behave. Life is very unfair. I feel like God didn't give me enough stuff.'

'He shorted you?'

'Yeah. Do you have anything for that?'

He laughed. 'Your mother in the picture? Your father?'

'My mother, yes, my father, no.'

He wrote something on a notepad. He looked up and gave me another electrifying smile. I noticed, for the first time, that his pupils were absolutely enormous. 'That's always the way,' he said. 'Mae, you know, I saw a movie with you in it once.'

'I've never been in a movie.'

'This girl,' he said, putting his hands on my shoulders, 'looked just like you. I think this movie was made-for-tele-vision. This little girl wanted to ice-skate. But she injured herself.'

'And what happened?' I asked desperately.

'Nothing good,' he said. 'The movie, I think, a lot of people would find it crude. These things are judged very harshly these days, but it had some fantastic ideas, from my perspective. You know, how good people become shrunken and distorted when their emotional, inner world doesn't match the people they're with. You hope that wouldn't happen now, but I've seen it happen.' He went quiet. 'I forget the name of the movie.'

I was aware of how close he was still standing to me.

'Many young girls like yourself believe the world to be a safe, comforting place,' he said.

'I guess,' I said.

'And that's why it's so shocking when you end up with boys like that Daniel, in his awful bedroom, in that dreadful apartment – that apartment is one of the worst places I've ever been – with his lizard tongue licking your little fingers and toes.' He put his hand on my knee. 'Young girls do that, they seek the wrong kinds of love, for a moment of being wanted, for feeling seen. When a boy like Daniel calls you on the phone, Mae, you should say you're busy.' He snapped his fingers. 'I don't think you need pills, I don't think it will help you. You're a moody, prickly girl, I can tell, and I admire that.' He wrote something on a prescription pad. 'You're not the type to wait around for some boy to save you, it's so easy to see that. No, you're a modern girl, you want to make your own money, your own way.'

'Yes,' I agreed, energetically.

He handed me the paper. 'Did you see the girl in the waiting room an hour ago? A mess. She was doing a job but I don't think she'll be going back there. I believe her parents are coming to get her.' He placed his hand on

his chest. 'It breaks my heart when the parents arrive.'
He took my hand and placed it over the paper. 'Don't
lose that address. My friend has an art studio, an expand-
ing business, over on East 72nd Street, and always needs
girls to go and do errands for him. Go and see him after
Christmas. Have you ever met any artists?'

I shook my head.

A pause. 'Do you like to do errands?'

'I love to,' I said.

'Can you type?'

It was the one thing I'd been better at than Maud in
school. The only thing really, the one class where I forgot
myself. I nodded.

'I bet you'd like to earn a little money too, wouldn't
you?' He tickled under my chin. 'You'll be good, discreet,
creative. I can tell that. Write your number down here so
I can find out how you do.' As I wrote my number down,
he put his arm around me, his mouth close to my ear. I
extricated myself from his grasp.

'Thank you,' I said. 'Thank you for this opportunity.'

'Mae,' he said, before the door closed, 'when I call,
make yourself available.'

At Christmas, I gave nothing away. My mother gifted me
a hat I hated, and I smiled pleasantly. I tried it on, and
she admired me in it. We didn't fight because there was
nothing to fight about. She was vanishing. I was leaving
her, and so every decision I made took on an air of melan-
choly. I let myself enjoy the warmth of various moments
we shared – tree decorating, my mother and Mikey
laughing and playing in the kitchen, unusual displays of
happiness. When everyone in the apartment was asleep,

I looked through Mikey's newspapers and magazines for information on the studio. A man with an impenetrable face, standing beside a series of girls with small breasts. I was happy about the size of their breasts, one thing I didn't have to compete over. Already, competition was on my mind. Tiny columns about heaving parties, reproductions of the painting I'd seen in the doctor's office, a girl with long legs, dark eyes. No big deal, I told myself. Just after Christmas I shoplifted a shirt for the day I'd introduce myself. The photos had made me more nervous than I admitted. The confidence, the beauty, the radiance, the easy charm.

The night before I planned on going to that address, Mikey came into my bedroom where I was lying face down on my pillow. Mikey was always alert to my moods. Maud told me she thought Mikey would be homeless if he didn't live with us, which struck me as true but wasn't something I wished to concede to her. When he moved in, I was eight. With the addition of Mikey, we were even less like a family even though we had all the suitable parts. My mother had met him at the diner. She said he sat at the counter and drove everyone but her insane. She thought this was because of her patient temperament, but I knew it was her attraction to the bizarre, the unstable. I figured they were together, but only sometimes. On her conditions. Mikey coming out of her bedroom with only a towel around his waist, his t-shirt balled up at the end of my mother's bed. He worshipped her, that went without saying. I kept my face buried in the pillow, even when he stood over me.

'Mae,' he asked, 'do you want to come to the movies?'

I turned around and gazed up at him, as if this was my last opportunity to do so. I'd been giving in to my dramatic impulses. Evening light filtered in through my bedroom window. It always surprised me how he looked in certain patches of light, how old he appeared. Already I was assigning him a different role in my life.

'Stop looking at me like that,' he said.

I didn't ask what was playing. This was what we always did together: sat in the dark with strangers. Since I'd known him, I liked going places with Mikey. He had a large number of enemies and acquaintances in the city, was recognised easily in certain neighbourhoods, the same man, the same big belly I saw rising and falling on the sofa every morning. But he was unforgiving, always had arguments with people who hired him, could never hold down a job for more than a few days, was constantly broke. This aura of failure followed him wherever he went; I considered him one of the smartest people I knew.

Out on the street, the air was cold.

'Do you think it's good to find out who people are?' he asked me.

'What do you mean?'

'Do you think it's better to find out exactly who people are, flaws and all, or to hold on to some idea you have of them in your head?'

'You need to get a job, Mikey,' I said. 'You're having too many thoughts.'

'I have every right to have numerous thoughts a day,' he said. 'Answer me.'

'I think it's good to find out. But I think it hurts too.'

'That wasn't so hard. It's funny,' he said, 'I'm so entirely the person I am—'

'—you are,' I interrupted him, 'you very much are.'

'—that I don't think I could be someone else if I tried.'

'Are you trying?' I asked.

'Nah,' he said.

'Good,' I said, 'I wouldn't want you to be.'

At the movie theatre, there was a line. We stood at the back, waiting, with our hands in our pockets. 'I think your mother would like me to be one of those men who can do everything,' he said.

'You really shouldn't care what that woman wants,' I said.

'She keeps talking about this guy who comes into the diner who can do everything – Alec can fix a radiator, Alec can run a business.'

'If you left,' I said, holding on to his arm to fix my shoe, 'she'd go crazy. Crazier.'

'It wasn't that important, the question,' he said. 'It didn't mean anything.'

'Right.'

'It was just a general question.'

'A general question,' I said.

I scanned the crowd for Daniel. It seemed like this was somewhere he would be, still in the same ironed shirt, still with the same seriousness of purpose. My mind sometimes flitted back to him kissing me, and I forgave him everything. If he was there, I'd blossom in front of him, at a grown-up movie. And the movie would prompt a change in him too – a reversal of his lying and seducing. After, he'd be waiting for me outside the theatre when it ended with a look of absolute contrition. The line snaked forward. No familiar face emerged.

Mikey paid. We didn't buy anything at the confectionary stand, but watched the boy carry out his tasks with rapid efficiency. As we turned to go into the dark, Mikey said, 'You've been quiet lately. Since that night you didn't come home.'

'Have I?'

'Yeah, it's not like you.'

We eased ourselves into our seats. I could feel his pointy elbow beside mine. I wanted to tell him where I was going the next day, he might be supportive, if I wanted to work, let me work. 'It's stupid,' I said, eventually.

'What's stupid?'

'Everything. Me, mostly.'

He was quiet. 'Don't let anyone make you feel worthless, Mae.'

'Yeah, right,' I said. 'You say your dad used to make you feel worthless all the time. It can't be helped. It happens.'

'It happens,' he said, 'but I don't want it to happen to you.'

The lights went down and on screen everything was glossy, ultra-real. It was all fun but there was something about the main actor's expression that didn't fit the story. His camera flashed on women who lay sprawled underneath him. His face was like an open wound, a dreadful pit of despair. He wanted to find out the truth, he got closer and closer, but the moment he grasped a single answer, everything dissolved. The film had started in black-and-white, and then colour seeped in. The colour made the sets look bright and fake. The colour concealed everything that should have been exposed.

mean big paper.
1967

The next morning, I went to the address the doctor had scribbled down. It was in Midtown and all around me, a still, uncertain figure, people moved decisively. They knew where they were going. There was always the possibility I would be turned away, of course. I could get a no, I wasn't needed or wanted. There was the chance of that. I don't know if the idea had any effect on me. My whole life up to that point had been a series of refusals, of being turned away in some form or another. It wouldn't have caused me any great pain because I didn't yet know what was at stake. I wanted my whole life to be disturbed. I was eager for it. There were other people just like me all over the city: I saw them on the trains, in the lines for the movies, standing in the trenches of the department stores. My mother often had the same look, plunging her hands in and out of dirty dishwater, like some great obligation hadn't been fulfilled. I was aware of my hands in a way I'd never been before. In the elevator, they hung limp and empty at my sides. I had cleaned underneath my fingernails, scrubbed my ears until they felt tender. I don't know what sort of inspection I was anticipating. I didn't believe there would be a job. It seemed like an idea manufactured by the doctor to get me in here – and then what? Did it matter? Wasn't just being here the point? When I opened the elevator cage, I felt a surprising amount of anger towards everyone who had underestimated me. Only I had perfect knowledge of myself, and only I knew what I was capable of. I remembered what I had read and straightened my shirt. I was entering a life unlike my own, unlike any normal person's, and I felt grateful to the doctor for giving it to me. Maybe I was on the same plane as everyone else on earth, but I was also somewhere entirely different.

It was daylight in the loft, and cold. A room covered in demented silver paper, tacky and peeling. The light poured in and reflected myself back at me. From certain angles I had a halo of light, like an angel. From other angles I looked ridiculous. I was concerned by my own appearance. Anxious, ridiculous questions. I wore the shirt I'd shoplifted. I'd stuffed it in my bag and waited for my life to collapse. The stress and pressure had ruined my reasonable taste. I had only realised it was terrible when I put it on that morning. If you want to look good you have to fight for it in this ugly world, my mother always said. But I'd fought – and I still looked bad. The silver confirmed it for me. I had eaten a single grapefruit for breakfast which I couldn't finish, sickened by the thought of Daniel's mother's mouth covered in the pale pink liquid. On the couch, some young people were stretching, yawning as if waking up, although it was the afternoon; their slim bodies spread out, their faces sleepy. A girl stood in the middle of the floor, unmoving, with a wide red mouth. I couldn't hear any noise from outside, and the noises I could hear were slowed down, as if time itself had stood still. A shirtless man stood by a silver payphone, turning the dial aimlessly, seemingly no one on the other end.

A girl with the long legs of a dancer laughed and her laughter reverberated, seemed to reflect off the walls.

My presence here was pitiful, but it was too late. I kept walking. I couldn't go back. At the far end of the room three girls who appeared miniature were gathered around desks: three drifters in a parking lot. As I approached them I braced myself for an onslaught of judgement, but the group barely acknowledged me. If it wasn't for my silver reflection I wouldn't have known I was there. I could tell one girl was slightly older than the others. She was tall, not made-up, tense. I still gravitated towards adult authority, and she seemed more like a grown-up than anyone else I'd seen in the building. She had a harried air of responsibility as if it was her job to make everyone else's dinner, put them to bed. Her appearance was sober, comforting in a room where everyone else was a blur. She slouched in front of a typewriter, papers piled on either side of her. Several of the pages were covered in coffee stains, a pattern tirelessly repeating. I watched her experienced hands move across the keys.

'Could you die from inhaling paint fumes in here?' I asked.

'Excuse me?' she said. She didn't look up.

She looked tired but that could have been an affectation. I glanced at her handwriting on the paper, an unhurried, bluntly organised print. She pressed the keys of her typewriter deliberately. There was the whisper of a click.

'It just seems like something you should be concerned about.'

'There's worse things for your health,' she said.

I picked up a paperclip from her desk. 'Is that why you all go to the doctor? I'm Mae, by the way.'

'Aren't you funny?' she said. 'Where are you from? Hey Dolores, this little girl knows the doctor. Would you believe that?'

'The doctor,' a short-haired girl repeated. She sat a desk away and didn't turn around. She and the third girl kept their fingers moving, their backs rigid, their attention far away. 'The doctor, our hero.'

'Hey, can I please have a cigarette?' the older girl asked. For the first time she looked at me directly. 'What did you do for the doctor then?' She smiled. 'What did you do to get him to be nice to you?'

'Nothing,' I said. I placed the cigarettes on the desk. I'd taken a pack of Mikey's that morning. I'd tried to buy my own but I'd been overwhelmed by choice. I knew one of these brands would define who I was. There was very little I could do in life except get dressed, smoke the correct cigarettes. I slid them across to her. I wanted to act above the job. I wanted to act above explaining myself. But my body wouldn't comply: it moved in jerks and starts as if each part was being helmed by a different captain. I cleared my throat. 'He was impressed by me. He said this would be a good place for me to expand my horizons.'

She reached gracefully for the pack, tucked her little feet underneath her. A pair of Mary Janes lay abandoned beneath her desk. The sight of her bare feet startled me. 'Aren't you just fantastic,' she laughed. 'I'm glad the doctor stopped bragging about his sex life for long enough to spot your enormous potential.' She put a cigarette in her mouth and lit up with a pale, bony hand. 'My name is Anita. Do you have any skills or are you one of those girls that just hangs around?'

'Girls that don't work,' Dolores supplied.

'They come here,' Anita said, 'their parents pay their rent, they have these nice fucking dresses, they smell of hairspray, the perfume counters, they congratulate themselves for just getting up in the morning. I'm tired of listening to them.'

'And they can't answer the phone,' Dolores said.

'I'm tired of that smell,' Anita said. 'It's very acrid. It's air pollution.'

'They don't last long because Anita bullies them,' Dolores said, laughing.

'Something about them makes me want to bully them. It's the smell.'

I could hear Dolores and the third girl clacking hard on their keys, working efficiently and without passion, producing reams and reams of paper. There was something familiar and tranquil about the act.

'I can type,' I said. 'I mean, I learnt in school.' I said it as if it meant nothing to me. 'I found a lot of what I learnt in school pointless, but that was useful, I guess.'

'Be a secretary,' Anita said. Her voice had a note of approval. 'Or be a slob, go to bars all night.'

'Those are not the only two options, Anita,' Dolores said.

'You look too young to have left school. Did you drop out?' Anita asked.

'Yes,' I said, in what even I recognised as a hideously affected voice. 'I dropped out because of external pressures.' In a few, short minutes, I told them about the girls at school, the dance performance, the fit. The ostracism after what I thought was a simple remark. I was high on self-pity. I'd been trying to communicate a complicated feeling to these schoolgirls, one that they didn't understand, and they hated me for it. A feeling about death, about God. I knew from the way that Anita and Dolores inclined their heads that they were listening, and it felt good to be around women who understood me. All my life, I'd been looking for that. I found the girls in school banal, and perhaps here was evidence that they were banal. I knew immediately that I could show these women who I was privately, underneath it all, and they would understand. The silver made us look like we were shining, like we were already in the future. I was running away with myself, embellishing, misrepresenting. I explained the part my former friend Maud had played – I highlighted her immense betrayal – but also how it didn't matter because she was a phony who needed to grow up. I recognised her falseness. She was living in a fantasy. I said all of this with total, immovable conviction.

'Stupid bitch,' said Dolores, when I finished. Her voice was soft.

'I can't tolerate people like that anymore,' Anita said firmly, 'I just won't tolerate them.'

'High school girls can be hateful,' said the third typist. Her face was fixed on the paper in her typewriter which was filling up. Her feet moved in time with her confident, impressive technique. She pulled out the page and placed it face-down on her pile. She reminded me of women I'd seen in adverts about housework – full of brisk, dead-eyed efficiency. Her hair was wrapped tightly in a bun. It resembled a coiled snake resting on her head. Her mouth was a thin, forbidding line.

'Who's the stupid bitch,' Anita drawled, 'the girl who had the fit or the one who made the fuss about it?'

'I don't know,' Dolores said, already bored. 'Both of them?'

'People don't like it when you talk about death,' Anita said to me. 'It's not a big hit here either. You should know that.'

'Or God for that matter,' Dolores added.

'I try not to hate those girls and Maud.' I paused. 'Even though they attempted to ruin my life,' I added dramatically. 'I forgive them.'

Anita started laughing, a great braying sound that didn't suit her. 'You are really something,' she said. 'Where did he find you? First of all, you can move to San Francisco if you plan on forgiving people. Around here we're quite attached to our grudges. And don't be pompous either, forgiving people pompously. That's really ugly.' She paused. 'Speaking of ugliness, Edie is going bald.'

'What does that mean?' the quiet typist asked.

'It means she's losing her hair,' Dolores said. She looked at me. 'Don't mind Anita. She has a limited mind underneath it all. Niceness horrifies her. Feel however you want about those girls.'

'Limited?' Anita said.

'What really matters is how you make mistakes. Let's give you a try.' Dolores stood up and put her hand on my shoulder. She manoeuvred me in front of her chair. She was commanding – it reminded me of Daniel leading me into his bedroom. It was so easy to follow someone. I didn't want to go home. I would have done whatever I was told. I took her seat.

'Once we figure out how you make mistakes, we will know how productive you can be,' Dolores said.

'Do you have a CV?' Anita asked. 'Have you committed any crimes?'

'How you make mistakes,' Dolores explained. 'If you're fast, chances are you're sloppy. You're not thinking. If you're too precise, you're slow or excessively cautious. You won't meet any deadlines. If you're full of ego, you're likely making errors you don't even notice. If you're shy on the page, that's no good either. We give everyone a quick test to figure out their weaknesses. We've had girls here, girls that made a lot of blunders.'

'Not that it really matters if you've committed crimes,' Anita said.

'It's fine,' the quiet typist said. 'Everyone has weaknesses.'

The turn of her face, the lift of her long neck, like a little pony announcing itself. She reminded me of hundred things at once – a Christmas ornament of a child, the carving of a young girl on a soap, a face pressed to a store-front window.

'Shelley is young too,' Dolores said. 'Your age.'

'But at least she files her nails,' Anita said, roughly grab-bing my hand. 'Gross.' She took Shelley's hand and placed it beside mine. The curve of her short nails, the softness of her palms. She was the cleanest person I'd ever seen. 'Neat, very neat,' Anita said. 'Get an emery board. It will make you a better person. Do you have a boyfriend? We can get you one if you want. People are always breaking up around here. A cool guy. An asshole. Would you like that?'

'Not particularly,' I said.

'Give it a rest, Anita,' Dolores said. She took my hands and placed them on the keys. It was a newer model than I used in my classes, a typewriter that a hundred girls had known, trying to improve themselves, trying to improve their lives, with worn keys and broken springs. This machine was more impressive – the silver keys trans-formed it into something modern and powerful. I took a small breath, a whoosh of air. Dolores's shirt was open and

I could see her swaying breasts, but she was already sexless to me. Her flat practicality wasn't appealing.

'So,' she said, 'at the beginning it might seem like you're not in control, that the typewriter is working independently of you, but you can control how you react to it, OK?'

I thought of the chair therapy Daniel had talked about, picturing the typewriter as Maud, screaming at it.

'I won't shout at it or anything,' I said.

Dolores nodded politely.

'If you make a mistake,' Anita said, 'you can start again patiently or you can tantrum and destroy everything. Be warned – if you throw tantrums no one will respect or like you. There's enough people doing that here already.' She was writing in a little grey notebook. 'Or you could be like Shelley and be a perfectionist.'

Shelley's smile in our direction. A row of uneven teeth.

'You know, Anita,' Dolores said, laughing, 'I used to tell these girls that they would like you if they got to know you but I'm not even sure that's true anymore.' She handed me some pages, scraps of unimportant paper. 'This is just practice, Mae. Don't think you can't ask me questions.'

Then I was alone. I felt nervous when my fingers first pressed the keys, as if I was embarking on an intimate relationship, which I suppose I was. I remembered my old typing teacher – an elderly woman with her hands clasped behind her back – strolling by, instructing, correcting. It felt good, after months of nothing, to be constructive, to have a purpose. The inside of the typewriter resembled an escalator, hitting the keys was like taking one step and then another and another. The radio played a simple, cheerful song at a low murmur. The clock hands moved, twisted round each other. The clock felt useless, as if it could spit out any time it liked. Around the room, people worked in pockets of concentration, groups of two or three, but the mood was languid. Two men came in and spread photographs on a long table. When they spoke to Anita, she turned silent and calm, her whole body angled towards them. The men were sucked into Levi's that showed their hip bones, and one of them touched Anita's cheek carelessly. She smiled back up at him, her face a beam of happiness. Everyone looked like they belonged in an advertisement. I tried not to watch the door. I worked quickly. I was faster than I expected to be. Nothing I typed was interesting or compelling, and it was easy too. From what I'd read I had expected it to be about art, scandal. I was already greedy for insight. The light changed. I was both relaxed and concentrated, and the typewriter moved in my hands like a toy. A man swept the floor in a strange back and forth way, as if he was engaging in an artistic method. 'This place really is filthy,' Anita announced to no one. She banged her typewriter like she wanted to win an argument. Shelley, on the other hand, looked like she and her typewriter were together, as if they were a couple. Where had I seen a look like that before? It was the way Daniel had looked at me on the train. Underneath the noise of the machines, I could hear the sighs of the couch as people sat down, as they removed their jackets, the creak of the floorboards as they moved across the room. I could hear Anita and Dolores gossiping. It was mostly real estate, who was living where. Who had ended things with who. The events were exciting but obscure, like a soap opera that kept flashing on and off. Someone was too good for someone else. Someone treated Anita poorly. Their voices were clear and intelligent. At one point, Anita took out two pills and put them in front of her.

She swallowed them without water, and returned to her crossword puzzle. She filled in every small square. Shelley sucked on her fingers as if they were part of the machine and needed lubrication. For the last hour, I didn't let my attention waver. I wanted to prove that I wasn't slight or superficial. I was fixated on my typewriter, my mind moving like a ribbon. Here, no one could touch me. I could see everyone in my life moving out of sight, blurry, inconsequential. I watched a woman with long blonde hair get a haircut. She took the scissors to the ends herself. The strands hit the floor. She showed no emotion, as if the act was in service of some greater purpose. I knew the same transformation was available to me. I could become someone of my own invention. It was possible that I could kill the person I had been by doing the right work, by producing, by impressing these people. It didn't occur to me that every girl in that room had the exact same ambition.

At the end of the day, Anita took my pages. I held on for a second and then let go. I was already possessive. 'I'll get back to you,' she said. I wrote my number on a napkin and set it underneath her coffee cup. I was terrified they would lose my information.

Anita licked her lips and picked up her grey notebook. 'So, last question, do you want to be an actress? Is that why you came here – the doctor told you you would get your big break? Do you want to be in movies? Do you want to have your picture taken? Are you lazy and selfish?'

'Not really,' I said. 'I mean I probably am lazy and self-ish but I don't want to be an actress. As for the crimes, I stole this shirt.' I pulled at the buttons. 'So just normal crimes, regular ones. I was told I should look cool when I came in today.'

Anita pulled out the napkin and put it on top of her crossword. She wrote something on it. 'Thanks Mae.'

I stood beside Shelley as we waited for the caged elevator. Neither of us spoke. It would have felt too sudden and strange after a day of being silent. She held a briefcase into which she had placed all her typewritten pages. The briefcase was solid and brown, with a gold clasp. It was a stuffy, uptight and pious object which I would have been embarrassed to be seen with. She was wearing a long green coat and high boots. I'd been stealing small glances at her all day and now she was in front of me, every part of her visible. Her face was vast and plain, and she had spread kohl inelegantly around her eyes. The music in the room had changed. Everything was in motion, and it felt shameful that Shelley and I had to leave. I glanced at her hands. They were smooth and, unlike my own, not covered in ink stains. Earlier I'd watched her replace her typewriter ribbon, the parts lying on her desk. There was something vaguely seedy about how I watched – as if I was seeing her get undressed without her permission. She didn't have a single broken nail.

'I scrub them,' she said. 'Every night, I use soap. Firstly gently, then aggressively.' She mimed the action. 'I've never lived like this before. I've never used so much soap.'

We stepped into the elevator and she pulled the cage across. She put her hand on my upper arm. 'You won't believe some of the stuff you're going to hear in there.'

I felt the levels drop and thought of ropes tightening and loosening, the insides of every machine. 'If I come back.'

'You will,' she said. 'They care about people like you.'

'Who are people like me?'

'Remarkable people,' she said. 'Don't be Anita's slave. Don't let her smoke all your cigarettes either. She's unbelievably cheap. She can buy her own, OK?'

We emerged on to the street. It had rained, the sidewalks were a wet slick with the occasional puddle of light. 'I spilled a cup of coffee on a paperback of hers and she had a fit. She's very square, underneath it all. She hates anything she can't control.'

I looked at her briefcase. 'She only wants you to think she's a monster,' she continued. 'I've been coming here for a month and I do a lot of the typing. You'll like it here. You'll be very comfortable. It won't be like school. People will respect you.'

'Well, I might like that,' I said.

She laughed. 'That story you told, the one about the dance performance, it made me feel...' She struggled for the word.

'Pity,' I offered. 'Desperation?'

'Compassion.' She had alert eyes and her features were pretty but disorienting, as if they were constantly being arranged and disarranged. 'School is a long time ago now. Everything seems like a long time ago since I got here.'

I blinked and was reminded that we were on the street. The idea that the city was still here was preposterous – people walking briskly, people sitting in the back of cabs, scared of their attraction to each other, measuring out the distance between them, people making genuine and unforgivable mistakes on every street corner. 'What brought you here?' I asked.

'I couldn't use my abilities where I'm from.'

'Typing?'

She smiled. 'And listening. There's not a single thing
to listen to where I grew up. The life I would have had if
I stayed there, it really filled me with terror. It made me
feel like a freak. That's the only way I can put it. So here
seemed like a good idea. Everyone is on my level here.'
She stretched her arms excitedly over her head. 'Hey,' she
said, 'are you any good at buying things?'

'I would be if I had any money. I think I'd be incredible
at it.'

She let out a giggle. Her uneven teeth were appealing.
'I need to buy a belt. I know the exact one I want. I'm
going to look.'

I didn't know if this was an invitation. It was easy to
picture her in a department store, her overwhelming joy
at even just being here, in this city, in this new life she'd
chosen for herself. 'Good luck,' I said.

She nodded. 'See you.' She turned and walked away.
When she was halfway down the street she shouted back,
'Don't let Anita smoke all your cigarettes, Mae. She'd
smoke every last one if she got a chance.'

That night, I concentrated on my hands. I washed the ink
off in the sink – the sink where I often watched Mikey,
his huge back to me, shirtless, mid-shave. Staring into the
mirror at his own reflection, the blades of his razor moving
across his cheeks. His shaving always had an anticipatory
atmosphere to it: he had a job interview, he was giving
a poetry reading, he was meeting a unique personality.
A look of almost violent concentration as the razor met
his face. I took a nail file from my bag. I'd bought it on
my way home. In the line, a mother in front of me was
telling her daughter that she was getting fat. 'I don't care,'
the daughter said, 'that's just the way it is.' Her sullen,

bored attitude reminded me of the typists. Young people everywhere were treating adults with bare contempt. Girls with ugly haircuts smiled condescendingly. They were trying out new facial expressions that their parents didn't understand. The adults weren't in on the joke at all anymore, and the thought made me happy. In its plastic case, the file resembled a tiny knife. I wondered if I could do damage with it. The ripping plastic sounded like a secret being revealed. As my nails became neat moons, my own life seemed to recede into the distance. I could pull the whole apartment apart – the damp, furry carpet, the cream walls – and reassemble it, like I'd watched Shelley do with the typewriter. I examined my hands for so long they seemed to blur and disappear. I thought about what they could produce that would separate me from thousands of other girls, and I waited for Anita to call.

That night Mikey and I watched a television show where a devious woman plotted; you could almost see her mind moving through horrible mental calculations. At around twelve, my mother came in and started dancing. She stood in the middle of the floor and swung her hips. She pointed her chin to the ceiling, and her face away from us, as if lost in her own ecstasy. Mikey and I didn't react but she persisted. By the end, she was sweating. I knew she'd been drinking for a few hours.

'Where did you learn that?' Mikey asked.

'That's how everyone is dancing now. I've seen them.'

She collapsed into Mikey's lap and I looked away. When I looked back, the dirty soles of her feet were upturned and staring at me.

'Gross,' I said.

'Do you think she'll be beautiful, Mikey?' she said, looking absently into my face, as if trying to locate something.

'I don't think it matters,' Mikey said.

'A feminist,' my mother said, smirking. 'Not that it does matter anyway.' She cupped my face. 'Unless you like torturing people. Do you like torturing people?'

I watched Mikey's studied, blank face. I wriggled free of her.

'It's like anything else,' I said, 'I think I probably want to try it once or twice.'

'She'll try anything,' my mother said, kicking her feet up in the air.

'Yeah,' I said. 'That's me.' She was still lying in Mikey's lap when I left the room.

Anita called that night. I thought it might be Maud. I was in and out of sleep: dreams about ice-cream parlours, tunnels, dreams in which I could feel every emotion. When I answered, it sounded like she was at a party – rushing voices in the background, overeager laughter. I couldn't picture Anita at a party, in a pile of bodies. My mother sat on a kitchen stool, watching me take the call, as if trying to process a grievance. The phone was her territory, the link to her life outside. How dare I? When I spoke, I could still taste the soda I had had earlier in the evening: overly sweet, unpleasant. I didn't take this late-night call as a sign of my overwhelmingly winning personality. Anita would need a buffer – someone in between her and the party. That's what I was. I remembered what Shelley said about her hating anything she couldn't control. Anita separating herself from anything sordid, announcing that she had to make a 'work call'. Always on an elevated plane, always apart.

'Mae,' she said, 'do you want to come back in here next week?'

I could see her on the silver phone, straight-backed, the party nothing but a humming noise behind her.

'Yes,' I said, determined.

'A clever girl.' She sounded amused. 'And you really can type, you know that?' She sounded drunk, the receiver in one hand, a drained glass in the other. 'Do you know I get the train in every morning? It's a long journey and the seats are uncomfortable but I do it to get here because it matters to me. Some of the girls here think the train is a fucking joke, but I get it every day, Mae.'

'I understand,' I said. 'I like the train anyway.' My mother sat listening, her small, bony shoulders slumped, a posture of indifference.

'You should,' Anita said. 'A word of warning: don't become invested in how good you are at this, and don't do favours for anyone here.' She laughed. 'Anyone except me. That story you told about the girls in school, you can forget about that, that sort of immaturity. Friendship is the most important thing here, it's number one. When you're working, don't stare at anyone. And don't answer the phone to his mother if you can avoid it, allright?'

'OK.'

'And I'm only asking you to come back on one condition: you don't answer the phone to the doctor, you don't talk to him ever again.'

'Why?'

'Because he embarrasses me, because I can always see him portioning up my body in his mind, looking around the room to see what girls are cute or not. It's not respectful.'

'I'm not as innocent as you think,' I said, turning to stare directly at my mother. 'I'm not even a virgin.'

My mother would never be provoked into a reaction. Watching her was how I learnt to shut down so effectively. She stared briefly into space and then, without even glancing at me, she stood up and left the kitchen.

'That's just great, Mae,' Anita said.

'Why are you asking me to come back?' I asked.

'I don't really know. I guess I liked your shirt,' Anita said, and then she hung up.

February was colder than anticipated. My mother wasn't speaking to me, and stomped around the apartment as if I'd wounded her in unspeakable ways. This was one of her most unattractive habits. She stopped wearing make-up. Her vanity lessened as mine grew. Spiritually, I was separating myself from the apartment. Here is the kitchen of my childhood, I told myself, here is the dark, ugly hallway of my childhood. I didn't go to school: I thought of rows and rows of girls studying small, cramped text in books and it made me feel sorry for them. The weather was interminable, as if the whole city was under a sentence. I sat by the typewriter most days and did whatever Anita asked me to. The city was the same as ever; people disappeared into subway stations shuddering with the cold, treacly new songs on the radio. The first few mornings I walked into that building were the most vivid of my life.

It took me several days to realise what the room reminded me of: a doll's house, with girls arranged everywhere, spread on every surface, lying across the couch, the faded carpets, looking exactly like Maud and I used to position them in our games. As I sat by my typewriter,

I felt like I was finally surrounded by genius, by grace, by people who had made decisions about their lives. It was often so dark in the room that I didn't see these people: I felt them. But even amongst them, Shelley took on a special significance. I think it was because she was the same age as me, and maybe something else, the resolved set of her jaw, her strange aura. A lot of the other girls were runaways too but, in my mind, she had come furthest, she had the most energy, she showed the most promise. She worked with purpose. I kept my eyes trained to the back of her flawless hands. I wanted to be friends with her but my only template for friendship was Maud, and what good was that?

Shelley was always there before me, she always left after me. I never saw her typewritten pages. She placed them directly into her briefcase. I was told she'd been working on something else for a little while, something separate from Anita and Dolores. She had a gentle authority, which was somehow further confirmed by the briefcase, an object for which she had an enormous amount of affection. I searched for evidence of her parents on her face. Well, I guessed they must have been pretty awful. My mind, raised on nothing but soaps and my mother's hard-luck tales, was capable of all kinds of sinister invention. It would have been logical; something more than curiosity had made her get on a bus, made her work her hands over those keys. Already, I admired her for refusing to accept her life. Already, I was amazed by her single-mindedness, by the force of her desire. The decisive, daily slam of her briefcase. I wondered what she was doing that gave her such divine purpose, that made her so remarkable even in a room full of beauty. Of course, she had the mythology of the runaway.

As my mother sat in silence with me at breakfast, I often tried to picture how Shelley started her day. She'd wake up in some dreary apartment, mattress on the floor, the full set-up. She likely had roommates. To me, that was exotic, an accomplishment, real life – faucets running, stumbling upon grey faces in the hallway, unfamiliar cigarette butts in the ashtray. I imagined her tender attempts at decoration, pictures ripped from magazines, magazines promoting beauty and self-improvement. The models were new now, I saw them in the magazines. My mother pointed at them and said they were too skinny, they were vile, what had happened to voluptuous women? I thought they had an appealing look, something accessible about their faces and charm. Shelley's morning routine, and mine. Both of us bent over sinks covered in other people's toothpaste and spittle. Both of us inspecting ourselves, determined to shed all traces of where we'd come from. I pictured Shelley's morning so often – what direction she travelled from, what steps she took, what caught her eye, the city's illicit thrill that was already lost on me – that sometimes I thought I might arrive at the building as her, and she might arrive as me.

I was doing nothing – typing up a few letters, invitations, walking to the post office, sometimes glancing in the silver to see if I was acceptable, if I could find a way in. Occasionally, I realised I should be in school, and the thought frightened me. Or else, I feared being hauled out on the street like an ugly piece of furniture that no longer fit. I sat upright and ready to take dictation at a moment's notice. Or I sang along quietly to the records that were on, my voice quavering at the high notes. I was doing nothing, but I was still doing more than the others who sat cheerfully disagreeing and smoking and relaying their personal lives. The buzz of their idle chat: moments in hotels I'd only heard of, their car rides home, their trips abroad, their love affairs. Made-up girls who came in with dead leaves accidentally stuck in their hair, who sat by the windows flicking ash onto the street below. This wasn't a problem: this was their job. They talked about parties for hours. I hadn't been to many parties – birthdays for girls in school that ended abruptly and without warning, celebrations that were memorable for only how repetitive they were – but I was under the illusion parties were relatively simple. You had a good time or you didn't. Now, I discovered an array of vast complications, a way to dispassionately evaluate a party's worth. The basic topography, the banal surface, the hard, dark centre. Who was fun, who was fun, who was fun. They talked about parties as if they were sweets they were trying to suck dry. I tried not to look at them, just as I'd been instructed. Not far from me, Shelley sat with a pair of huge headphones on. They made her look like a creature from another planet, as if she was receiving signals from across the galaxy. She was mostly ignored. What I liked about her – the commitment she had summoned from within herself – marked her as abnormal in a room where no one cared. Her defiant and insistent typing. If she felt left out, it didn't show. When I got home, my neck ached from staring directly ahead. After being in the studio, the conversations I overheard on the subway, about dinner, about restaurants, about work, seemed dull, worse than dull: devoid of any life, unreal.

I never saw him come in but I felt the atmosphere change when he did. I felt it brighten as if suddenly everybody knew exactly where to direct the beam of their attention-seeking. His presence demanded a response

although he didn't do or say much. When he walked across
the floorboards, people were quiet. Anita had explained, in
a bored way, who he was, but I'd already seen the pictures.
He worked further down the room and no noise, no
disturbance, seemed to irritate him. His concentration was
vast and untouchable. He appeared several times in my
dreams, where he was much friendlier; he smiled or patted
the top of my head, looked at me with adoration. I was
never even introduced to him, but I knew his soft voice,
his quick, soundless steps. Whenever he spoke to someone
they stood up as if they were more alive, more human, in
that moment.

After a few days, Anita showed me how to answer the
telephone. She held it out to me, its long cord unfurling
like a confrontation. I took it uncertainly. 'Uh, hello,' I
said into the mouthpiece. Suddenly, the act of my mouth
pressing to the speaker seemed outrageously intimate.

'Anita just discovered the telephone,' Dolores said.

'I want her to get it right. First impressions count.'
Anita was in a little raincoat with the hood still up. It
made her head appear shrunken.

'Sometimes the simple way is the best way,' Shelley
said, slipping off her headphones.

Shelley, whenever she spoke, seemed repelled by Anita's
dominance, her gestures towards discipline. Her neat
desk, her paperbacks, her whole idea of efficiency seemed
to oppose everyone else who came into the building. I
knew what Shelley was thinking: if Anita had to work
so hard to wield her power, it probably meant she didn't
have much. If you watched closely, this was easy to figure
out. Sometimes, I caught Anita reading at her desk in
the mornings. At those times, she resembled a different,
happier woman then.

Shelley always breathed huskily down the phone when she answered. A tremendous amount of effort to appeal to someone she might never see. I felt a flush of embarrassment whenever this happened. She wasn't sexy, and her attempts were hopeless, pitiable, like my mother striking poses when she was drunk. Anita shook her head slowly back and forth whenever she did this, an expression of physical discomfort on her face. Shelley always made her voice unnaturally high, almost comically sexual, but it came out sounding groggy and confused. I think she liked to think of herself and Anita as total opposites, but Shelley, too, always looked most pleased with herself when engaged in some accomplishable task: typing, listening to her headphones, gathering up her papers to place in her briefcase. Sometimes, in the mornings, in the few minutes before she put on her headphones, Shelley's face had a stranded, lonely expression that terrified me.

In those first few days when I sat at the desk Anita had appointed me, school and my life before became incomprehensible. I couldn't believe I had spent time in that unsophisticated place, with girls who solved their problems by pulling each other's hair, scratching at each other's eyes. Because I didn't want to go home, I often stayed longer than I needed to. I liked the dark room when it was nearly empty except for Shelley involved in her mysterious task, the sound of concentration.

Late one evening, Anita dictated a letter to me asking someone's parents for money. It was the first time I'd ever taken dictation. I got the impression that any number of these letters were in rotation at any given time. I'd posted envelopes to formal-sounding addresses on the East Coast, houses that had gates and titles, manicured lawns.

It was hard for me to even picture the insides of these houses: in my mind, they resembled the bland, white expanse of the department store. I wondered if the recipients knew what grimy requests they contained before they even opened the envelopes. Were they expecting them? Envelopes hitting the floor from wayward children all over the world. Anita sat beside me painting her nails as she dictated, stretches of blue that matched the bright sky in the morning. I typed carefully as if in conversation with the parents I wanted to impress.

'Do you have rich parents?' Anita asked me. She was applying one slick coat after another, then holding out her hand in admiration. She knew I didn't; everything with Anita was a test or a challenge. I don't believe she harboured any actual goodwill towards me, but she knew we were alike. A cold apartment, the aggression of one parent or another, the ambition that kind of environment can sometimes produce. For that reason alone, she kept me around, even if there was nothing to do.

I shook my head.

'A lot of the girls here do. You're not allowed to get mad with them about it because it's not their fault. Isn't that right, Dolores?'

'That's right,' Dolores said, laughing. 'It's a disability.'

'Yeah,' Anita said, laughing now too. 'It's a cosmic punishment so we have to be nice to them.'

'Sensitive souls. They don't enjoy it.'

Anita pressed a hand into my shoulder. 'It doesn't really matter what you type, you know. All that matters is it's clear we need money. OK, I'm starting now.'

'Her favourite performance,' Dolores said.

'Daddy, since I left,' Anita called out, 'I haven't asked you for anything. Would it be painful to send some money? I know I have my allowance but New York is so very expensive when you live a certain way.' Dolores laughed loudly. 'There are a lot of costs here, Daddy. Please have some mercy. My friends are doing important work and I'm sort of depressed. You know how I get! Let's keep the lights on, let's keep everyone happy. Love to you and Mother. You probably won't care but I was on the cover of a magazine recently. Please whatever you can spare, love, your beloved Snuggles.'

I felt faintly sick as I typed, as if I was intruding on something personal, but everyone around me acted like it was no big deal. I passed the sheet of paper to Anita. She placed it in an envelope and licked it closed.

'I will send this one,' she said. She shook the envelope close to her ear. 'Hey, what does this say? Let me guess – Oh, Daddy, Daddy please love and forgive me, I fell in with some degenerates.'

After she left, Dolores came and sat on my desk. 'Anita despises Susan. I mean she despises most of the girls but especially Susan for some reason. She thinks she's snotty.'

Shelley's headphones were off and she was alert and listening.

At home, Maud called a few times, calls that were predictably irritating. Teachers had been asking for me, not asking for me, people missed me, people didn't care; she was torn, as always, between punishing and praising me. There was a note of outrage, as if she couldn't believe I'd actually done it – left school, left her. She was sorry, if I wanted to know, for everything that happened with the dance performance. If I wanted to know. The clammy hand of her friendship reaching out through the machine. I could feel my face twitch involuntarily as I listened. I started idly writing down the things she said, testing my powers of transcription. I typed them up late in the evenings when Anita and Dolores were distracted. I don't think they would have cared if they caught me. I only did it out of some remaining loyalty to Maud. They would have got too much of a kick out of her plaintive, girlish tone. I read over these phone calls on the subway. I never typed up my side. Everything looked worse when committed to the typewriter. They were like missives from another life. Underneath it all, there was the threat of a real love and friendship that I didn't know Maud was capable of. She missed me, and that only convinced me further. I was right to exchange school, Maud, all of it to sit in a room where I was largely ignored. I was right.

Shelley and I hadn't spoken, not directly, since the first day, but because we turned up at the same time, because I felt we were both working towards having our own small independence, there was an invisible thread running between us. We both sat behind our typewriters, mute, secretly watching. I'd caught her looking too, squinting around in the darkness for whoever was interesting that day, whoever she could learn something from. We were both trying to absorb – I don't know what. Their social victories? Their beauty? I knew instinctively when the focus of her attention wasn't on whatever was being piped through her headphones. I knew she felt the same way as me – that behind our typewriters the walls were opening out to reveal the whole world, to reveal people that lived differently, who lived without consequences. One afternoon, as we stepped out of the elevator, into the evening air she turned to me and asked, 'Do you want to get something to eat?'

We went to a nearby tea-room, a place I'd heard mentioned. Shelley's ease suggested she'd been many times before. All around us sat fussy, old ladies wrapped in winter coats, still like gargoyles. There were plastic tulips on every table, a board announcing the specials.

When we were seated, Shelley moved the salt and pepper shakers shyly around the table. I knew she was preparing for us to sit in silence. She had only asked me out of curiosity.

'Are you enjoying yourself since you started?' Her voice was flat, sort of disinterested, as if she was reading from a script. She had no particular accent, her voice had no particular shape – she was unidentifiable, she talked like nobody I'd ever met in my life.

'Sure,' I said. 'The work you're doing, is it hard?'

'Not really.' She sat up straight with a look of avid concentration. Her dress was distinctly unfashionable. A woman took our order, a single slice of chocolate cake. Neither of us had money for anything else. Two glasses of water. We both looked out the window. The streets were busy, despite the cold. A night like that was beginning to feel open to me in a way it previously hadn't, like there wasn't a straightforward routine anymore, no linear path to follow back home. Shelley leaned across the table with an audible sigh, as if I was her fallback plan, although it had been her suggestion.

'How is your typewriter?' she asked.

'It works fine,' I said. 'Some keys are stiff. I had some trouble at the start but I got over it.'

'Did you have classes in school?'

'Yeah.'

'Naturally, I hoped you were having problems so if they had to pick between you and me, they would pick me.' She was smiling as she said this. 'I've always been competitive, from a young age.'

'Sorry,' I shrugged. 'Sorry for not having more problems.'

'I don't think they need two of us, you know.'

'I'm not sure they need one of us.'

She laughed. Awkwardly, she took a forkful of cake. She wasn't graceful or precise like she was at the typewriter. 'Lord, that Anita, what a dummy. What an arrogant dummy.'

'She seems intelligent to me. I always see her reading.'

'You think that means she's smart?' There was chocolate at the corners of her mouth. She put her fork down. 'She's only smart in one way. Besides, there's a lot of intellectuals there. Not that anyone recognises it.' She paused. 'They probably want you and me to be enemies.'

'Why?'

'Because a feud would be fun, and Anita would enjoy it.' She smiled conspiratorially. 'I want to tell you something.'

I picked up my own fork. 'Tell me what?'

'I heard Anita on the phone to her boyfriend. They were having phone sex. There was a pause on the tape I was transcribing and I swear it was happening before I even noticed. She must have thought, because I still had my headphones on, that I couldn't hear. What could I do? It was too late to stand up and leave the room.' Her posture grew defensive as she watched me. 'She was the one who did it. It doesn't make *me* a creep.'

'And what happened?' I asked. I was aware of my own interest, it was so naked.

'I could only hear her side obviously. And I felt like doing something – you will probably think it's disgusting. I transcribed it.' A big, goofy smile. 'I figured if I transcribed it I would understand it.' She took a sip of her water. 'Your face, you look horrified.' She put her briefcase on the table between us and popped it open. She removed a page. 'Do you want to hear it?'

'Are you going to blackmail her with that?'

'Blackmail? Aren't you adventurous, Mae. No, she's such a prissy little bitch. She's so unpleasant about the other girls. Making up lies. It's about time someone did this to her. I enjoyed seeing her being demeaned. I mean that's probably why the guy on the other end enjoyed it too.'

'You're going to read it to me anyway, even if I ask you not to.'

'Yeah. I am.'

'Go ahead,' I said, 'I'm experienced.'

'Are you?' she said, pulling her hair away from her mouth. Then she cleared her throat and began her Anita impression. 'I'm here right now. No, I'm in here right now. I can't talk. I said, I can't talk.' Shelley giggled and looked up from the page. 'She's clearly uncomfortable here.' She returned to the page, returned to her fake voice. 'I want your cock? Are you happy? Is that what you wanted me to say? I would suck your cock right now.' She smiled. 'I think she was enjoying herself by now. I think she was having fun. I wondered if she was going to touch herself.'

'And did she?'

She took another forkful of cake. 'No, she hung up.'

'It would be hard to transcribe an orgasm,' I said. Something about the way she was speaking made me nervous; there was a gap between what she was saying and how she thought she appeared. Her avid interest made her innocent, naïve.

'Have you done it? Had phone sex?'

'I'm not big into the phone,' I said. 'Who's the guy?'

'Some weenie. He's married.'

'How do you know that?'

'It's known,' she said. 'Anita would need that, wouldn't she? Some extra thrill or drama, to make her feel special. A dweeb to compare her to the moon or whatever. She'd be desperate for attention like that. I think it's terrible the way some people are so transparent.' She turned her focus to the pool of cream on the edge of her plate. 'I like to annoy her. It's something my father taught me. Find what someone is most proud of and undermine it. My father is in business. You can do this in a polite way. The other day we were talking about another couple and I said, "I didn't even think people *had* affairs anymore. It seems very unfashionable."' She licked the underside of her spoon. 'She got quite embarrassed. You know what? I don't even like cake.' She put the spoon down. 'I don't usually eat sweets. It's childish.'

I had the feeling that everything Shelley knew about what was fashionable, and what wasn't, came from magazines, articles she underlined, gossip she memorised. 'Where are you from?' I asked.

Her glassy, unnerving stare.

'What do you mean?'

'I mean where's home?'

She continued to stare at me when I asked this. We were both probably thinking the same thing: home was starting to feel like the heavy front door, the familiar sight of the curved couch, our stations behind the typewriters, wandering in and out of conversations. 'Home,' she said, thoughtfully. 'Home? Is that a good question? Hey, I was thinking I might dye my hair actually. Would you come with me?'

'Why won't you tell me?'

'Because it's none of your business,' she said. 'What is it to you? What does it matter? I think you want to hear some tragic story of a girl coming from a small town who ends up blowing guys at the bus station for five dollars. I'd think you'd be interested in smut like that. Your saintly face. It doesn't fool me.' She wagged a finger in my face. 'I was warned about people like you. You've got a dirty mind, Mae.'

I snorted. 'That's stupid. I don't. A dirty mind? Really.'

'A dirty mind isn't always a sex thing. You can have a hard-on for suffering, punishment. That's your bag obviously.'

'Just tell me the place you're from.' I was annoyed now. I'd have liked to reach across the table and take a swipe at her. I wondered if she brought out this behaviour in other reasonable people.

'No.' She stuck out her tongue. 'Problems. What problems do you have, Mae?'

'Well, my mother drinks.'

She started laughing. 'That's great. What does she drink?'

'Anything,' I said.

'Wow, an alcoholic, and there I was thinking that drinking was over and drugs were in.' She propped herself up on her elbows. 'Maybe I was just bored, that's why I left. Maybe I was so bored I thought I might die. Is that not enough?' She briefly closed her eyes, as if exhausted by herself, her own charade.

'So affairs are over, drinking is over. What's left to do?'

'Go to the movies.' She took out a few rolled-up bills and placed them on the table. 'Come with me,' she said.

I hesitated. 'I've seen them all.'

She held the door of the restaurant open.

I gathered up my coat and I once again followed a relative stranger through the street, letting her take me wherever she wanted. She had a funny, old-fashioned walk, like a woman in a small town running errands for her husband before he returned from work. A frantic, wifey purposefulness. It was dark and everywhere smelled like wet garbage. A huge garbage truck loitered on the sidewalk, and as she passed under its shadow, it made her look even smaller and more fragile. She was short and compact, yet there was nothing desirable about her. I wondered if, like Anita, she hated being around so many women that were wanted, yearned for, written about. We walked in silence for a while before she turned to me and asked me to explain more about the fit, the girl in the dance performance.

'I heard you talking about it on your first day,' she said. 'What was it like?'

She was rabid for any kind of experience. Through her eyes, even the worst streets weren't ugly, but transformative, full of possibility.

'The girl's head hit the floor. It made a massive smack and her eyes – they rolled back. Far back. There was a little bit of blood. Everyone in the audience was frightened, agitated. Don't get me wrong, I didn't find it exciting, like everyone said I did, like everyone accused me of. But I found it interesting.'

'Right. The human body under stress, the physical reaction.'

'I found it interesting,' I repeated. 'That's separate from finding it exciting.'

'Absolutely,' she agreed, 'people act so virtuous, as if they don't find watching others get hurt exciting. Of course they do! That's what most cartoons are about. In my opinion, everyone is repressed as hell. Or they were in my house. But I guess they are less repressed here, than other places,' she said, happily. 'It kills people, where I'm from.'

'So you don't think I'm a pervert?'

'Oh, I do.' She touched my arm. 'I do think you're a pervert.'

Her laugh then made me want to tell her everything. I wanted to move obsessively through the details of my life that I found sad or shameful. She didn't seem like she would, like every other girl I knew, turn away from vulnerability, as if it could infect her. Unlike Maud, who sat with her eyes closed, her textbook open on her lap, as she pretended not to hear any of my complaints about my mother's loopy behaviour. Shelley didn't seem bound by a social code she didn't even understand. I think she was interested in all aspects of life, even what scared or disgusted her. She'd come here to confront it all. In that way, she was like nobody else. I could tell her everything, and she'd make it right. About Daniel, his mother, her still wearing her wedding ring, how degrading I found it all. But in the retelling, I wouldn't find it degrading, I would find humour in all the right places. You poor soul, Shelley would say, laughing hard. You poor soul.

The rain began again and she hoisted her umbrella over both of our heads. Then we stopped in front of a movie theatre. A small line was forming. Shelley greeted all these strangers as if she knew them personally, smiling and nodding. The crowd treated her with reserve. The street, the grown-up crowd, all gave me the same feeling I had when I talked to Daniel's mother, that I was finally seeing parts of life that had been hidden from me. Shelley shook out the rain from her umbrella. She took a lipstick out of her pocket and passed it to me. 'This picture means a great deal to me,' she said. I applied the lipstick hurriedly while she asked for two tickets from the man in the glass booth. She slowly peeled off some more bills from her roll of money.

Inside, there was no lobby. We walked behind a curtain into the screening room. A few couples were slumped in their seats, only half of their faces turned towards the light. A bag of candy was propped open on one of their laps. An elderly man smiled at me. The smile made me feel disgusting, but I returned it too. Most people stared straight ahead at the screen. The theatre was shabbier than the ones I'd been to with Mikey. Shelley's legs tripped up the aisle in excitement, and we took two seats at the front. As we waited for the movie to begin, she leaned over.

'You shouldn't care about what other people think of you, or let other people's opinions stop you from becoming the thing you want to become.' Her voice was quiet.

I didn't say anything for a second.

'What thing do you want to become?'

I waited for her to say actress, or singer or dancer, thinking of her voice range on the telephone. I imagined she had ambitions and those ambitions were mostly obvious. 'I am the thing I want to become,' she said. 'A typist.'

It began. There was a shaky title card. I turned to look at the projectionist up in his God-space, deciding what we would watch. The film opened on a kitchen, a woman lounging on a countertop. I knew one or two of the faces, the most striking, the biggest, roundest, most plaintive eyes. I recognised some of the voices from the calls I'd answered, although they were lower in the film, almost unintelligible. I turned to Shelley and she smiled knowingly, as if she had planned this, as if she'd made the film herself. The camera was still, like an animal getting ready to pounce. I could feel Shelley breathing beside me, her eyes following every single body movement. There was no narrative – a hotel room, screaming, voices vibrating into the void – yet Shelley laughed along as if she had private knowledge. I sat watching the first hour as if paralysed, feeling a type of fear that was inexplicable. Girls in heavy eye make-up lounging on a bed, looking up at the camera as if expecting it to tell them what to do, who to be. Looking at the camera as if it was inevitable it would be there. They were being insincere, silly, but underneath their games there was the suggestion of real aggression. Every so often the phone rang and it was like an emission from hell. All action seemed dictated by the phone. Torture, the phone, couples close to copulating, the phone, false laughter. A gleeful woman stuck a needle in someone else. The bizarre and extreme personalities on display could have only been brought out by one person; I knew from the interactions I'd watched. I knew by the way I watched them perform for him in the studio. I could almost feel Shelley's heart beating beside me, as if she wanted to climb inside the screen. Yes, her eager body said, this is the direction I want my life to take. There was one distinct, beautiful girl on screen. 'Susan,' Shelley whispered in my ear. Snuggles. As she sat on the bed, her shoulders hunched, amiably taking abuse hurled at her from the other girls, it was hard to believe she came from money, security. If she wanted to forget that, here, in front of this camera, was the right place to do it. The camera could erase all evidence of the person you had been. A good-looking boy had his pants pulled down, his genitals fondled, his pubic hair revealed. There was something unreal about his handsomeness, so much more than that of the girls. Their faces said, I would do anything for you, and they looked right into the camera. Their viciousness, their mouths uttering cruel words, their forked tongues twitching outwards. The entire city distilled down to one single hotel bed. We sat for three hours, longer than I'd ever sat with Mikey. Near the end, there was a young man who spoke more fluently, more intelligently than the others. His use of language moved me: he seemed less interested in impressing the camera than conversing with it. He referred to himself as The Pope and anyone could come forward and confess, he would relieve them of their sins. His flock was composed of homosexuals, perverts of any kind, thieves, criminals, those rejected by society. When he said, 'Perverts of any kind,' Shelley elbowed me in the ribs and mouthed, 'That's you.' I was attracted to him but not in any sexual way – I was attracted to his eloquence, the turbulence of his emotions which he spoke about so easily. I wanted to get on my knees and cry, press my wet face to his legs, feel his forgiveness flowing through me. 'May God forgive you,' he said, 'for you don't know what love is.' That seemed like the truest thing I'd ever heard. It was the only thing you would need forgiveness for.

When the lights came up, Shelley clapped her hands. She was the only one. Smack, smack, smack. It was the only sound. The air was thick with cigarette smoke. I thought of other people sitting in screens, watching what they thought was life but wasn't life at all; images that were fixed, unvaried, nullifying and meaningless. They had no idea about the ringing phone that sounded like a scream. I felt like my face was pointed closer to the sun than these people. I'd veered off the intended route and found something better.

'I've never seen a movie with people I knew in it before,' I said, when the lights came up.

'Cool, isn't it? You know what I like about them?' Shelley asked. 'They're willing to go far. Really far. You should be grateful, you know. Lots of people would kill to be living in their mess.'

On the street she took my arm. We ran through the streets, and all the faces we passed were slack and unknowledgeable.

'How did you come to get in with us again?' Shelley asked.

I thought about the doctor. His fake kind attitude, his straight posture, how he read me, his disconcerting stare. I hadn't been able to think of him in the same way since what Anita had told me. 'I think they just liked me. There was no reason for it. What about you?'

'I got a job in Serendipity and I waited.'

'Waited for what?'

'To be found.'

I wanted to laugh but she was quite serious.

When I got home that night, my mother was up. Mikey was out. These were always the worst times, when there was no barrier between us. After the film, our home only looked even more like somewhere where nothing would ever happen. It was characterless. My mother didn't care about design or art or anything like that. She just wanted to get through every day. She didn't care about possibility.

NICOLE FLATTERY   103

I sat on the couch, and she loomed over me, huge and, in a new way, unrecognisable. There was already distance between us. Everything that had meant a great deal to her was disappearing. I caught her looking at me sometimes and these looks said: it will happen to you as well. I was so alert to all her little unhappinesses. I had to carry it all around with me. I could see her facial creases, her sad eyes, the crusted mascara. I thought she was going to hit me and I welcomed it, as it would confirm everything I already thought – I was the victim, she was the torturer. It would take surprisingly little effort for her to hit me: she just had to lean across and do it. Instead, she wiped at the corner of my mouth where the lipstick must have run.

'I could have shown you how to do this properly,' she said.

'No more silent treatment?'

'Got bored of that.'

'Goodnight,' I said.

'A man called for you,' she said. 'Said he was your doctor.'

'Do me a favour, next time he calls, tell him I'm not around, tell him I moved.'

I'd done this hundreds of times for my mother, brushed off men who called for her with outrageous excuses that we'd make up together, howling with laughter at their desperation. This was the first time she'd done it for me. 'No problem, darling,' she said, and turned back to the television.

Nothing of any true significance had happened. I'd seen a film – three hours in a dark room. But in the days that followed, I felt vibrant in a way I didn't expect. Although Mikey had always tried to impress the idea on me, I didn't know a film could open you up like that. It seemed like everyone who was in the film had fought for something and won. Later, when I saw some of them sitting on the fire escape, lying on the couch, they were exalted, immune to daily life, immune to anything conventional. When I got up in the morning, I thought about those girls and how they looked both ugly and beautiful at the same time. It seemed incredible to me that you could be both at once. Behind my typewriter, I practised being blank, impervious and assured. I no longer cared about anything else. I started watching my mother, really studying her before she went to work – standing in the kitchen, her expression morose, rummaging in her cluttered handbag. She moved like a woman trapped, but trapped by what? I'd inherited some of that – a tendency towards self-pity, an ability to see limits everywhere – and I wanted to shake it off. It felt urgent and necessary for my survival. Here was the place to do it. Shelley came and sat on the edge of my

desk every morning, and asked me what my evening had
been like. She listened with such intent. There were other
friendships in the studio – they laughed at each other's
jokes, they lay on top of each other, their slack bodies,
touching in a detached, gentle way – but I didn't think
they had what was developing between Shelley and me.
She was interested in me in a way I was unaccustomed
to. She asked me so many questions, but was cagey about
herself. Still, I liked being the centre of attention for once.
I felt I'd never been listened to so closely by anyone. Every
day, there was the constant metal-on-metal sound of the
typewriters.

   I answered the phone only once – an act of utmost
courage. Hello, I said, and the voice on the other end
said, I want to speak to Andy, get me Andy. I approached
him. All our interactions still consisted of me seeing him
across the room, painting or talking. On the phone, curl-
ing the cord around his fingers in the dark, or standing
still in contemplation. Then I was in front of him and he
was like an apparition. He barely responded when I told
him there was a call for him. He rested his hand on his
cheek to obscure his pimples, a trick I knew well. He gave
a nod, an assertion that he had seen me before. He didn't
ask where I came from, or what had brought me here.
And why would he? I was just another young person in
a room full of young people. He had absolutely nothing to say to me but I could see him assessing, deciding:
harmless. Bad skin, bad hair, hiding even when he was
in front of you. The effort he put in to make it seem like
he had no power at all. He took the call, his arms folded.
Even when he was in a room full of people, he was apart
from them. Totally separate, though he was connected
to everything. I appraised him like Shelley would, with

the same probably misplaced confidence, refusing to be intimidated. Without even noticing, I'd started to think like her. I'd always been inclined to follow.

One morning, I came in and my typewriter was gone. I touched the cold surface of my desk where it had once sat. At first, I felt only slight annoyance as if someone had rearranged items in my bedroom. Then: a rising panic, I was being thrown out, useless, like the bags of grey refuse that were removed weekly. I'd been caught out. I thought about other things I could do. I could make coffee – the family trade. My mind seized on the coffee pot as my saviour. As I stood there looking bewildered, Shelley placed a box on my desk. She swung her legs over towards me, a cigarette extending from her hand.

'Do you want me to take dictation? I can't, someone has stolen my typewriter,' I said. 'Was it you?'

'Was it you? Was it you?' Shelley mimicked me. 'Look inside.'

I was already reaching into the box. I held a cassette up to the light, as if expecting it to reveal something. I turned it over a couple of times in my hand.

'I'm always surprised these are made out of plastic,' Shelley said. 'It seems like it should be something more durable.'

This was what Shelley had been doing, and now because she wanted me to, it was what I would be doing too. So she told me, I was to sit at my desk, and type every single noise, every utterance, that appeared on those cassettes. I was to go in order from 1965 to 1967, as the cassettes were labelled. I was to be extremely meticulous. Shelley explained all of this slowly with an absurd amount of eye contact. This was what she'd been doing for a while. Her caresses of the tapes, the authority with which she spoke, all of it implied it was a job only she was capable of. That was how she worked: she put herself in a place where she wouldn't normally be welcomed, or accepted, and she made herself, through her own rigid determination, invaluable. Her letting me in was an admission of utmost trust. I spun one of the cassettes around and around in my hands. I held it up between my eyes, as if looking through binoculars.

'Sounds boring,' I said.

'It's a lot more stimulating mentally than what you've been doing,' Shelley said. 'It's not the same made-up garbage Anita has been giving you. It's noble.'

'What's it for?'

'A book. You can't trust just anyone with this sort of work. The girls here... I can tell you've a different sort of appetite than them. And I need someone to help me if I ever want to sleep again. I've looked through your pages, you're careful. And I'm fast.'

'So, together we make one good typist.' I laughed. 'You know I'm fast too, right?'

'You're arrogant.'

'Sorry.'

'No, no, don't apologise. It's a good thing.'

I followed her. I followed her again. I was in a continual chase. At the back of the room, sound equipment was set up, two reel-to-reel tape recorders placed against the brick wall. My typewriter was already there. There had really been nothing to agree to. It was better than the set-up I'd seen Shelley working with recently and she stood beside it beaming, like a proud employee. I looked at the tangle of wires, as if trying to absorb details. She ran her fingers over the keys of my typewriter. She had no qualms about touching other people's possessions. She ran her fingers along the recorders.

'Aluminium,' she announced.

Shelley mentioned the name of the guy who supplied the equipment, someone who used to be around a lot. This part of the room was the most sparse, away from the couch, away from the paintings. There was one small square window: the dimensions of my new life. There would be no more gazing at the people who entered, no more looking for deep, obscure signs that these people even knew I existed. We wouldn't be required to answer the phone because presumably we wouldn't be able to hear the phone. All those voices that somehow vibrated at a higher level than our own, we would never hear. This set-up marked us as alone, and I didn't know how Shelley couldn't see that.

'Let me show you how it works,' she said.

She scrambled through the cassette box. It was un-labelled, nothing to suggest it was in any way important. That was standard – no objects in the room received special treatment apart from the phone. I'd seen paintings left on the floor, tripped over expensive furs, everything gathered the same dusty silver sheen. She pulled out a tape with a handwritten label that indicated it was from 1965. She slid it into the machine and pressed play. The wheels started spinning increasingly fast. I felt my heart-beat quicken, as it sometimes did when Mikey put on music I didn't recognise. Shelley stared up as if transfixed. She put on a pair of headphones and leant forward on the desk. The bottom of her shirt had become untucked from the waistband of her skirt, and it trailed behind her. She bent closer to the machine, like she had done during the film, as if she were having an especially charged, private experience. I watched her back tense. After a few minutes, she turned around and placed the headphones on my ears.

'Listen,' she said.

I pressed the headphones closer to my right ear. I could hear the click of a dial tone, then loud street noises, ambulances, the city babble. They were the same noises I heard every day except now they seemed amplified, clearer. Then, a man's voice. He was talking about what he had done the night before; I immediately knew the knowing, ironic lilt, the speed. I knew the sermon.

'The Pope,' I said, aloud to no one as Shelley already had her own headphones on, her tape moving. I stopped the tape I'd been listening to. I turned it on again, and listened to the torrent of The Pope's language, all the words pouring out of him. I stopped it, I shut him up. I examined the machine for something to do, as if inspecting it for defects only I could identify, turned the switches on, turned them off again. I was scared to begin, but I couldn't admit that to Shelley. It would seem like an admission of weakness. I put my headphones back on. I didn't press play but I cocked my head in a fake listening pose. Nothing – white noise. Everyone in the building felt too close, as if they were watching me, but too far away also. We were unmoored from the rest of the room. Outside the window, the sky was a clear and cold blue.

That afternoon, Anita invited us to a party. 'Maybe,' Shelley replied, while gazing over her head. She'd put on a pair of large, oversized glasses I'd never seen her wear before. They seemed to signify the enormity of the task she was involved in. When evening came, Shelley stood up nonchalantly. Anita had left before us but we had the address. Night had come through the window, a perfect black square as if cut from dark material. As we stood by the elevator, Shelley rolled out her wrists. She took off her glasses and put them in her briefcase.

We walked to the subway station. As we walked, I told Shelley about how I'd started working. That, on first listen, I had only written down a few words and then gone back to retrieve the rest of the phrases. On the platform, Shelley leaned against a pole, her eyes fierce and shining, taking everything in. She was careful to never do anything that could be accused of being touristy, but she was like a tourist in the way I could see her projecting herself into imaginary scenarios from films, songs. She was a tourist in reality. As much as she tried to give the illusion of experience, there was something naïve about her, something too open on her face. I had learnt to shake that off as I got older. You couldn't be walking around like that, yet it was endearing on her. I knew I appealed to her for the opposite reason – my familiarity with the city, how blasé I was to the insanity of it all. That gave her some protection too. In the studio, she was nobody, no money, no wealthy parents, she wasn't a knockout, she wasn't horrible in a funny way. These were the measurements. Still, I liked her because, despite her strangeness, she seemed to be living honestly, more honestly than anyone I'd ever encountered. I liked the sight of her face appearing from the huddle of her heavy green coat, like a tentative animal emerging from a cave. I liked her small tremor of delight at the whoosh of the train. I had no idea where she got her clothes – the pleated pinafores, the starched collars. All of it implied a virtue that other girls were desperate to be rid of. It was all mini-skirts, the tops flimsy but tight; virtue was passé, virtue was obscene. I think she enjoyed her ridiculousness – the gap between how she looked, and who she spent her days with. And yet, she seemed more open to connection than I was. The world kept telling us we had never been so free, but it was only when I was with Shelley, alive with her excitement, in her dream that had taken her across the country on a bus, that I believed it.

The train bumped constantly as Shelley carefully dissected Anita, as if figuring out exactly what was wrong with her was a public service. Anita was the enemy.

'She is the kind of person who would have been proud of getting good grades in high school if you know what I mean. A person who finds the merest hint of failure disgusting. Being surrounded by what she sees as fuck-ups probably cheers her up. Boosts her self-image.'

I didn't say anything. I didn't feel the same way about Anita as Shelley did, and I felt tired from sitting at the machine all day, from the difficulty of the project, how tiny I felt positioned in front of the wall. Behind me, things kept happening and I couldn't look. It was devastating to me that I couldn't look. The bare scraps of sunlight falling across the keys. I changed the subject.

'Did you get good grades in high school?' I asked.

'Who honestly cares? I left before they figured out if I was a slob or if I was smart. You have to know how to get yourself out of situations you don't want to be in.' She took out a large silver flask from her coat pocket. 'I'm writing a book now so what does it matter? I'm a writer.' She laughed. 'He's nothing really, is he? I could tell you were thinking that when you spoke to him. He's just a pair of blue jeans, that's exactly what you were thinking. Why do so many people like him? It's not immediately apparent why they would.'

'He has a bad complexion,' I said.

'So what?'

'So do I,' I said, 'that's something we could talk about.'

Shelley gave me a look. 'OK, Mae. That's a good idea. When I first meet someone I often ask what does this person love? I mean what would they die for? It's something my father taught me. It's a good way to figure them out. What do you think he loves?'

'I couldn't possibly say,' I said.

She took a long swig from her flask and passed it to me. 'You could be attractive if you tried, you know. You've a lot of potential with your hair and face.'

'I feel that way about a lot of things.'

'What way?'

'That I could be something if I just tried.' I took a sip and coughed discreetly. 'It's the trying I have a problem with really. I don't like trying.'

She attempted to light a cigarette. The first go was imperfect. She went again and inhaled. 'It's not so hard.'

She frequently spoke offhandedly like this, as if she had reached the pinnacle of female perfection. Her unfashionable clothes, her often agitated face, her boxy shape: nothing was an obstacle. She acted like she was the sole proprietor of all the beauty in the world and so, in her company, against your better judgement, you started to believe it too.

'What's on your tape right now?' I asked.

'Nothing. Talking, sounds,' she said, somewhat guarded.

'Yeah, mine is the same. It's dull, right?' I said, thinking of the rush of adrenaline and fear I felt as I watched my tape begin its rotation.

She nodded and pushed her hands in her pockets. She kept her mouth glued to her cigarette. She had an

unnatural way of smoking, self-conscious and eager, a way
that was recognisable from other girls who were trying to
invent themselves.

'Did you have friends at your school?' she asked me,
suddenly.

'Yeah, one,' I said, 'Maud.'

'I'm jealous.'

'That could easily be solved by meeting Maud.'

'Well, forget her. So long, Maud,' she said, when the
train doors opened. She linked her arm in mine and we
walked out like that together.

The party was a gallery opening in the West Village. When
we got there, it was later than we had realised. We had
missed the formalities. Only one man was left pacing in
a room full of balloons. Shelley picked up a red balloon,
and rubbed it across my arm, making all the hairs stand
on end. Kneading his forehead as if from a headache, the
man told us that everyone had gone upstairs. We had to
walk up three flights of stairs and by the end, Shelley was
out of breath and irritated. She held on to the balloon the
whole way. She looked at me before we walked in.

'Hey, change your face,' she said. 'Being terrified won't
help anything.'

In the apartment it was almost too dark to see. The
only light came from screens playing flickering images. I
moved closer, and I saw they were of men on their knees
and other men assuming position in front of their mouths.
They were funny, I guessed, but not in any way that made
me laugh. There was something troubling about the
involved expressions of the men on their knees, the nothing expressions of the men being pleasured. The crowd

was fashionable and self-absorbed, and didn't notice
Shelley or me. It was like we weren't there at all. I stood
beside one of the screens, as if the images didn't bother
me, as if I was lost in my own thoughts which were deep,
deeper than parties or cocktails. This was an attitude I
often cultivated, even at school. Shelley disappeared into
the crowd and I spoke to no one. I worked on my own
impenetrable exterior. People moved in and out of the
light of the screen, changing shape. When they were illu-
minated underneath the flare, I could see many of them
were ordinary. Broken, yellowing teeth, irregular features,
bulging eyes. But all of it was overshadowed by whatever
confidence and sexuality they projected. Occasionally, a
delicately beautiful face appeared out of the darkness, like
a dream. I saw Susan; I recognised her from the film. She
was dancing with a tall man, his hands fixed to her waist,
her heavy earrings swinging jauntily from her earlobes.
She kept blinking and smiling as if even she was surprised
by how desirable she was. Hey, I wanted to say, I type
your letters, Snuggles. Around her, everyone danced energetically like planets moving around the sun. I watched
a suited man stroke the cheek of another man, as if they
were in the middle of a reconciliation. It was too intimate
and I turned away. Anita stood across the room, talking
to someone, her dark hair covering her face. She waved at
me. Dolores stood beside her, lit by the red tip of her cigarette. Anita didn't look like someone who would whisper
filth down a phone line. I was scrambling to relearn everything I knew about people. Every so often, as if part of a
performance, a woman took to the middle of the floor
and sang over the music, projecting her personality into
the room. The music was low and thoughtful, the type
Mikey said could save your soul.

He was there – a leather-clad elbow, his head bent low. People put their hands on him, rubbed him fondly like a beloved dog. His head was permanently slightly to the side, as if he was always receiving information. It reminded me of how I looked when I was pretending to listen to the tape.

It felt like my eyes were covered by a film, that my vision was blurry, as if there was an actual physical reason why I couldn't fully enter the party. I must have stood like that for an hour. I saw Susan making out with the same man she'd been dancing with earlier. His shirt was open, his face frank, his body an invitation. It was logical, their coupling. It made sense. Shelley came back and spoke much too loudly and frantically in my ear. She had a butterfly painted on the left side of her face. No other girls I could see had a butterfly. It was rushed and child-like, no sign of artistic talent. I couldn't even see someone face-painting.

'Who did that, Shelley?' I asked, touching it softly.

'I like it,' she said.

A photographer took our picture then, not like he wanted to but as if there was no alternative. My wan smile, Shelley's strained beauty. He didn't look happy with his subjects; there was probably something wrong and lonely about us, something the camera turned away from. I couldn't take it after that. I didn't want to see it end, glass on the floor, huge displays of emotion, good-byes, disappointment, people moving on somewhere we weren't invited.

'Let's go,' I said.

Outside, my head throbbed and the night seemed impossibly bright. The colours on Shelley's face had already run and leaked.

'This isn't nice,' I said, tracing the wings. I knew some of the others thought Shelley was a joke: the air of the small-town, her sturdiness, her resolute face underneath her headphones. She'd never even consider someone's friendliness to be deceptive.

'What's not nice about it?' Shelley asked. 'It's a butterfly.'

'Forget about it,' I said.

Shelley pulled me close and crushed me to her chest. Her hug was warm, obliterating, the same as my mother's when she was in an outrageous mood. She smelled overwhelmingly of alcohol. 'You worry too much,' she said. 'You even worry about face paint.'

We went to a diner on the corner and sat at the counter. The smell was reassuring after all that unfamiliarity. It smelled like my childhood. Two girls in sweaters sat in a dark panelled booth. Shelley had leaned on me the whole way. I put her on a stool and she rested her feet on the silver bar beneath her. She was still holding the red balloon, and placed it on the counter between us. 'I hate this coat,' she said, 'I don't feel light in it. I don't feel *breezy*. We should go shopping.' She pressed her mouth to the counter, kissing it, leaving a little ring of steam. 'I want to dance,' she said, her voice muffled.

'Susan was there,' I said.

'Edie wasn't though. I looked. I don't believe what they said about her hair falling out. They should apologise... Anita and Dolores. They're angry at her for no reason, probably because she's so divine.' She banged her hand on the counter.

I wondered if someone had slipped something into her drink. Shelley would have allowed it because she would have no understanding that it was possible. I ordered her a burger, a hunk of red meat she almost had to unhook her jaw to eat. Her eyes were full of expectation, the meat hanging from her mouth.

'I've met nobody but great people since I came here. Except Anita. She's a bitch. But mostly, it's been generous spirits. And all of them absolutely crazy about me. I have this charm here that I didn't have at home. Nobody liked me at home. Everyone does here because they're more sophisticated.' She was speaking so passionately, her teeth showing, the back of her throat visible.

I swallowed some water. 'That's good, Shelley.'

'My parents,' she said, with the wide, plaintive eyes of the confessor, 'they were overbearing, especially my father.'

'That tends to happen, with parents. They think they own you.'

'Yeah, that's it,' she said, through mouthfuls of food. 'He thought he owned me. Isn't that dumb?'

'It's not surprising.'

The waitress stopped to ask if we wanted anything else.

'No thanks,' she said cheerfully. 'I'm drunk.'

I glanced at the waitress as she passed. She was older, frazzled hair, dark circles under her eyes. 'My mother, she's a waitress. She comes home every evening and just talks about how tired she is. It's pathetic.' I sipped on my soda. I could say whatever I wanted, I could betray whoever I liked, because Shelley wouldn't remember in the morning. 'She'd probably be jealous of my job.'

'Professional job,' Shelley said, spitting flecks of meat.

'Yeah, her daughter has a professional job and she's still cleaning slop off tables.' The night I'd had, the regard that everyone in the room held themselves in, the bewildering opportunities opening up to me now: it all had an effect on me. 'Slop,' I said again, relishing the way it sounded.

'Does she get good tips?'

'She does OK.'

'I've a tremendous amount of respect for her.'

'Why?'

'Because she raised you, and you're nice.' She gave me a sweet, sloppy smile. 'I'm going to be sick.'

It took some effort to heave her off the stool and out the door. Outside, she threw up in a trashcan for three to four minutes. She tried to do it with a certain elegance. Two men passed and looked at us like we were despicable, like they had heard about people like us and now we were here in the flesh, doing what they expected. I no longer cared. I was wearing a cloak, I wasn't myself. I was a person that exuded confidence even as I held Shelley's hair back, even as drops of vomit hit my feet.

'Oh my goodness, oh my goodness.' Her breath was staggered, and the colours had leaked further down her face. Out of her hand, the red balloon flew up into the sky and away from us. I watched its journey for a few seconds. I could feel her finally straightening her body beside mine. She was finished. 'Damn,' she said. 'I really loved that balloon.'

As soon as I got home, I washed my hair in the tub. I stank of smoke and vomit. In the kitchen, my mother sat opposite a man I didn't recognise. Her hand was coiled around his. Every man my mother brought home, except Mikey, had a sneering, contemptuous look to them, filling the room with their scorn. My mother never sustained their interest, or they never sustained hers. I stood in the kitchen doorway, in my nightgown, my wet hair dripping onto the floor. The man looked away. My mother took in my appearance. 'Are you stressed or something?' she asked.

'Yeah.' I paused. 'School.'

'You should do your exercises.'

'What exercises?'

She turned back to the man. 'The ones you're supposed to do.'

When I left the room, I heard her say, 'She was the cutest baby. She won competitions.'

On the couch, Mikey was pretending to read a novel, ignoring the seduction in the kitchen, his mouth curved downwards, leafing through the pages as if trying to find the source of his unhappiness.

In my bedroom mirror, I smeared kohl around my eyes. I tried to make it more alluring and mysterious than Shelley's efforts. The dark eyes of a stranger stared back at me. I piled my hair up high like Susan's. I thought about putting myself in the middle of a party, in front of all those people and singing an important song, one that could change your life. I examined my body for the first time since I'd been with Daniel – small breasts, large hips, short legs but, for the first time, it seemed surmountable, not a problem to be solved. I did some poses in the mirror, talking poses, laughing poses. Finally, I lay down on my bed but I didn't go to sleep. I thought about the party. There had been no particular scenes to remember, but everything returned in pulses, in beats. I was aware of my hands, my fingers, how they had gripped Shelley's hair when she vomited. I heard my mother and the man go into her bedroom. When it was light, I left the apartment.

The front door was open. It always was. Anyone could wander in and anyone often did. Even that early in the morning, I wasn't alone. When I walked in, Shelley's hunched back was the first thing I saw. The wheels of her machine were already in motion. Five or six paintings

were leaning against the wall in a row. It was the first
time I really looked at them. It was quiet enough to allow
it. They were lurid, electric colours, like the streaks on
Shelley's face the night before. I recognised the famous
woman from the painting. I'd seen up her skirt, I'd seen
her in a swimming pool, but I hadn't seen her like this.
She looked preserved, embalmed. I thought of the bright,
pink flesh of Shelley's burger. Her face again and again,
but the attention to detail didn't make it more lifelike,
only rendered her inhuman, as if she was just one of a
million animals being sent off to be slaughtered.

   'Hi,' I said and Shelley nodded at me. Her shirt was
buttoned right to the top, as if she wasn't the type of girl
to throw up on the street, as if she constantly walked
around being shocked and astonished by impropriety.
She smelled heavily of drugstore perfume. Outwardly,
she looked like she always did. The cassette box had been
upended as if she had been searching for something. She
beckoned me closer. One finger. Her cardigan tightly
buttoned. She placed the headphones over my ears. I could
hear the voice of a young woman, high, flirty, joyful. 'It's
Edie,' Shelley whispered into my right ear. She took the
headphones off me and put them back on. She looked
thrilled, as if she had found exactly what she'd been looking for, what she'd suffered for. Her face, which had been
so open the previous night, now concealed everything,
all her history. She was nobody but a woman at a typewriter. She sat and started taking furious notes, working
with an intensity I couldn't imagine. I reached into the
box and took out a cassette labelled 1965. For my own
sense of purpose, I felt it was essential I went in order.
I flicked on a switch. I put on my own headphones. I
started listening.

There was no silence. If I wanted silence – and even after the first few hours I came to crave it – I had to take off my headphones and pick a point on the wall. I had to stare directly at that point and imagine silence flooding in. Picture a green meadow, breathe in and out, imagine an empty room filled with light. But quickly even my empty rooms were invaded by the people I had to listen to. There were pockets of silence on the tapes, but these were only the prepared silences before someone else began to speak, before language poured out again, ugly and vulgar and unstoppable. In these pockets of silence, the times when they were pausing, taking their breaths, the city made itself known. Honking, blasting, violent. In the background of the tapes, New York sounded like a shrieking cartoon hell. When I travelled home in the evening, these noises – street arguments, sirens, subway screeches – were amplified to me. They were almost tangible as if I could reach out and touch them. In the evenings I ate my dinner in silence, as if the act of conversation was too much for me. I didn't have the energy to navigate more words. I tried not to stare at Shelley during that first week. She moved with such ease it unsettled me. It was as if she was

born to do this. Her face occasionally gave away what she
was listening to – an expression of tenderness, a look of
indignation, all expertly played out as if she were a silent
movie actress. It felt intrusive to even look at her. Her tape
was her own secret, and I didn't want to see her reactions.
Instead, I moved closer to the window, to have another
point of focus. Our scrap of sky showed the beginnings
of spring.

I knew that in comparison to Shelley I was already
behind. She had a neat stack of finished tapes piled up
beside her. She was probably many conversations ahead. I
had no idea when we had to hand our pages in – Shelley
never told me – but something competitive kicked up
in me. I was always surprised when this happened, but I
welcomed it. Shelley's ambition was catching. At the start,
I tried to be good, beginning again if the margins weren't
in the right places, balling up the paper and throwing it
away if there were typos. I was precise and precision was a
problem. Those early attempts felt like a struggle between
two different parts of myself. The typing itself was physically exhausting, every key demanding huge effort. Some
evenings, I felt broken. All that was left to do was eat some
cookies, crawl into bed. Then I remembered my will and
determination. Where had it come from? I let my subcon-
scious take over. I hit the keys instinctively. It was hard
even for me to believe that I hadn't taken much dictation
before. When I sat down in the mornings, I no longer felt
like I was beginning a slow descent down the void. I was
controlled, invincible. The room fell away. Nothing but
Shelley moving a pen in and out of her mouth. In and
out, in and out, spittle covering the lid. Then the carriage
bell would ring to indicate the end of a page, and I was
back up, out of the water, resurfacing.

But learning to type was nothing compared to learning to listen. I barely moved when I put on the first tape, as if any movement of mine might disturb them, as if I was in the room with them. The first tape I put on started with sounds and I dutifully typed them. Rattle, gurgle, clink, ring. Then the sounds of a phone. Click, pause, click, ring. I was so careful. I didn't leave anything out. After that it was nothing but an outpouring of language. I rewound often to capture exact meanings, to try and figure out who, amongst all that noise, was speaking. Their voices never matched what they were saying, their emotions were all wrong. They were sick, broke, depressed, but always laughing, always amused, always energetic. The disconnect was enormous and I couldn't understand it: the gap between how badly they felt, and their energy and commitment to keeping going. Like at the party, I was waiting for a mist to clear. Then I realised it didn't matter. I didn't have to say how they were feeling; I just had to get the words down. I simply had to absorb it and regurgitate it onto the page. It was an act of trust, more than anything else. I had to make their private words public. It was often dark by the time I finished. It was, I realised, the first time I felt total connection to the work I was doing.

As the weeks went on, I didn't wonder about Shelley's technique but it bothered me that she was ahead. We talked every morning and evening, but about other things: music we had discovered, films that were playing, physical hang-ups that I had. How could I make myself longer? Where could I get my hands on low-cut dresses? We didn't really talk about the tapes, but we were together, a pair, heroines in our private drama that everyone else was excluded from. Our work was worth something. Shelley rarely talked about herself. If I asked

her any direct questions about home, she scrunched
up her face, as if trying to remember and then changed
the subject. She made me talk and talk, and I didn't mind
it so much. She wanted stories about the apartment,
about what Mikey was reading, how my mother drove
me half-demented. Secretly, I think she enjoyed casting
herself into these domestic scenes. If I were you, this is
what I'd do: that's how her advice always started. She
listened to me carefully but when her headphones were
on, Shelley's default expression was beatific, saintly, as if
she were hearing voices sent from Heaven. She looked
relaxed somehow. I didn't. I constantly felt the pressure
of time because all they talked about on the tapes was
time. What to do with it, when to move on somewhere
else, when to keep the night going. Sometimes, when I
took my headphones off at the end of the day, the clock
seemed to tick louder. When I bought a muffin or a
subway ticket, I half-expected to hear the voices from the
tapes travelling through these strangers. After a while, I
accepted that it would take me a few hours every evening
to return to reality.

Behind us life was technically happening, but we had no
part in it. We were trapped in their world from two years
ago. The red couch was no longer in my eyeline, but I saw
girls march in, wearing high leather boots, full of determination, and exit meekly, cowed. They often sat rigid,
having their picture taken, only their profiles visible. A
film camera sometimes circled the room. Everything had
to be recorded. There were always boys who didn't seem to
know what to do with themselves, who sat awkwardly on
stools, or lay on the floor, smiling stupidly.

I watched him standing in the busiest part of the room, constructing, looking small and distant. His life had such momentum that even what had happened two years ago must have felt far-away. Whenever the silver phone rang he was summoned.

At the end of the month, Anita took our pages to check them. She'd been away, planning an exhibition in Europe. I got the impression that things were happening now in a way they hadn't before. Before she picked up the pages, she slid a pack of French cigarettes across the table to me. She gave Shelley nothing. Dolores sat watching us, peeling an orange slowly and placing the rinds in the bin. Anita balanced on the edge of my desk.

'It's incoherent,' she said, leafing through the pages. 'Not your fault. I think he wants it that way.'

'It's lively,' Dolores said, 'you can feel it.'

'It's lively and you don't want anything to do with it,' Anita replied. 'Dolores doesn't like the dirty words. That's why she couldn't type this up. She doesn't like filth.'

I felt momentary panic – had I only been drafted in because Dolores didn't want to do it? I looked at Dolores sharply, categorising her faults. There was nothing she could do that I couldn't.

Dolores shrugged. No retort, nothing could ever shake her. She was the most solid person I'd ever known.

'She has ideas about God,' Anita explained.

'It makes me strong,' Dolores smiled tightly.

'It makes you sanctimonious,' Anita smiled back at her. 'I don't care if you're a God botherer. I love you anyway.' Her eye was caught by something on one of my pages. 'No sanctimony here though.'

Dolores's eyes moved across Shelley's manuscript. She flinched. 'No,' she said, finally.

'You're a good speller, Mae,' Anita said. 'Jesus, it's as bad as Henry Miller.'

'Does he work here?' Shelley asked. She didn't help herself. Perhaps she enjoyed playing the part of the uncultured hick for her own amusement. Her sense of humour was bizarre, and she seemed to derive happiness from bothering people in only slight, insignificant ways. Then again, she never tried this with me. She moved stuff carefully around her desk as she waited for an answer. She picked up a pencil and started sharpening it.

'Maybe I should quit,' Anita said, 'maybe it's time I found people more on my level.'

'Poor Anita,' Dolores halved her orange and stared at it contemplatively. 'Poor Anita, she gives too much.'

Anita continued to read. I was nervous: I was finally being evaluated on something I cared about.

'Is Edie on this?' Anita asked.

I saw Shelley stiffen. 'Yeah but I haven't typed her part yet, it's complicated.' Shelley always stressed how nobody but us understood the project. 'What do you care anyway? You're always so horrible about her.'

Anita moved off my desk. 'Grow up, Shelley. There's worse things happening in the world. Read a newspaper, listen to the radio.' She put down the pages and I watched her walk away.

Dolores remained seated, as if in a trance. She gave me a look of incredible understanding. 'Ondine. I don't envy you listening to that all day, Mae.'

He was O on my pages. O was for Ondine, also known as The Pope, and he was the main talker, words tumbling from him in a ceaseless monologue. If I hadn't seen him in the film, a Coke in hand, I'd have thought he was born on the tapes. No family, no history. He existed only to be

recorded. After the second week of nothing but his voice
in my ear, I knew how he finished his sentences. I knew
his favourite curse words, the onsets of his mania, when
he was tightly wound, in a fit of rage. I knew when he
was especially high. I think I knew when he was lying. He
knew a different New York than I did; he walked through
a different city, a city I'd only heard of, seen headlines
about, a city as sharp as a razor blade. He was able to move
seamlessly from red-brick buildings with doormen to the
darkest, filthiest rooms where he fulfilled all his fantasies.
All the girls I knew in school had worked so hard to make
one boy fall in love with them. Make one boy fall in love
with you and then control him forever, that's what we
were taught. That, like everything else, was being revealed
as a big fat lie. Ondine was promiscuous and I loved
to hear him talk. I rewound his tapes several times so I
didn't miss one moment or a single punchline. The sexual
frankness with which he spoke embarrassed me at first. I
felt everyone must know what I spent my days listening
to: Mikey, strangers on the street. Then it started to thrill
me. Everything was more available to him, because he was
brave, selfish and volatile enough to take it. The jangle of
pills being shaken into a hand. The sound of swallowing.
He talked about men the way I'd only heard men talk
about women. He reduced them to parts – how big his
dick was, how tight his ass was. He was not without
his own tenderness. He could be goofy and whimsical, and
he made me giggle. I often typed slowly, with one hand
covering my laughing mouth. Who knew it could be so
much fun? To think I'd looked to my mother's dreary love
life for inspiration. I imagined Daniel from the escalator
looking over my shoulder as I typed, a look of disgust on
his face, but aroused too – of course, aroused. I imagined

Ondine grabbing his hand on the escalator instead, what they would do together as his mother slept. The flippant way O talked about sex made him powerful.

I knew how O would treat a man like Daniel – a person to be used, to be sucked dry, a twenty here, a fifty there, every available free drink that could be placed on a beer mat. To be laughed at too, laugh at his asinine dreams, cut him, flay him with his wit, turn him into a cruel anecdote even when he was sitting opposite him. O was invulnerable. Nothing could touch him, nothing could hurt him. I wanted that for myself. Who wouldn't want that? At the start, I thought his power came from some idea I possessed about coolness, about art, from his irony, from his humour, but after a few hours with the tapes, I knew that his strength came from his willingness to be ugly. How enlivening ugliness was, it cut right through the bullshit. He told me everything and I typed it up as if we had a special connection. By the end of the first week, it felt like friendship.

One Tuesday, in the late afternoon, I turned around and O was across the room. The place was quieter than usual. Sometimes there was a mass exodus for an event Shelley and I weren't told about and we would find ourselves fully alone. Nothing but the steady sound of Shelley's type-writer, the haze of afternoon sunshine. I recognised him straight away from the film, but we also shared a greater intimacy: I'd heard everything he'd done, I felt everything he'd done. Nobody knew him like me. He was dark-haired, louche in a t-shirt and jeans, and I was hypnotised. His skin was pale against the walls, which in the daytime were more grey than silver. The pink of his mouth. It was hard to believe it was the same mouth. I'd just turned off the tape where he was speaking, taken off my headphones, and there he was. He moved like he had something on his mind. I watched him flip through pages on Anita's desk as if searching for something. He moved on to Dolores's desk. He didn't look like a junkie, what everyone called him, but I had no idea what a junkie looked like. He turned up the record player. I didn't want to believe it anyway: I was sure an addict didn't walk with such confidence, I was sure an addict didn't jam their hands in their pockets in that precise way. I was sure of a lot of things. For a second, he stopped searching and stared across the room at Shelley. He was muttering to himself. Even when no one was listening, he was still talking. I could see how he got his nickname, The Pope – even when he was frenzied there was an imperiousness to him, like he could forgive you and it would really mean something because he'd done it all, everything bad that could be done. As if his forgiveness could make you happy and strong. Maybe I was in love with him. I felt something like love towards him. Still, when he turned to face me I could see he was older than the voice I'd been hearing, although only two years had passed between now and the first taping session in '65. He looked like a vital part of his armour had been removed. He raked his hand through his hair, and went back to Anita's drawer. He raised his closed fist in greeting to me and I raised one finger back. When Anita returned later I watched her open the drawer and rifle through it.

'Jesus Christ,' she said.

Andy's voice was on the tapes too. It was the first time I'd really heard him speak. On the tapes, they called him Drella – Cinderella and Dracula. His voice was so quiet and unassuming, I often had to turn up the volume.

Everyone else forgot about the tape recorder, happy to talk about their physical disappointments, to scream, fight, rant about who they wanted to beat up. The point was to forget about the tape recorder. Drella never did. He was the one who was going home with it. I wondered if he put it on the table between himself and O, obvious and unapologetic. Why bother to cover it up? It was the whole reason they were there. Or if he kept it hidden, behind the curtain. His tone betrayed a lack of investment which I believed was faked. Hmmm. Oh, perfect. Noncommittal. His only job was to keep everyone talking. When others drifted in, when the clamour became louder, he seemed to recede even further away. All that talking and I don't think a single person was listening. I guess that's what we were there for.

It was only on the tapes with Ondine that he was enraptured, warmer. There was real affection there, their laughter ugly, coarse and shared. There was excitement too, the excitement of people who thought they were separate from everything else, who had somehow, despite everything, managed to make their own private world. Their conversations reminded me of early times with Maud, tears of laughter streaming down our faces, before things went wrong.

I was possessive of all of O's tapes. I wanted to be alone with him. I wanted to tell him everything, explain how terrible I was capable of being, but there was no evidence that he even knew I was on the other side. Except once. He was lecturing on business, on how to get a reception-ist: 'We've got to find a moron girl for the phone. Luckily, Queens is full of these little girls, just pick out one, drag her here... and she's at the phone.' I didn't feel disre-spected. I just smiled, a broad, moron-girl smile plastered across my face. Here was confirmation that we were better, more important, than Anita and Dolores. Not just anyone could do what we were doing. Any idiot could answer the phone. I wondered how Anita would react, in her Mary Janes, her novels piled on her desk, if she knew they were referring to her like this. It was sad, the gap between what her purpose was and what she thought it was. I felt sorry for her. I did. But Shelley and I had real and rare authority; we had the words we put on the page, the book we made. It wouldn't – it couldn't – happen without us. And we weren't allowed even a moment of illusion. Every day, the tapes made sure of that.

Now, when men in thin jackets with wild, ravenous eyes looked at me on the subway, I met their gaze. My imagination was overpowering. It happened quickly, unexpectedly. In the mornings, I took long, cold showers to avoid speaking to my mother or Mikey. I put my normal school clothes over my dimpled skin. It was a costume now. I don't know whose benefit it was for – my own? It felt like committing to a fiction. A performance I took part in every day. I always changed before I went inside and started typing. I'd begun to feel about typing the way I once felt about the escalators: it was the only thing worth doing. It was going to transport me. When I started my machine, the reels moved like film unspooling. During the day, when I removed my headphones, the only sound I could hear was Shelley clicking her tongue in concentration. I zeroed in on it. That little push against the roof of her mouth. Click, click, click. She was always in side profile: the long curve of her neck, the familiar jut of her jaw, the prissy spring of her curls. I thought about the bones underneath her face. I couldn't help it. I had had these thoughts since I looked at the paintings – that all faces were masks that hid something vicious, unbearable.

One morning when I was running late, I started to get changed in the subway carriage. I was hidden from view except from one man in a raincoat. I took off my sweater and I was just in a vest. I felt no embarrassment. A situation that would have seemed squalid to me only a few months ago now had no effect on me at all. I slid the straps of my vest down until my bra was visible. The man was still, but he looked at me as if he could barely understand me. But he wanted to. His entire life might depend on understanding me. I stared back at him, vibrant, energetic. How much further would I have gone if the train hadn't stopped? I'd have stripped naked in front of him. There was no reason why I wouldn't have done it. When I got off the train, I laughed and laughed and my laughter echoed Ondine's, as if we were in an opera that we were making up as we went along.

Shelley's and my days were full of tasks we had to accomplish, but that wasn't the same for everyone there. The studio was starting to get more and more attention. I'd seen it in a few abandoned papers that I'd picked up. It was no longer mere gossip – it was talked about in conversation in the right circles. It was where you went if you wanted to feel no shame. And people came every day to look, to see what all the fuss was about. I could hear them striding determinedly behind me, observing the place as if it was a circus. They did this under the guise of art, but nobody believed that, least of all themselves. Then they went back to their dinner parties and said that place on East 47th street – well, it wasn't so great. It was full of homosexuals, layabouts, nothing intellectual. But quietly they burned with resentment. The beautiful women, the freedom, the vulgarity of it all. They were pissed off about it. That was their problem.

When Shelley and I went to parties, we danced, our arms frozen above our heads. Our deliberately slow movements, the tiny jerks of our feet and knees were just like how we worked at the typewriters. We were, in comparison to everyone else, thoughtful dancers. Even our dancing was our own little project of two. I took her to Central Park Zoo and showed her the lions, the zebras. When we were walking around, she clung onto me as if she were delicate and weak. This was something she liked to project when we were in the outside world, but it bore no resemblance to the person she was in front of the machine. It was all an act; it reminded me of how Maud wept in front of her father to get what she wanted. I was always disgusted by unconvincing displays of girlishness, probably because I never had a father to perform for. With Shelley it was different: the act was so highly strung, so ridiculous, it just became silly, another one of her nonsense jokes. Besides, it didn't correspond to the way she spoke about herself: with total confidence in our shared future, in our creative gifts. She believed we were engaged in a project of huge importance. We were going places, could I not feel it too? She mocked the actresses who strolled in and out of the studio. It was such a waste, wasn't it, to want something so banal? She mocked the girls from her town who'd married young; she was quite hostile towards them. Her story about leaving home, which she told often, was one of absolute triumph: she alone had done it. I too became more forthright when I was with her. I wanted her to see me the right way, with an ambition as huge and

bottomless as hers. I'd been in that distressing apartment
for so long, I'd forgotten how to want things. Shelley was
teaching me how to remember. We never talked about the
actual content of the tapes because the work had taken
on its own myth in each of our minds. The people on the
tapes were so perfect, so alive, that I didn't want Shelley's
assertions ruining them for me. I wanted all that charming spontaneity for myself, to play again and again.

On a Friday evening late in March, we went for something to eat. We made chit-chat on the way there, paused
and discussed store windows. We sat at the counter. We
already had our routines. Shelley swung herself onto a
green vinyl stool and placed her briefcase beside herself.
She ordered an ice-cream sundae with a cherry on top,
and I had a Coke. I was watching my figure, I said. In
truth, I was broke. There had been no mention of payment
and I'd stolen too many bills from my mother's wallet.
I could only do that for so long. Shelley had dyed her
hair that week, a dark blonde. It was weirdly shaped and
static, and I didn't comment on it. The diner was full –
just babble to a clumsy ear. I knew that with a certain
amount of effort I could discern conversations, sounds,
separate them from the surrounding noise. I was proud
of the intense concentration I had learned over the last
few weeks. The diner seemed grey to me, or maybe that
was just how the outside world felt now. The day-to-day
places of ordinary people in their suits and good dresses
now seemed gutless, mediocre. Situations that were once
adult to me now seemed the opposite. There was life on
the tapes, and it was better than the one everyone else was
living. Privately, I felt superior to every single person in
that room. Maybe Shelley was thinking the same thing.
She had a sweet, dreamy smile affixed to her face. The way

she was looking around the diner: it was as if she expected people to recognise her. She kept moving around in her seat, her hair fluttering into my face. I knew it because I felt it too. It was as if just by listening we had absorbed some of their charisma and now expected heads to turn for us. Turn and look, turn and look. But we were just two girls, one with an unfathomable expression, in an unseasonably heavy green coat. She swallowed some of her sundae and then seemed to forget about it. Her hands shredded a napkin. The pale blue veins, the tiny freckles. Sometimes, I thought I knew Shelley's hands better than I knew my own face.

I didn't feel the same around Shelley as I felt around other people I encountered in the studio. I didn't have the same advantage, the same secret knowledge. She was listening to the tapes too. Besides, I was too fascinated by her. My life had taken a new direction and I had Shelley to thank for it. She had chosen me for the project, after all. Still, I needed to know what she was listening to. It was grotesque, my need. I'd never been good at pretending indifference. She was several taping sessions ahead of me, she'd encountered more hotel rooms, more conversations, new people. I felt this gave her an advantage and it was terrible that I didn't even know what this advantage was, and what it could be used for. Shelley only told you things she wanted you to know; with anything else, she got disagreeable. She sat there, licking ice cream from the back of her hand, like a cat, totally impenetrable.

'Imagine if we were still answering the phone,' I said.

'It's hard to know how Dolores and Anita can be happy with that, in this day and age,' she said. 'Do you want to get a drink? I know a bartender who will serve us. He's made sexual advances towards me.'

'So,' I said 'you're ahead of me. What's on your tapes?'

She looked at me as if seeing me for the first time. 'The Duchess. Brigid.'

I remembered her from the film, a large woman wielding a needle. A wide, frightening mouth. An indefatigable personality. 'What does she talk about?'

'You look crazy,' she said, 'your eyes all rabid like a dog, your hair sticking up. Don't stare at me like that again, Mae. It's Friday evening. Enjoy yourself.'

'You're not being fair.' I sounded whiny, childish.

'Fine. If you must know, it's the same as all the others. Brigid, the way she goes on, you'd swear she was the first ever ugly woman. She's a pioneer,' she laughed meanly. 'She's a good sport. She's sick but it's a joke, ha-ha.'

'A joke?'

'She's in the hospital but it's a lot of fun, I think. It's hard to know what means anything when nobody is being serious. I think they could just have a good time anywhere, you know. Also there's some interference on the tape.'

'What do you write for that?'

'Interference.' She added air quotes.

'No sense in being too creative.'

'Hey, I'm a pro.' She smiled and banged her spoon against the side of her bowl. The crack it made when it collided: even these tiny sounds were becoming more pronounced to me. A flicker of annoyance passed over her face, which she tried to conceal. We were both withholding, but for whose benefit? Her eyes were bleary. She was always at her desk before me. She could have been sleeping there for all I knew. To spend all day listening to the tapes and then go home to nothing. She told me she didn't like her roommates, that they were uncivilised and sloppy. She spent a lot of time sitting on her bed wrapped in a blanket. Her roommates hated her too. To me, all of this sounded incredible – a deteriorating building, rats, roommates that had the energy and time to hate. It sounded like living.

'What's on yours then?' she asked, playfully.

'Ondine,' I said. 'A lot about his ass, his kinks, his difficulties, the drugs he takes. He's pretty amusing when he's not fully out of his mind. A lot of restaurants, girls, movies.' I could hardly believe my own dismissiveness, as if the tapes weren't the most startling thing to ever happen to me. 'It's just talking, so much talking. They love to hear their own voices.'

A waitress came over and asked if we needed anything else. 'You never speak to the waitresses,' Shelley said. 'I had a friend at home and her mother was a waitress. She used to, you know, always talk to them, make them laugh, get to know them. Like the waitresses all over the world were one big, happy family. You don't do that.'

It was a habit I knew I had. I kept my head down when waitresses spoke to me, my eyes averted. I didn't want to see them, and recognise something severe and lost in them I knew from my mother. I realised then that when I'd been watching Shelley she'd been watching me too. I'd become lazy. I looked around the studio, at what I enjoyed, what I was interested in, but Shelley was always observing. She had the innate alertness of the interloper, of the new in town. She was an expert voyeur in a way I could never hope to be.

I took a sip of my Coke and placed it back on the counter. 'They don't like it. The conversation. They just have to act like they do. It wastes their time.'

'Every profession has its secrets. It's fine Mae, I hate my mother too. You don't have to lie. It's important not to lie. You should be comfortable with your true self.'

'—I'

'Do you like this briefcase? It was my dad's. To wake up and find your daughter gone? Pretty bad. But your daughter *and* your briefcase?'

'Why did you leave, Shelley?' I had asked her the same question so many times. She always gave different answers. It had become a sort of game between us.

'Because,' she stuck her spoon in her sundae aggressively, as if marking a spot, 'because I saw a picture of Edie in a magazine. And I couldn't focus on anything else after that. She made life look really something, really magnificent. Also my dad didn't want me around anymore. He didn't even have to say it. A selfish man. Like all of them, huh? That's like a little joke your mother would make to her favourite customers.'

I wondered what Shelley's experiences with men were. Probably nothing much, dirty pictures, Anita's phone-sex tape. But it was easy to picture her, starstruck, doing whatever was asked of her. Sucking someone's dick, sticking her hands down a boy's pants as long as he promised to respect her afterwards, getting pushed around, becoming restless because someone refused to love her. The tapes had firmly planted these ideas in my mind, ideas of humiliation and cruelty. They were making me think it was what some people deserved. When I closed my eyes, films in blue and red, flesh puckered and imperfect, mouths opening and closing, sucking and swallowing, played out on the screens of my eyelids. 'Probably,' I said. 'Probably.'

Nothing could separate me from my typewriter now, not sickness, not exhaustion. My body was lengthening, becoming part of the machine. I knew each individual spring under each key; my life reduced to the alphabet. It was true that I'd been plucked out of nowhere, but it was equally true that I was the only person who could do this. The more time I spent in front of the typewriter, the more I understood Shelley. Anything that threatened my new life had to go. I put further space between Mikey and myself. The fact that we used to be close didn't seem to matter anymore. Shelley was secretive, even with me, removing the sheets from the typewriter and placing them straight into her briefcase. I never even caught a glimpse of her pages. She wouldn't tell me anything about her work and grew annoyed when I asked. So I stopped asking.

I got everything I needed from the tapes anyway. Listening to them was like falling down a trap door. Time was fractured, nonsensical. What a strange world they had made for themselves, full of scorn and rage and competition, with moments of giddiness. I made long lists of names that appeared and memorised those names as if it might be useful for me in the future. I tried to use punctuation and then abandoned it. I made errors, of course I did: many of them. I was writing down the sludge that seeped out of their drug-addled brains late at night. There was not much room for patience. There was not much room for beauty. I had to be quick – I was constantly reminded of this. There was a timeline for the book, which I resented: I watched other young girls lounge around the studio, unbothered by the idea of work, uninterested in any pursuits. Their obscene entitlement. I was constantly aware of my own breathing: ragged, fast, nervous. If Shelley had any doubts about what we were doing, she didn't express it in her efficiency. She never once slowed down. In the beginning, people didn't speak to us because they weren't interested. Now, it was we who were the problem. We had become too remote, focused on the evolving theatre of the people on the tapes. We couldn't have been found even if someone had come look-ing. I was high on how much I knew: every hour people confessed directly into my ears. The truth was I did think these people were special, and listening to the tapes didn't disabuse me of this notion. They were above the law, above the humdrum dailiness of life, above hurt. There were blue days when I felt none of it meant anything, that I could pull the ribbon from each tape, watch the pages disintegrate in my hands. Then there were days when I felt like God.

One April afternoon, I watched as Shelley removed her headphones and stared, defeatedly, in front of her. I'd never seen her stop so abruptly before. Her face was twisted and tired. I slipped off my own headphones. 'You OK?'

She pointed at the window. 'Does that thing open?'

'You can try.'

'No point in trying. Jesus, I can't breathe in here.'

The paint was flaking constantly off every wall. There was no reason in trying to find the source anymore. Girls complained that it ruined their dresses and Anita told them to fuck off then, but she said it in a light way. She was good at that – hating people in a way that kept everyone happy. She was always absurdly nice to me, like how a child might treat a hamster they had just received. 'Nobody but Mae can keep up with me in here,' she declared. She looked ghostly though, the way my mother always did when she was fighting through a love affair. Around us, girls auditioned, changing into lingerie, squeezing their tits, waiting for the recording devices to roll. All time was suspended until they stood in front of the camera. The moment so hotly anticipated. The studio, although it was open-plan, was full of secret pockets, parts I didn't understand. It didn't help my pride that he never acknowledged Shelley or me, not in the same way he did the girls who queued up to be in his movies. Shelley watched these girls, her face exasperated, as if they were a distraction from her work, something she'd return to once she had the time. Those big stars.

Ondine still dominated my tapes, but something had changed. It was to do with how he sounded. I'd always taken special care with his words. Out of everyone, I wanted to get him right; I constantly rewound his sections, looking for inflections, what was hidden. What could I say? It was a demonstration of my love, my dedication. I was more like an actor playing him than someone transcribing him. But the more I listened, the more it seemed like being Ondine was a lot of work. There were new feelings emerging: pain, horror, embarrassment. It was unbelievable to me that he could feel embarrassed, a person for whom there were no effective limits, who could, and did, consume anything. But there were moments when I had to stop the tapes, moments that felt appalling, that shook me awake at night. Stop recording, he said, at first, like it was a joke because everything was a joke. Then, more insistently: stop recording. He asked for that, a great tiredness obviously sweeping over him. I could hear it in his voice: tired of playing himself, moments of paralysing doubt about the point of any of it. Too many substances. But there was never any response from the man holding the tape recorder, and the red recording light stayed on.

There were parties that had no precise beginning or end time. If they hadn't existed, I'd have dreamt them. I came home at three, four, five, didn't come home at all, and my mother screamed with rage. She told me I was a slut, and I told her she was just pissed because I reminded her of her own decrepitude. Where did you even learn to speak like that, she asked in genuine astonishment. I wore miniskirts when I had the courage, tight and emphasising my ass. I got compliments. 'There are men here that are more attractive than you, Shelley,' Anita told Shelley one night. They were always either ignoring, or antagonising each other. Shelley just gave her the finger. I saw my own face up close and, under the lights, I was not disappointed. Could I be fascinating too? I didn't touch anything that was going around. I was frightened; frightened of the prospect of losing even the modicum of control I had. The person I presented myself as at these things: I was seductive, disinterested. The practised disinterest was something I learnt from the tapes. I was fluent in it now. Of course, I'd never known poverty. I was a whole new girl. Shelley and I danced obediently, we danced for hours, as if we stopped, something might devour us. We were not in demand. The usual evening: at the beginning, someone sat beside us on the couch, took a pill, bad-mouthed somebody else, complained about all the dishonesty in the world and didn't ask our names. Then the mornings after: our fuzzy heads as we reached into the box to take another tape, as we placed our headphones over our pounding ears, our eyes stinging as they began their usual spin. On the couch, there would still be one or two people left over from the night before, looking like they had been spat out of a giant mouth.

I only felt alive at these things, when I stood beside the people I'd heard on the tapes. I knew Shelley felt it too. The private nature of what we knew lent even the smallest moments intensity. The Duchess glancing in our direction. Ondine's head in a crowd. His fingernails tapping a glass. Familiar voices overlaying the party, as if we were listening to a tape, as if we weren't even present. Sometimes when I caught Shelley's eye, it felt unbearably intimate, like we were the only people who knew anything in the whole world, and what luck, we had found each other.

One night, we were celebrating. Our successes were obscure to me, but I knew they were happening rapidly. Sometimes there was a limousine now, white and absurd in front of the studio door. We skipped lightly through the streets, as if we owned them, and arrived at a town house. Their successes were our successes too. We really believed that. There were high bookshelves, wooden floors, a chandelier, a long, cavernous hallway, expensive trinkets on the fireplace, paintings I recognised from the studio floor, constantly full wine glasses. A collector. At the door of the building, Anita greeted us, a cigarette extending from her hand as if it was physically attached. 'Fresh air,' she explained.

'You'd make a good doorman, Anita,' Shelley said, 'but could you handle the responsibility after being a secretary?'

'Nah,' Anita said, 'too neurotic to be a doorman.' She smiled in my direction.

I laughed but Shelley simply straightened her dress and walked in. That night, as it was an occasion, Shelley wore a lavender dress that reminded me tragically of pampered mothers, of meanness disguised as generosity, of something unshakeably suburban. She was always peculiar before these events: nervous, discreetly trembling like a volcano before it erupts. Her was hair was cone-shaped and frizzy. It never settled. The style touched me tenderly. It's wrongness moved me. When I tried to run my fingers through it, it was brittle with hairspray. Shelley had her mysterious going-out routines. She didn't seem to notice that every other woman in the room looked completely different to her. She was exactly what they didn't want to look like. Although I, who had seriously weighed these things, comparing our eyes, lips, cheekbones, considered her less beautiful than myself, she had her own charm. All I did now was judge myself, other people. I often tried to point her in the right direction – had she ever tried off-the-shoulder dresses, some jewellery? No, and why should she? I think I wanted there to be some competition between us. To feel anything other than the trance of the tapes, to give these nights more momentum. I wanted to win. I'd learnt from the tapes that there were only winners and losers in life, that somebody else had to be pulled down for you to rise. But Shelley wasn't Maud: she didn't engage in pettiness. She had no interest in it. She took friendship seriously, she took me seriously. Even

in my most ungenerous moments, it was impossible to
consider her the enemy. Despite her oddness, she might
have been the most graceful person in the room. She sat
alone, chain-smoking in her exaggerated way, and people
gravitated towards her. Fringe characters of all descriptions, drunk, high and self-righteous, dribbling on her,
or staring at her with glassy, unseeing eyes. People who
wanted to unload. She represented a safe, loving space
because there was nothing threatening about her. And
she listened intently. She listened as if her life depended
on it. If I was sometimes shocked by what I saw – men
fucking in front of us, girls done up like decorations –
Shelley's face remained still, impassive. And it hadn't even
been that long since she said goodbye to Mom and Pops,
the dreamless girls, the grabby, pimply boys of her small
town. There were times when I thought she might have
been the most brilliant person I'd ever known, because
she understood her role so much better than I did. These
people needed an audience and we were it. They needed
someone to sit and watch them spin out in all different
directions, and wait for them to come back. All the better
if we were efficient and forgiving and invisible.

Recently, I had been on my own mission. Sex was
what I thought about when the sound of the typewriter
stopped. I constantly surprised myself with my drive. At
the start, I looked indignant when anyone tried to cop a
feel. Stop, I said, but my voice was a lie. It was so easy to
let them pick me up, but the trick was to make it seem
hard, so they felt they were getting something worthwhile. Men didn't like naked desire. I wanted to become
sexually experienced in the same way I'd become better at
the tapes. All of it was a process of improvement, all of it
was learning. The act itself, and the fact that I often did

these things in front of crowds of strangers, didn't matter
so much. There had been something horrible about the
way Daniel saw my vulnerabilities – and how swiftly that
allowed him to hurt me. I didn't want it to ever happen
again. I wanted my experiences to be machine-like,
impersonal. Like Ondine, I pledged allegiance to my own
pleasure. 'I'm glad you're having fun,' Shelley said firmly,
as if trying to convince herself too. She was always thoroughly supportive, as if she had read in a magazine that
this was required of her. But behind my flighty actions,
there was the same wretched need I had felt on the escalator: I wanted one of the boys I went with to notice me,
to really see me, realise I was extraordinary, take me away
in a car with tinted windows, to become the wife or girlfriend of someone important, or even just a woman in his
life whose remit was unclear. When the night was over,
when I was back in my bedroom, I felt humiliated, like
a child again. The tapes were right: being ordinary was a
torment. And why did I have this sudden lust for degrading experiences? There was no one reason for it. Maybe I'd
been listening to Ondine for too long. Maybe I'd replaced
my personality with his.

The bright lights of the chandelier showed up what was
wrong with us, the regulars. Our filthy, torn clothes, our
matted hair, their large pupils, their needle marks. The
vastness and wealth of the place made us seem weird, like
a freak show, and I didn't enjoy it. There was always awe
and suspicion when we were brought to places like this.
The boys shifted around uncomfortably, as if they were
only killing time before they'd be dragged out. An impec-
cably dressed couple smiled at us with fondness. We were
self-conscious, like we never were in dirtier places. There
were vast quantities of food and alcohol. As the night went

on, everyone wore the same looks of regret, but none of us knew why. It was an uneasy exchange – had we been fun enough, madcap enough?

That night, I left Shelley alone and wandered around. I wanted to know whose apartment it was. I walked in on a girl who was leaning over a bathtub, her underwear around her ankles. I rifled through the pills in the cabinets. There was a closet with clothes of all different shapes and textures. I thought about stealing something but nothing was cool or modern enough.

The hallway was thick with smoke and bodies, and that's where I met him. He was a visitor, I could tell by his hyperactivity: he had the joyful disposition of someone who had gotten in. He said ridiculous things. I guess, in his excitement, he saw me as a further way to gain entry, to become part of something. Or at least have a story to tell, kissing one of those art girls over on East 47th, something him and his friends could have a long, masturbatory conversation about. I didn't mind. I took his hand as he fired jokes in my direction. He seemed like a liar, his tongue was quick, long and nimble. It had been so long since anyone told me the truth about who they were, I don't think I would have recognised it anyway. We went to a bedroom and laid down on silk sheets. The apartment was familiar to me but, at the same time, sealed off from the world. His mouth was on my ear when he pushed two fingers inside of me. He started saying dirty things, seemingly unconsciously, and I lost myself in those words. I didn't know what to say in return. I wondered how I'd transcribe his staggered breathing. It didn't seem like we were reacting to one another but moving through a series of poses we'd seen before. When we were finished, I lay on the bed, rubbing the silk through my fingers.

Back at the party, he asked me what I did. I said I did a couple of different things. I used to answer the telephone, now I did the typing. He had a large wrinkled forehead and that was what I spoke to. He seemed disappointed that he hadn't captured one of the stars, or even one of the talkers. He stood with his hands clasped as if in a posture of grief.

'But she's very good at typing.' Shelley appeared from nowhere. 'She's really more of a writer.'

Later that night, I watched him leave hand-in-hand with another woman. Maybe he had picked her up after me, or maybe they'd arrived together and she was his wife. Shelley didn't comment. I thought about vicious things I could say about him on the walk to the subway.

We stayed late, stayed after the crowd thinned. Around two in the morning, I found out whose apartment it was. I felt his presence before I saw him. The doctor was standing in the kitchen, in his suit and tie, like he'd just come home from work. I watched him talk to a girl – she was receptive to him – touching his arm. She was looking at him the same way I'd seen them look at Andy: silently asking his permission to do something awful and him saying yes, that's fine, go right ahead. The sight of him conjured the memory of the innocent chatter of the waiting room, a needle piercing skin, his hands forcing themselves down my back. His face was ugly to me now. I didn't know how he hid his ugliness the first time we met. I heard him call my name. He walked over to me and put an arm around my shoulders.

'Mae,' he said, 'you're not returning my calls. Let me make amends, even though I don't know what exactly I'm making amends for.'

I shrugged him off and walked away laughing crazily, as if I were high. These were terms I knew he would accept. You have to meet everyone on their terms. 'No time to chat, Doc,' I shouted back. I didn't want to be in his apartment any longer. Suddenly, I found it disgusting. If I stood there for a second longer, I felt I would be obliterated. Everyone else was smiling at him like he was a teen idol.

I hid under the kitchen table and pulled my knees up to my chest. I wasn't thinking rationally. I was doing things now, not even really of my own volition. After thirty minutes or so, Shelley's wide face appeared through the legs of a chair.

'I was looking for you. What are you doing?'

'Hiding from a pervert.'

'Oh. Will you be doing it for long?'

She crawled in beside me and I whispered, 'Don't say a word.' We watched people's footsteps go by: elegant heels with dirty soles, the occasional bare foot. We sat for an hour communicating in hand gestures. It was a grand adventure. It was being a kid again. Eventually we slithered out on our hands and knees.

'Gimme one second,' I said to Shelley.

I ran back to the wardrobe and took a fur coat. I put it on. I was rescuing it; I was giving it a better home. On the bed, two boys were kissing. I didn't recognise them. In the glow of the lamp, they looked like they belonged in a movie.

Shelley and I emerged on to the street laughing hysterically. There weren't many people remaining when we left. After these things everyone seemed to move on somewhere else but for us there was no somewhere else. When the parties ended, we went home.

On the train, I conjured up horrible memories of the doctor, stuff that had never happened as if to justify my behaviour.

'Who was he?' Shelley asked.

'Just your average jerk.'

Our subway carriage was empty. I didn't have the energy to dissect or strategise with Shelley. She must have felt the same way: she sat opposite me with her head leaning against the metal, and closed her eyes. I still didn't exactly know where she lived. She concealed a lot, but it didn't seem sinister, just another step in her big reinvention. It wouldn't have surprised me if I had found out she'd been sleeping on the trains at night, like so many others. I'd see them in the mornings with rumpled faces, waking up with a brisk, jerking motion, remembering where they were. It was easy to imagine her on a floor too, her balled-up dress underneath her head. She had to be relying on someone, something. All of the trade-offs that happened out of sheer terror, all over this city, all of it unmentionable, under the surface.

'Do you think my clothes are stupid?' she asked me.

I was taken aback. She rarely showed any insecurity, even if I gave her an opening. 'I like how you look. You look put-together. Not like a big mess. There's too much sloppiness these days.' I was, when I wasn't being careful, suddenly my mother.

'Am I wearing too many clothes?'

'No, the other girls just aren't wearing enough.'

'I don't understand the music either.'

'Nobody does. Don't deceive yourself.'

'I guess that apartment belonged to a big shot,' she said. 'Things are changing. Aren't they changing?'

I thought of the limo, the same white as the doctor's coat, its door swinging smoothly open. I shrugged.

'Did you like that guy? The one you went off with?'

'Not particularly,' I said, 'it was just easy.' I pushed the fur up and down on my arm. I was getting used to the idea of being this person. 'Did you find my behaviour outrageous?' I smiled.

'I don't find anything outrageous anymore.' She tapped her head lightly against the metal. 'Nothing outrages me. Did you swallow?'

'No, I had sex with him this time.' I had, up until tonight, been limiting myself to blow jobs. I was an amateur. It made me feel more in control. And I didn't have to take my clothes off. Shelley always asked for the most unnerving, specific details as if conducting a field study.

'You have no plan, a lot of the other girls have a secret plan for the men they sleep with. It's all some big logic or scheme. But I guess they want to be actresses.'

'A plan? Gross,' I said. 'I don't want to be an actress, as you know.' I saluted the sky. 'Somebody has to do the typing.'

She started laughing, and I laughed with her. Both of us laughing and laughing, although I didn't know what the joke was. She didn't say what she'd been doing when I was gone. Shelley often seemed like she had been attending a different party than me. These were not the occasions she thought they were. She was a girl from another time but she'd have been hurt if I'd tried to explain that to her, and I didn't want to hurt her. Everything she knew about sex seemed stolen: Anita's phone call, gossip from girls in school, pages ripped from romance books. I think every party she went to was an attempt to prove something to herself. I often felt her withdraw from me afterwards, as if she had disappointed herself.

'I'm beat,' she said.

'Yeah, me too.'

She smacked her lips together in the matronly way she had. We were not quite sure what to do when the residues of the parties were still on us. The conversation never flowed afterwards, as if we had forgotten who we were. In truth, some of our confidence evaporated when we stood up from the typewriters. No matter what we did at the parties, we couldn't get any closer to the people on the tapes. For several hours a day we had all the power. Then we stepped into the real world and had none. I think Shelley was more sensitive about this than I was. I had grown up here, I knew what it was like to walk by thousands of strangers every day, to take what I wanted. I wasn't inflexible. I had watched my mother: I could use people too. If you didn't have your own private agenda at these parties, you could feel lonely, abandoned. What was special about Shelley? Nothing in the context of the people we listened to every day, not her sense of humour, which wasn't brash or obnoxious enough, not her intelligence. She wasn't a great talker. Everything she valued, everything we both valued. The one thing she had which nobody else did was that she never made me feel like an appendage to her story, the story she told herself. She treated me like I was real. This was an incredibly rare and virtuous quality. When she got on a bus to make herself new, it was the one thing she couldn't shake. I knew she thought it was going to hold her back. Again she was right. It probably would have.

'Tell me about it,' she said, 'tell me about the guy.'

'No, mind your own business.'

'Oh, typical you. You like to listen, you like to look. You don't want to actually talk about anything.'

The stations we passed through were quiet, as if recently shushed, movie ushers patrolling. It was early in the morning and people climbed on, ready for work. I pulled the coat tighter around me.

'You just think you know me so well because you sit next to me every day,' I said.

'I've examined you.'

'And tell me, Shelley, what have you learnt?'

'Less than you think,' she said. 'It's not so easy.'

'Come on, you know me, all the dreadful parts of me. You don't even seem to mind them, really. I think that's what friendship is, knowing each other inside-out, even the rotten stuff, especially the rotten stuff. That's what I can't believe when I'm listening to the tapes, that all these people found each other. How he brought them all together.' I shut out the hiss of Ondine's voice when he begged for the tape recorder to be turned off. 'It's better than romantic love, you know. It's purer because it asks nothing, it's life companionship. They're just together, happy. I think a lot of people look for love like that their whole lives and never find it. So they stop trying.'

Shelley was looking at me like she felt sorry for me. It was the same way I sometimes looked at her, like she was impossibly simple, uncomprehending. Her eyes moved to the window, just past my face. 'What year are you on?'

'Still '65.'

She leaned forward and touched the inside of my wrist. 'You'll see,' she said.

The train shuddered and she stood up. A wall of lavender. I noticed a fading bruise on the inside of her arm. She always got off at different stops. She said she liked to walk, it cleared her head. I didn't want to say goodbye like this. I wanted to be pleasant, easy-going. I strived for pleasantness in all things.

'Any dates this week?' I asked, indulging in one of her fantasies. 'Seeing any friends?'

She drew her coat up to her neck and turned to me. 'You're my only friend in the whole of New York, Mae. I'll see you tomorrow.'

The train doors closed.

When I got home, I ran into my mother on her way to work. She walked by me with total contempt, not saying anything. When she passed me on the stairs, she shouted, 'Your life is never going to work out, Mae.'

'You're such a fucking baby, honestly,' I called back.

The apartment no longer seemed real, only a recon-struction of an apartment, like a place a host would show me around to display how far I'd come in life. The televi-sion was fixed on a sea view, and Mikey sat in front of it. He gestured to me to sit down and I did. The last time we had sat side-by-side was at the movie theatre, and every-thing had changed since then. On screen, perfect blue water lapped in the sunset.

'That woman is destroying me,' I said.

'Me too,' Mikey said. 'Maybe I should have tried that, living beside the sea. It's depressing after a while, this city.'

I felt too exhausted to bring any charm to the conver-sation, the easy rapport between Mikey and I had disappeared. Our discussions amounted to nothing now. His face looked older, and all I felt for him was a limited amount of sympathy. This hopeless man's problems didn't involve me; maybe they never had.

'Nice coat,' he said.

'A friend gave it to me.'

'Nice friend.'

I watched the screen. 'Fish have a lot of dignity,' I said. 'No problems.' A wide-faced fish that reminded me of Shelley pressed itself right up to the camera.

'What problems do you have?' he asked. 'An intelligent girl like yourself?'

'City problems like everyone else.'

He nodded knowledgeably, like he was now back on familiar ground. 'You need to get out. Fresh air. That's why they have parks, green spaces to do your thinking. Make sure you're talking to the right people. Interesting people.'

'Yeah,' I said, 'I take walks.'

In the shower, the water cascaded down on top of me, filling my ears, drowning out every noise, every thought. I watched the water roll off my back, down my legs. It was tranquil. It was a relief. I put the fur coat on and fell asleep.

In the weeks afterwards, there was a change in how I treated the tapes. If you had looked from the outside, you'd have seen no difference. I arrived at the same time every morning, I sat in front of my typewriter as usual, I placed my headphones over my ears, I didn't move for eight hours. The same clang, the keys in the position they always were. The right letters, the right words. The ding of the bell. But because of what Shelley had said, I was deliberately moving more slowly. Our conversation on the train had made me nervous, as if there was something waiting for me on one of these recordings that I didn't want to know about. I told myself that it was carefulness. I spent the longest time pretending to work, and then I had to take a new tape out of the box. Its cold surface, never listened to. It was the worst one, by far. Ondine asking for the tape recorder to be turned off, the nasty things they said which their irreverent tone didn't try and hide this time, the barbs, the limitless savagery, the attention-seeking at a frenzied high. Worst of all – the quivering, fearful pitch of their voices. Some of them were poor, and getting poorer. Some of them depressed, some of them regretting ever setting foot in the studio. They weren't having fun anymore. The tape recorder, always on, always taking and taking and taking. And my job, to record their suffering. I told myself it was only a job. It was only the best thing to ever happen to me.

Shelley was far ahead of me: she was on the second half, the last taping session, recorded earlier that year. This was our agreement. She had given me the easier end of the bargain, but we didn't know it at the time. She hadn't rebelled, she hadn't turned away from the tapes, but there was a new reluctance. One afternoon, I looked across at her, the headphones resting on the table beside her. She was eating a sandwich, carefully removing the lettuce and pickles.

'Mae,' she said, 'do you ever feel like you've made a big mistake?'

'What sort of mistake?' I asked.

She looked at me blankly. 'Got the wrong sandwich.'

There were new people coming in every day, and they were different to the people who made up the tapes in '65. New performers. I could tell by just glancing across the room. They were assured, possessed an unfamiliar intentionality as they stalked across the floorboards. Their desires were straightforward, and their every visit followed the same pattern. They wanted to have their picture taken by him. They always ended up in front of the camera. They weren't needy; many of them were already rich or famous. They didn't want love or affection or healing or conversation. As soon as the camera was turned off, they moved out. They went back to their apartments, their restaurants, their nightclubs, their real lives. They appeared flat to me. They looked unfairly healthy, their trim and perfect bodies in direct competition with the lives I listened to every day. A lot of the people on the tapes were sick. I mean they had their obvious addictions, but they also had hepatitis, rotting limbs, open sores. They discussed them frankly and not without humour. They didn't give their bodies a second thought, actively enjoyed punishing them.

Out of loyalty to people who had no clue who I was, I decided the new people weren't interesting. Their trips to the studio were only about getting somewhere else. They were incurious about us and, in turn, I was incurious about them. I didn't hide it. I stayed plugged in and mostly stared at the wall, even if there was excitement about a certain visitor. Shelley would usually talk afterwards about which one of the famous actresses wasn't all that great. Anita too stared straight ahead. She resented having to go out and fetch things for these visitors, she said she wasn't a fucking receptionist. Outside the window, the sky was terribly bright, summer coming soon. No, the new people weren't my kind. They were too controlled. People whose desires were that naked weren't any fun to figure out. I imagined the tapes they would make. False, pandering recordings to which I'd feel no connection. Tapes about their journeys to fame, the great destinies of their lives. I wouldn't want to hear it.

But it was taking me a long time to uncover what the people on the tapes desired. It took me months. I had to peel back layers and layers of surface. I had to wade through their muck. What did they want? Normal things, as much as they pretended otherwise. Security, dignity. More than anything, they wanted to be loved by the tape, by the man holding the tape recorder. A lot of the old people didn't come around during the day anymore, but there was still the odd straggler, nervously hugging their paintings, their plays; their hair greasy, their faces unbearable. But their wants were drowned out by the new people, and the new people kept arriving.

On the first Friday of May, I stood in the elevator beside Ondine. I shouted at whoever was in there to hold the elevator for me, an uncharacteristic move. I was usually quiet in the studio, talking mostly to Shelley. When I stepped in, he pulled the elevator cage closed in one single, strong movement. It was almost dark and I could only see his side profile. It was astonishing to me how all of this had come together. Someone had fixed the elevator so Ondine and I could stand side-by-side. Someone had arranged the pulleys. Someone had made this machine just for us. He looked fatigued. In person, I wasn't intimidated by him. I wanted to protect him, console him. He was counting a few grubby bills that he'd clearly just stolen from Anita's drawer. When he turned to face me, I couldn't believe how fragile he looked up close.

He waved the money in my direction and said, 'You won't tell anyone, will you?'

I shook my head. It was the only thing he ever said to me. We both got out of the elevator and I watched him walk down the street, still counting.

At dinner, Mikey noticed my hands were red, cut and worn. He picked up my left hand, held it for a minute and then let it fall limply. He picked it up again and I moved it out of his grasp. 'I'll live,' I said. My mother was in a good mood and unusually energetic. I don't know what had prompted these changes. I guessed: a small, inexpensive gift from a guy, a compliment or two, a comparison to a young actress. All the meaning you could conjure from these small gestures. I'd started being like this too. It was an ominous sign. I'd started drinking more from Shelley's flask at the parties. That too was a sign of something but so what? I wasn't thinking a whole lot about my behaviour, or even considering it behaviour. These were just things I was doing.

'That guy called for you again, Mae,' she said. 'He says you stole a coat from him and I said a daughter of mine would do no such thing. We had it out over the phone. Is it true?'

I was wearing the coat. 'No,' I said.

'Tut, tut, tut,' she said, 'it's not good to steal from someone unless it's really funny and they deserve it.'

'What if it's both?'

She rubbed under my chin. It had been so long since she had shown me any affection that the effect was disorienting, shattering. I felt near grateful. 'That's alright then. Under those circumstances, it's allowed.'

It was May and for the first time in a long time, I was jealous of the people on the subway. The first sighting of a summer dress, women discreetly displaying themselves, vacations being discussed at a loud volume, homes on the beach. My secret had, with the last tape, lost some of its allure. It now carried a weight, like I was traversing the city with a weapon. These people no longer seemed dangerous, outlaws, but unstable, and I had to spend all summer with them, in the dusty silver, at my desk. There was a song that I heard constantly on the radio, a banal and cutesy melody that reminded me of Maud. The lyrics were about stolen caresses, a man falling for a sweet, simple girl. That's a song for Maud, I thought every time I heard it. Then, as if I had summoned her, I saw her in a restaurant window. I stopped abruptly. I rapped on the window and she looked up. She sat for a minute smiling at me in a dumb way, but offering no invitation to come inside. She was sitting with three other sweet, simple girls. Was this who had taken my place? Maud explained something to the table, gesticulating, as if she had just seen a distant but troublesome relative. In that moment she looked like she had won, and maybe she had. I was the one standing on the street, tired, hungover, covered in ink and sweat. I watched her fold her napkin for a long time before she stood up. I wondered if she was describing this as 'confronting' me to the table. The thought of giving her that level of satisfaction made me sick. My head was thumping. When she finally stood in front of me on the street, I asked, 'Did you need three different girls to replace me?'

She rolled her eyes, and I followed her inside. I was introduced to each of the girls. I sat down and immediately stood up again.

'I'm sorry, Maud,' I said, with all the authority I could muster. 'It's too bright in this restaurant.' I walked out.

When I relayed this encounter to Shelley, she just said, 'I hate brightly lit restaurants.' In the evenings, Shelley and I went to the movies. We queued around the block. People were impatient to find out who they were, and they wanted the movies to tell them. We sat in the audience and filled our heads with noise. We saw comedies and laughed a lot. We laughed when anyone had bad luck, or got married, which we considered a form of bad luck, imprisonment. 'If I had a husband, I'd shoot him,' Shelley whispered to me once. Her commentary made the movies more varied, because really they were all the same. The music always built before the man and woman kissed. Everyone wanted good things to happen to the really beautiful people. Everyone wanted horrible things to happen to the bad guys, who were always obvious to discern. Afterwards we sat in the park and drank from Shelley's flask. Homeless people asked us for money and we truthfully told them we had none. None, we said, pulling out our pockets. Anita had paid us only twice. 'It would be awful to be like that,' Shelley said when we met someone down on their luck. Her compassion extended in all directions. During these evenings, we often didn't talk for long stretches. We were tired of talking, of listening to talk. Shelley mentioned, casually, that she had lost some interest in the project. It was true that she was at her desk less regularly now. When she did appear, I watched her sit with her headphones on, her eyes closed, examining her fingernails, picking at the hem of her skirt. This is what she must have been like in school – daydreaming, removing herself from her surroundings, flicking through her magazines, and then finally making plans to escape. In the afternoons, she typed slowly, pausing her tape often, taking breaks where she walked around in small circles. Throughout, she talked to herself in a whisper-voice.

I went to parties alone then. Shelley made excuses. I turned eighteen at one, the clock striking midnight, and I prepared myself for something to happen, for them to know somehow. I expected to see Ondine, for the crowd to part. Shelley was right, the parties were changing. There wasn't the same illicit excitement. The apartments were more luxurious now. Expensive rugs on the floor, piles of records, respectable dresses. The atmosphere was brisk, business-like. I felt judged at them, like I hadn't before. I got the feeling I was turning into a faintly ludicrous figure, this little girl that did the typing. I told a passing man that it was my birthday and he patted me compassionately on the shoulder. He slipped me a pill that only increased the chattering in my mind. I went home, feeling jittery and sick. Mikey had left a novel and card on my bed. Shelley left a gift on my desk too, carefully wrapped. It was a silk scarf and when I put it on Anita told me it looked expensive. 'Wow,' Anita said, when she saw me wearing it on the street. 'Who loves you that much?' I put it on every morning. The sight of me in it seemed to bring Shelley pure happiness.

Then, one morning in late May, Shelley was back to her old self, working at a more committed rate than ever. I was given no reason for the immense change. Her back was straight, her face deeply serious. I remembered her locked-in mode, her ability to slip into the tapes. All her cynicism was gone. I knew what she was like in that flow: if they breathed on the tapes, she'd transcribe it. It pained me to think of how good her pages were, how accurate and real and colourful. How she could probably make you feel like you were in the room with them. Whereas I was getting careless and I didn't do anything to stop it. I was still interested in them but something else had crept in: an interest in myself. I put more and more of myself in the book – misspellings, pauses where there weren't any, my own emphasis, my own in-jokes. I had to leave a mark. You couldn't be around egos like that for so long and not develop your own. It was my own performance.

And it was a distraction from what made me uneasy. I'd moved on to 1966, the entire tape set in one apartment. I felt hemmed in, suffocating there quietly, at my desk. Put the mike down, Ondine said, I have a secret. Then later, his familiar voice, a voice I knew better than anyone's: what goes down with the tape recorder is HORRRible. As soon as I heard that, I ripped the headphones from my ears and walked out, as if I'd just developed a conscience. I could feel Anita looking at me. My determined stride, like I was never going to go back. Who was I fooling? Who was this little show of integrity for? As if I hadn't known all along what was happening. Over that week, I made excuses to myself. There was nothing exploitative about it, these people were exhibitionists; if the tape recorder wasn't in front of them they would have found some other way to humiliate themselves. It was stupid of me to have any doubts. It was really pedestrian.

Anita started watching me. It was disconcerting to be the person who was watched. I was used to Shelley and I being in our own intimate corner, where nobody could

access us. Anita was sad now, and her sadness made her
furious. Everyone knew she'd gone to her boyfriend's
apartment in the middle of the night and woken up his
wife. She must have looked like a lunatic standing outside
his window in high suede boots, demanding love. I'm
sure it delighted him to see her so humiliated. Dolores
had to go and drag her into a taxi. She was suffering and
wanted everyone else to suffer too. She put pressure on us
about time. She requested my pages at the end of the day,
making her annoying, little mark-ups. I guess it made her
feel important. We all had to find our own ways to feel
important. 'Good job,' she said to Shelley. She was trying
to play us off one another, a trick I knew from the tapes. I
often caught her looking at me, her legs on her desk, as if
I was a puzzle she was trying to solve. She thought I was
going to do something reckless and foolish. Or maybe it
was only just occurring to her how limited her role was,
and she wanted revenge for it.

One morning I came in and she was sitting at my desk,
listening to a tape, checking it against what I'd typed. It
was bizarre, as if I was witnessing something genuinely
impossible. It was a reminder that I owned nothing:
not the typewriter, not the blank pages, not the chair I
sat on. It could all be taken away at any moment. The
way she waved at me when I walked in might have been
the most obnoxious thing I'd ever seen. She took off my
headphones.

'This isn't right, Mae,' she said. 'They're not an exact
match. What did I tell you at the start? Get it down and
get it right.'

'It must have been quite the exhibition,' I said. I
watched Shelley cover her smiling mouth with her hand.

'What?'

'The scene you put on in the street. I just didn't think
you of all people would want something as conformist as
marriage, Anita.'

She had it in for me then. I could feel her eyes burning
into my back. I wasn't sorry. She'd shit all over my work.
I thought a certain amount of freedom was what it was
all about, but it was only freedom on their terms. I knew
Anita would punish me then. I knew the cycle from the
tapes. Everyone else had been dealt with in one way or
another. I was surprised it had taken so long.

Anita called me over the following morning when I was
on my way to my desk. 'Not today,' she said. Where could
I go but my desk? I could see the back of Shelley's head, as
if from across a distant sea, and I couldn't reach her.

'Do you know where Bloomingdale's is?' Anita asked.
'Your mother ever take you shopping there? I bet she has,
a girl like you who wants the finer things in life.'

I nodded along, yes I knew it, yes I'd been there before.

'There will be an elderly woman waiting for you in the
restaurant. Don't let her leave without buying anything.'

Shelley looked nervous on my behalf. 'I was there once,'
she said, 'and it was a very contemplative and calming
experience, you'll like it.'

'I've been,' I lied.

'And don't mind anything she says, Mae. She drinks.
Your mother drinks too, right? You know the way it is,
how they get. You'll get on like a house on fire.' She picked
up some papers on her desk and turned away from me.

I walked. Then I was standing in front of a window
display: elegant mannequins in New Woman postures,
smoking cigarettes, answering the phone. There was a

mannequin positioned behind a typewriter, but she was
better dressed than I was. Many real-life women stopped
while I was standing there and we all gazed up together
as if looking at a religious display. An appreciative silence,
all of us longing for the exact same thing. When I stepped
inside, I looked at the first price tag I saw. So this was
Anita's idea of punishment – remind me of my own
poverty, don't let me have any ideas about myself, don't
let me have any aspirations. Or maybe it was simpler than
that. Maybe, despite everything, I still looked like I was
good with mothers.

'He sent a child,' the woman said when she saw me. 'He
doesn't have the time to come himself so he sent a child.'

She had a thick accent and even in the busyness of
the restaurant she looked like she inhabited her own
private world. There was a bag of candy on her lap, and
a half-drunk glass of water in front of her. She looked
odd and ridiculous in her surroundings, even though
she'd made a special effort – curled her hair tight, put on
lipstick, had buttoned her blouse up high. The department store didn't just look like it was unfamiliar to her,
it looked like it would be unfamiliar to her imagination.
She clutched at her coat, and I knew she was unwill-
ing to take it off even in the heat. The city didn't want
to watch women like this, it was finished with them. I
went to help her up, and she stopped me. She smiled at
me uncertainly. If I hadn't known who she was, I'd have
walked right by her.

'I'm not a child,' I said. 'I turned eighteen two weeks
ago. My friend Shelley bought me this,' I pulled at the
scarf.

'It's good to have a friend,' she said, rising from her
seat.

People were rude, shoving past her, growing visibly aggrieved at her slow pace, but she did nothing to rectify the situation. She was the first person I'd met in a long time who didn't understand and wield her power. She took my arm on the escalator. Escalators endured, escalators were the same everywhere. They didn't thrill me in the way they used to, they no longer offered the same possibilities. Everything I'd wanted from that time had proved disappointingly easy to reach. We sailed up and down. I felt guilty about something but I didn't know what it was. An unsubstantiated crime. I think it was because of how vulnerable she felt standing beside me, her size, that I walked by women like her every day and didn't think of them once. I considered that my own mother might be as defenceless someday. But my own mother would never treat me so kindly, wouldn't take my arm no matter how weak she was, would never relent.

At the beauty counters, I recognised products from Daniel's mother's bathroom shelf. I watched her take the lipstick she was wearing off with a tissue, and replace it with a bright, pink colour. She took the process extremely seriously. She glided it across her thin lips, the pink settling into the grooves of her mouth. Her giggle was like a little girl's. What was I supposed to do or say? Was I required to give compliments? I considered the possibility that she might report back that I hadn't given enough compliments. I plastered a large smile on my face. I was surprised she spent so long at the counters. The assistants all treated her the same way – brusquely and without affection, as if she were only occupying space. She didn't look wealthy, carried no trace of his status. Her posture was hunched, her breathing was loud, dragging her body around seemed like a torment. Every so often, she reached into her coat pocket, took out a candy and plopped it into her mouth.

She tried on shoes and let the assistants run their hands over her plump purple veins. The assistants looked momentarily sated when she opened her coin purse. She said very little. She was easy company. What a change. Nobody to suck up to, nobody to befriend, nobody to torture.

She tried on two blouses, the second of which provoked hopelessness in her. 'It's ugly,' she said, close to tears. 'It's ugly, like everything in this country.'

'It's not, it's good. Not this country, but the shirt,' I assured her.

She undressed in front of me, outside the changing room, and asked shyly if I was friends with her son. 'Good friends,' I said. I looked at her exposed stomach as I said this, the pale, sagging flesh.

She left with two pairs of flat shoes, the blouse she didn't hate and two cardigans. She clutched the bag containing them. She didn't strike me as at all flippant and they were thoughtful purchases. I wasn't sure how good I was at lying about outfits. They should have sent Shelley, who would have oohed and aaahed in the required places. The place must have seemed overwhelming to her: huge and too hot and full of potential disasters. Before we left, she slipped three dollars into my hand. On impulse, I gave her a hug. All around her, people moved, their coats flapping, with no idea of her life, no idea of who she spent her days with. I watched her depart down the street to her home. She told me I didn't need to go with her. She had a quick pace despite her size. Underneath her pleasure, her face had a permanent mask of fear.

When I returned Anita offered nothing but one of her patronising little smiles. A hair clip had come undone and was stranded in her hair. She looked better undone. That was the way her boyfriend liked to see her – desperate, disorganised. It was, I was learning, fun to watch things fall apart.

All afternoon, after Bloomingdale's, Shelley threw notes on my desk and I ignored them. I didn't want to deal with her good mood. I couldn't shake off the intensity of the morning. I didn't want to be myself, I wanted to be like the women in the store, dignified and distant. Again and again the notes landed on my desk. They were full of questions: What happened? Did you buy anything nice? I answered none of them. 'Shelley,' I turned to her sharply, 'leave me alone.' The second-last note read, 'Cheer up.' The last note asked, 'Do you want to come bowling?' I looked at it for a second too long.

'You do want to come bowling,' Shelley said, triumphantly.

'Where?'

'A bowling alley, you dummy.'

We left our paper in the machines, which was unlike Shelley. He was there when we were leaving, staying late, self-contained, totally detached. I wondered when our work was finished would he think I was intelligent, would he think I was brilliant? Everything I thought about myself, all my self-worth had become tied up in the production of the book. I watched his feet as we pulled the elevator door closed.

The bowling alley was both cosy and brash: a place with a different set of rules, something new to focus on. Of all the places to go to in the city, she always returned to places like this. Shelley's hair was big and it made her face appear tiny and plaintive. She was wearing an ancient floral dress, and her eyes bulged with excitement underneath her glasses. She paid for my shoes, waving her hands in agitation when I took out my purse. She had her own coin purse; she was more like an old woman than any of the girls she aspired to. Her posture was erect and her stare was long: she pretended frivolity, but she was deeply serious. She bent down and tied a precise knot in my laces.

'Big clown shoes,' she said.

'You know me,' I said, 'I'm a big clown girl.' I did a little curtsey.

'They suit you. Cute.'

Every lane was full of screeching competitive boys and the occasional bored-looking girlfriend fiddling with her shirt or sweater. So this was how everyone else had been spending their Friday nights. It was wholesome in a way I was unprepared for. It made me feel there was nothing good about my life anymore, that there was no way to go back to being a simple person with simple desires. Maybe it reminded Shelley of home, although I had no idea what that meant to her. I just had an amalgamation of images – Shelley sitting in a pink bedroom flipping through a magazine, figurines on a mantelpiece, a square school building, sadistic parents, a flash of green, her hair getting pulled in the schoolyard, necking in the back of some guy's car. These ideas were as corny and unimaginative as the ones she probably had about New York.

We picked a lane and watched a boy for a few minutes. He walked out in front of us as if he was on a stage. He caressed the ball tenderly. After he rolled, his eyes seemed to move everywhere at once. He had a thousand eyes. He missed two pins.

'Poor technique,' Shelley said. 'My father used to bowl, not a champion or anything, but good.' She lifted out a red ball. 'He used to take me sometimes.' She staggered down the aisle, weighed down by the ball, her green coat open and flapping behind her. I knew if I'd been watching from afar, I'd have thought that there was something unreasonable about that girl, something unrelenting and dangerous. She hit every single pin and raised her fist in victory. She noted her score.

'It would be nice to go one night without keeping score,' I said.

'You wouldn't say that if you were any good.'

I padded through the aisle. The ball was unnecessarily heavy. It landed with a foreboding thud, wrestled with the pins and flattened two. I refused to be embarrassed. 'This game is provincial,' I said. 'Is this why you left? Because they made you spend your Friday nights doing this?'

She stood up and took the same red ball. 'Nope, I left because none of it felt real to me.' Another perfect strike. 'Did you buy anything nice today?'

'Those places are full of crap.'

'Crap we can't afford,' she said, sighing.

'The crap some people need,' I said, 'it's really pointless, isn't it?' I lit a cigarette and swung my legs up on the table. 'She bought some unbelievably ugly stuff.' I paused. 'I liked her though. She reminded me of you actually.'

'Is she good at bowling too?'

'No, she was buttoned-up.' I stood up and did an imitation, standing stiff and rigid. 'Like this.'

'Is that how you think I am?' She sounded hurt.

'No, no, I'm just joking. She was serene like you, like she's motivated by a higher power.'

'What's my higher power, Mae?'

'The typewriter, of course.' I changed the subject. 'I think they have cats. Her coat was covered in cat hair. I bet their place is dirty, or maybe she cleans it every day, who knows. Boiling, sterilising. His little wifey *and* mother. That's my worst nightmare, cleaning stuff all day. I'd go insane. But she seemed patient.'

'Not the sort of thing your mother would do.'

I snorted. 'My mother only cleans when she's paid to do it. If it wasn't for that, she'd never help anyone.'

'Meow,' she said. 'Do you think she minds that her son fucks men?'

'You know what, Shelley, I didn't ask. Maybe I should have asked when she was trying on a girdle or whatever.'

Shelley laughed. 'Before I came here, I'd never seen two boys together before. And it's simple. Not that other people see it that way. It makes me laugh to think of my parents at home reading all about the depravity in New York and knowing I'm right here in the thick of it.'

I gestured around the bowling alley. 'Not right now obviously.'

'I never contact my parents. I never even think about them anymore,' she said. 'Everyone back home is ignorant.'

She was being surprisingly open, and I was feeling expansive: brought on by the benign lights of the bowling alley, his mother's forgiving expression. I turned to face her. 'You know what you said to me on the train. I know I'm not as far ahead as you, but I know what you mean now. The tapes,' I looked down the aisle to the black hole where the pins disappeared, 'they're horrible. I mean they're really horrible. It makes me nauseous now, the sound of that little machine being turned on.'

'They're not so bad.'

'You've changed your tune.'

'Well,' she said, 'my luck is changing. As soon as you stop wanting something, you get it. Take your shot.'

I stood up and aimed. Only one pin remained.

'Your luck is changing too,' she said, noting my score.

'You know, I think after we've finished, I might move to California. Change of scene.' I hadn't voiced this aloud before.

'Why?'

'Sunshine. The people are well adjusted there.'

'And what?' She grinned wolfishly, 'They're not here? My dad used to bowl in his sleep sometimes, mime all the actions.'

'No they're not well adjusted, of course they aren't. They're all here because their mommies and daddies didn't love them enough.'

'That wasn't my problem. Mine loved me too much.'

She hit another strike. Bang, bang, bang. I looked at all the pins lying desolate on their sides. 'Can we leave?' I asked. 'Because honestly, Shelley, it's scaring the shit out of me how good you are at bowling.'

That night, I came home and climbed into bed beside my mother. It wasn't something I'd done since I had been a child. I had fantasies of a proper reconciliation, of her touching my face, looking at me lovingly, like his mother had done in Bloomingdale's. She would finally understand me. I now had my own taste for maximum drama; I don't think it even occurred to me to think about what she might want. I stood on the threshold of her bedroom and willed myself in. My mother was unknowable to me in many ways – sometimes I felt no attachment to her, she could have been any woman trying on gloves, any pinched-face

on a park bench. Other times, my craving for her was as
deep and insatiable as a baby's. She'd fallen asleep with her
lamp on. Her bedroom had the familiar smell of grease
and lavender, which she dabbed on her wrists before she
slept. She had her minor luxuries. Her waitressing uniform
was on a hanger, alert and white and sentient, as if it could
decide its fate without my mother inside it. It was easy to
be sentimental about her as she slept, her mouth hanging
loose and open. If you couldn't love someone while they
were sleeping, you couldn't love them at all. I climbed in
beside her and pulled the sheets over us. I cuddled into her
clammy back. 'Mae,' she said, confused, her voice muffled
by sleep, 'go away.' 'Go away,' she said, again. 'Don't come
into my room, go away, go away,' she roared. She hit me
gently with her fists. I stood up and looked at her neutrally,
as if my calm demeanour only showed how crazy she really
was. I didn't have to love her. I didn't have to live in an
apartment with cheap linoleum. There was still hope for
me. 'Fine,' I said, 'I'll go away.'

I didn't take long packing a bag. There wasn't much I
wanted to bring. I took the fur coat, one or two summer
dresses, books Mikey had given me. I sat on the couch for
a long time, as if waiting for somebody to ask me to stay,
but Mikey wasn't there and my mother didn't budge from
her room. I wanted to remember every detail about that
night – the night I made a decision. Now, I'd be the same
as any runaway, the same as Shelley, except I promised
myself that no matter what happened, I'd remain strong.
Even if the surface was chaotic, underneath I'd be intact.
I didn't leave a note for Mikey.

I knew where I'd sleep. I'd caught people sleeping there
before, curled into balls or sprawled out on the couch. I'd

patiently shaken a man awake in the toilet before. 'She needs to pee,' Shelley had said to his limp body, 'she's *working*.' Every memory of my life before this moment was warm and bright and enveloping to me now: it was my life when it had some kind of order, before I became an adult. The train was full of drunk couples and it smelled foul. I watched a girl sitting happily on her boyfriend's lap, and I wanted to do something violent to her, punish her for her happiness, rip her eyes out. It was silly of me to be jealous, but I was. I had nothing. Maybe everyone deserved what happened to them in this life. That included me.

I expected it to be dark, nothing happening, because it was after twelve and I hadn't heard of anything planned. But when I pulled open the elevator door, I was struck by a blinding light. They were filming. I hadn't been around for much of the filming, but I'd heard stories. Anita said you always knew when a movie had been made because the studio was disgusting the next day: trash abandoned, the furniture rearranged, a lingering atmosphere. I put my bag down and moved closer. In front of a screen, sitting on a high stool was Shelley. The light gave her a saintly glow. She was eating from a bowl of ice cream, the strands occasionally landing in the glass dish. She was doing a curious thing: taking a scoop of ice cream, then looking up at the camera with her eyes looking huge and affected, pausing and then repeating the process. It was one of her uncanny seduction techniques. She didn't resemble the girl I'd seen only a few hours before. It was worse than anything I'd seen in my life, because she didn't belong there. She belonged with me, behind the typewriters. All this time, she'd been harbouring the same dreams as everyone else, lying awake at night, fervently wanting to be in front

of the camera, the rest of her life just a waiting room.
Was her whole act for me alone? Here was this woman
whose intelligence and dedication I was so impressed by.
This was the life I'd been trying to live up to. I felt both
betrayed and embarrassed. Her sitting on that stool was
worse than anything I'd ever imagined. It was all wrong.
She was strange on camera and not in a way I'd knew
they'd appreciate. She broke the spell by asking should she
take off her cardigan. The only sound in the room was her
spoon hitting the bowl: I wasn't breathing. The ice cream
was chocolate. When she removed her cardigan, I saw her
arms were covered in scratches.

I didn't need to ask why she'd done this. This was how
they had got her to stay, this was how they convinced her
to finish the tapes, a job she knew better than anyone.
She was needed, but not in the way she wanted to be.
Her audition, her eventual triumph over everything, her
past, her parents, those know-nothing girls at home. But
around her, the people watching made a mockery of her
longing. I saw a woman giggle, like the situation was
absurd. It made me feel ashamed that I was friends with
her, and I felt terrible for even thinking that. But no, I
wanted to say, you don't know her at all. She couldn't see
me because the light was in her eyes. Don't look at her,
I thought, don't look. God, don't look. Then a voice I
didn't recognise started asking her questions. I knew all
the voices – how didn't I know this one? It was low and
serious. Wasn't she a good girl? Wasn't she having a good
time? I watched her nod shyly, as if made self-conscious
by the extra attention. She was totally unfamiliar with
getting what she wanted. She looked out of frame for
a second, as if seeking assistance, was there anyone she
could call? The voice continued. Did she like to take her

clothes off? Did she not like to? Was she dumb? Was she frigid? I knew she felt cornered, pinned by the camera. Did her mommy and daddy put their loving hands on her and tell her she was beautiful? Why did she leave them? Was it because she thought she was better than them? Her face held a new hurt when her parents were mentioned. This was the bargain; if she wanted the spotlight she had to reveal everything. The camera, the tape recorder: it needed proof of desire.

I was paralysed. In another life, I would have grabbed her by the arm and we would have left. But I was incapable of moving even my hands. I stood in the darkness and watched her answer question after question. Her eating alone at a lunch table in the cafeteria, the hatred of her classmates, her walking down a country road, the life she didn't want to acknowledge. She said stuff about her father, his rolled-up shirt sleeves, his adoring little kisses on her forehead. How her unhappy mother had disappeared in front of her eyes. She loved her, she repeated that. She'd do anything, *anything*, for her. The silence in between each question and her answer was a pit that I felt I could tumble into endlessly. I watched her slip out of her dress. I watched her take it, withstand it all. She only asked one question: What do you want from me? I could have protected her. I could have stepped forward and turned off the camera. What would happen to me then? No more tapes, no more life, no more purpose. I was a coward: that's who I was. All this time I'd been wondering. I could have ended her suffering, but I just picked up my bag and walked out. On the street, I was dizzy. I told myself that nothing of any consequence was happening. I could do that easily. I had no problem lying to myself in that way. I kept walking. It was still cold, then. For summer.

It was July, and people were adjusting. I wanted my life as a runaway to be less revolting, less distressing. What did I expect? A series of lit candles in charmingly ramshackle rooms? Instead, I stayed in the studio a lot, listening to the tapes as late as I could. I'd drifted further into their world so I didn't have to deal with my own. Even the most degrading moments on the tapes now seemed natural, expected. And their lives were still more real to me than anyone I encountered. I began to resent that. I started to live my life at a higher speed, as if to compete with them. At night, I stayed with boys I met at parties, relying on generosity, a pretend coolness, good humour, luck. I don't think I left an impression on any of them but they were thrilled by my work, by my proximity to a life they wanted to be a part of, the novel I was writing. The rooms where we slept were often curtain-less, and the sun always rose in a disconcerting way, in a way that made everything funny. The boys fed me peach yoghurt they had stolen from supermarkets, and I got them to dispassionately evaluate my looks. It didn't matter what they said. I forgave them anyway. The guilt I felt since that night with Shelley didn't go away. It didn't even abate. I'd failed her, and now I had nightmares where she scratched herself with a razor blade in a dirty kitchen, others where she was lit only by a single spotlight. Since that night, I'd not felt clean or good. One morning I awoke to find a woman sitting on the edge of the mattress beside a man I'd slept with a few hours earlier. 'I'm his wife,' she said. She was nonchalant about it in a way that was entirely unconvincing. Eventually, she locked herself in the bathroom. I was finally part of my generation. I knocked on the door until she came out.

'You should call the cops on me,' I said.

'Why?'

'I don't know?' I said. 'For everything?'

It was in these boys' looks and lifestyles that I really saw the effect of *their* influence on the city – the leather, the smirks, the quiet aggression, the amused and cynical attitudes. All of it was second-hand. It was a way of being Ondine without being Ondine. You didn't have to actually be a maniac, you could just wear the clothes. Even when I left the studio now, there was no way out. I was watching one of these boys get dressed in the morning, propped up on my elbows, like I was back in the zoo with Shelley, observing. He was lacing up his dirty boots.

'Why are you looking at me like that?' he asked.

'You remind me of someone.'

My days were grubby, but not exciting. I dimly knew it was unsustainable. Everything I did, I expected to be refused. In a way, I wanted to be refused. For an adult to wag their finger, tell me I was a child, do their duty. But where were the adults? They couldn't be found. They weren't even identifiable anymore. The city was controlled by children. So I kept going and going. I caught the odd look of concern from Anita and Dolores.

I didn't tell them about Shelley's audition. I didn't tell them anything. My life had become a sort of endless comedy, and I think it was because I really hated myself. It was moving into late summer, and the men on the street catcalled openly. They catcalled with concentration. Nothing was demeaning anymore, nothing was pathetic: it was all open expression. My mind, already disciplined from the tapes, never flashed to Mikey or my mother. I sold the doctor's fur coat. Never mind, I told myself, pocketing the money. It was never mine in the first place. I needed money. I'd gotten money before by crying but now people seemed prepared for my tears. They didn't have the same effect. I refused to sell Shelley's scarf, even when sellers expressed interest. 'No,' I said, 'it was a gift.'

Shelley stayed by my side, her face not even resembling the girl I had seen that night, in the darkness. The morning after the audition, I came in and she was at her desk, in a turquoise t-shirt I'd never seen before, taking almonds from a bag and eating them slowly. She sat upright in her chair, writing in a black notebook. If her humiliation weighed on her, there was no evidence of it. When I sat down, she looked inordinately pleased to see me. 'Mae,' she said, as if I was all she'd been waiting for, as if I could rescue her. Well, I'd already proved I couldn't do that. I spoke to her in a new voice, softer, as if she might break. She hadn't seen me in the shadows. Everything I knew felt unfair, unearned. I waited for a sign that she was going to share it with me, but it never arrived. At the end of the day, I told her I'd left home.

'Ran away, what a ridiculous phrase,' I said. 'I walked away. Out the front door. Nothing is that hard.'

'No, nothing is,' she said. 'Of course, it isn't.'

For the weeks after, she escaped me. She never socialised. She looked lost, flailing. She joked about her insomnia, she joked about everything, her self-deprecating smile. 'Oh Mae, this work will kill me,' she said, but she was still vigorous. I guess she was upholding her end of the bargain, the audition, no matter how hideous, in return for the tapes. And what was I getting? Nothing. Rather, I had something to prove. I guess I saw myself as a writer now. That was the way I carried myself when I was out in the world. We often were the only people in there. There was no air conditioning so people migrated to the fire escape, or didn't come in at all. Around us, pictures were sold and replaced, even as he appeared less and less, commitments taking him away. The phone rang constantly with another invitation and another and another. I overheard Dolores telling Anita that Edie had been brought to an institution. Anita nodded at this information, but didn't move her lips. Nervous breakdown, overdose, suicide attempt, hospital, panicked, uptight parents returning. This news was always secretly celebrated, because if it happened to someone else that day it meant it wouldn't happen to you. They were defiant in the face of death. Death would always happen to other people. The silver flakes fell like snow to the ground. There was talk of moving to a new building when he got back. All that summer, the atmosphere was relentlessly sloppy, like someone's parents had gone out of town.

We knew we wouldn't be going with them. We were nearing the end. Every day, I lifted the tape box and it was lighter. Tape fourteen, tape fifteen. I took tape eighteen. Shelley took the final session, the one Ondine had come back to do, recorded the previous May. 'I'll take this,' she said, when I put my hand on it, as if she was executing an act of mercy. Then, no matter how slowly we worked, there would be nothing left for us to do. No machine to turn on, nothing to listen to, no confessions to hear. These people would go on living with no idea we had created them. What kind of work would we find after this? It must have crossed Shelley's mind too that when the last tape ended, so would our lives. Then again, maybe hers already had.

On a whim, I went to my mother's diner. My excuse was that it was air-conditioned. I wanted her to see how well it was all going for me, how I'd freed myself in a way that she was incapable of. The worse it got, the more pressure I felt I was under, the better I wanted it all to look. I tried calling home once or twice, standing on the street, holding the phone receiver. But I didn't like myself in those moments: there was something off about the image. I always put the receiver down before dialling the number. I preferred the company of strangers now to people who actually knew me. But I had woken up that morning, and decided it was a good day to tell my mother something about herself. That she was afraid of life, afraid of her own mind. She'd always be alone. She'd always be a minor romance in the lives of these men she brought home. I wanted to deliver a sermon. And I wanted a milkshake.

I arranged myself at the counter as if posing for a photo. The place was full of women I knew from growing up, women well versed in the language of hardship and work. I knew the clench of their jaws when dealing with customers, I knew their revulsion at the food they served. There were new girls I didn't recognise, young, maybe one or two years older than me, modern, their hair dishevelled, the job and the customers only tolerated in service of their night lives. They were willing to let the city exhaust them. I imagined their diaries, where they recorded every detail, because this was it, this was their lives starting. I knew my mother clucked over these girls. She considered them her very good friends: girls who she saw fleetingly when their shifts changed. I wondered if they pitied her. My mother had never done anything else. It was possible that she would want to be buried in her uniform, the top button undone to get better tips. That was the sort of joke she would appreciate, and I wanted to make it to her, make her laugh. I swivelled around in the stool, offered an inscrutable smile to the diners.

'Mae.' Rita, the oldest waitress, who I'd known since I was a baby, poured me a cup of coffee. She grabbed at my cheek. 'Your mother isn't here. Are you feeling better now? She told me you weren't going to school and were hanging around with some freaks.'

I smiled sweetly. 'I'm never going back to that bitch.'

'Hey,' she said, laughing, 'my own daughter used to say the same thing.' She came back and left a milkshake in front of me, my favourite. I stared at my two drinks. A single red cherry floated in the cream like a swimmer on its back. When I went to pay, she stopped me. 'Your mother is right about something,' she said, 'you were the cutest baby I ever saw.' I started sucking down the milkshake quickly through a straw. I thought about leaving. It was a mistake to come at all. When I looked across the counter, I saw Mikey. Gradually, with what seemed like painful slowness, he raised his coffee cup in my direction. I saw he was wearing a new jacket, leather and too small on him. I felt a rush of happiness when he came and sat beside me. I didn't look up. I wanted to feel his shape next to me, without having to speak. We sat facing forward as if at a secret assignation. On the walls of the diner were portraits of singers and actors, and I looked at them until my brain dissolved into their perfect, bland faces. Mikey's coffee cup left a faint impression on the counter. He stuck a finger into my milkshake and swallowed.

'Nice jacket,' I said. 'It's too small on you though.'

'Oh no, I'll have to be very careful in it.'

'Where did you get it?'

He smiled. 'Oh, just one of the shops.'

I shrugged. I knew my face was unreadable. He ordered another coffee with sugar, and took a sip: the smack of his lips, the ripple of his exhale. I wanted to record this moment with him, play it back later at my desk. The rustle of his cigarettes, his coffee cup hitting the counter, the fading screech of taxies, the spiky comebacks of the waitresses, the slogans of the city uttered by everyone daily, hourly, everyone trying to prove themselves, every private, hidden moment played just for me.

'Your mother misses you,' he said.

'Yeah, right.'

'She does. She plays all these songs that remind her of you.'

'And drinks. And feels sorry for herself. Nothing to do with me.'

'Where have you been?'

I turned to face him. 'Been around. Experiencing life.'

'And what's it like?'

'It's alright,' I said.

'Not in my experience. What are you doing every day? Going to the movies?'

I laid my hands flat on the counter. 'Typing.'

'Are they paying you?' He fumbled with his lighter. 'Or are they paying you in experiences?'

'Bit of both.'

He took a single drag. 'They better be some good experiences.'

'Why is everything a trade-off for you?' I pulled a face. 'Don't be cynical, Mikey.'

'Don't be a tourist, Mae.'

'That's not very nice,' I said. He looked at me directly. His face was soft, creased and slack. If a fight dispersed Mikey's face was the one you'd expect to see on the ground. 'I was wondering when I'd see you again. I kept thinking different men were you on the street.' I laughed. 'Less intelligent men, of course.'

'Of course. Well here I am.' He lit another cigarette off his own and passed it to me. 'What do you type?'

'You disapprove.'

'I disapprove of all work.'

I sat up straight. 'Typist is more of a word. I'm really more of a writer.' I paused. 'There are these tapes and I take dictation, but I've a lot of control too. It's me and my friend, Shelley. Friends, parties, open discussions. It's good work. And it's going to be a book.' I looked away. 'You should meet Shelley, you'd like her.'

'Are you ever going to speak to your mother again?' He exhaled smoke out the left side of his mouth.

'Probably not.'

'She's ruined my life more than yours.'

'Let's not be competitive about it,' I said, and patted his hand.

'So what happens,' he asked, 'you write up the tapes and what – they take you to parties and things, it makes you feel important?'

'It's not the money,' I said, my voice cracking a little. 'I'd do it for free.' I wanted to tell him everything. How nauseous I felt when I was listening, that it felt like my life had been reduced to nothing but the tapes, that I no longer recognised the sound of my own voice. I wanted to tell him about Shelley's audition, about how they had laughed at her, reduced her life to nothing, Shelley's hands on the typewriter, how she hit every single bowling pin, her blank, thoughtless face as she typed. Ondine's voice. But I didn't know how to say any of it.

'Who is on these tapes?' he asked.

'Friends, people like that.'

'Recording your friends.' He leaned back. 'That doesn't sound like writing, Mae. It's eavesdropping. It's surveillance.'

'Wow you really care,' I said. 'Look at you, the family man without a family.'

He flinched. 'I just didn't think you would be interested in stuff like that.'

'Interested in what? Meeting people? Having fun? Improving myself? Getting out of our shithole of an apartment?' I raised my voice. Other diners were looking, but pretending not to. I was making a scene. Any remaining warmth I felt towards Mikey evaporated. 'I should go.'

'Wait,' he said, taking off the jacket, exposing his round stomach. 'This is for you.'

'How did you know I'd come here?'

He laughed. 'You forget how well I know you.'

I stubbed out my cigarette. 'You should leave her too, Mikey. There's nothing left to do. You think you can save her? That's such horseshit. She'll never love you. She'll never even *try*.'

He handed me the jacket. 'For when it gets cold.'

I took it. 'You act like she was the only person I was staying for,' he said.

I grabbed his shoulder as I stood up. 'What do you want me to do?' I asked.

'Whatever you want to do, Mae.'

I turned away first. I left him sitting at the counter. Outside, through the window, he didn't look like anyone, he didn't even look like Mikey. From this distance it was easy to convince myself that I didn't know him at all. I gave a perfunctory wave goodbye. He was any man, drinking coffee alone.

Shelley was avoiding me. She was still there, at the perimeter of my vision. When I spoke to her, she met my eye. But there was something gone about her, something precious missing. The summer was ending. The music had stopped: no more records. I gathered my pages together, and it required a deftness the work hadn't previously needed. The shock of the material had disappeared. It was only my spine pressed against the back of my chair, sixty words a minute, the last of the summer sun hitting my face. I was past the point of even registering what I was typing. But it had shape now. I'd given them that – they'd given me life and I'd given the book shape. At the end of the night, I played one of Ondine's early tapes on repeat. I liked the flavour of it, it was like eating a familiar and comforting treat. One line I played over and over again, like it was holy, like he was offering himself up: my last words are Andy Warhol.

Sometimes, I looked at Shelley and I hated her. If I hated her, it made everything easier. How could I stay here, after seeing that display? But an ordinary life was now unimaginable. She'd robbed me of my dream too,

my desire to be part of something bigger than myself, all
for her own vanity. It was her audition that was grotesque,
not the people surrounding us. I felt violently towards
her. Then she would smile sadly, pathetically at me, and
I would ache with longing for our friendship, for the
person she'd once been. For the person she'd been trying
to become. I offered to take her out one evening to the
tea-room where we'd first gone together. I thought it
would jolt some happy memory for her. She sat opposite
me. She looked, for the first time, unprecise, careless, like
she'd gotten dressed in a hurry. She looked bleak.

'How's your life as a runaway?' she asked me.

'OK,' I said, 'a little lonely, if truth be told.' I could still
tell her anything, even if she didn't feel the same way. 'Are
you OK?'

'My nerves are gone. Something my mother used to
say.'

'Not much time left.'

She nodded. 'Are you still thinking of going to
California, off to do something different and important?'
she asked.

'Aren't we already doing something different and
important?'

I still believed in it. I couldn't have kept doing it if I
didn't. I couldn't have turned on the machine, I couldn't
have kept writing down every word they said. All that
effort, all that time. You couldn't persuade me it wasn't
worth something. I thought she felt it too. I thought that
was the unspoken agreement between us.

'Sure,' she said, stiffly. 'Hey,' she said, brightening, 'will
you telephone me when you leave?'

'You'll have to give me your number.'

'Gee,' she said, affecting his voice, 'my number, oh my.' In that moment, she was herself again. She glanced away, at the clock on the wall. 'Do you know, I auditioned for them.'

A pause. 'Were you good?'

'I was great.'

'I bet you were.'

'But I might not have the right look for their pictures.'

'It's a specific look.' I didn't want to have this conversation, I couldn't have it. I laughed. I had to maintain a lightness. 'Typing not enough for you anymore? I thought you were on my side. The two biggest artists New York has ever seen.'

She looked out the window. She stared for a long time, as if seeing nothing, as if the city itself were empty. 'Mae, do you think your name is going to be on this book? It's going to come out and it won't be your name on the cover and it won't be mine either. Do you know what the cover will say? I think you do.'

I didn't speak.

'There's a tape I want you to listen to,' she said. 'I'm tired. I get so tired these days.' She stood up and put some money on the table. 'I left it on your desk.'

When I got out of the elevator, he was the only one there, across the room, blasting rock music. There was an obvious gulf between us, but here we both were, alone together for the first time ever, two workaholics. Shelley's words rewound in my head. It didn't take me long to find what she'd left on my desk. The tape was placed on top of a pile of papers. I put it in the machine. I fiddled with the knobs

and felt a profound sensation of relaxation at the familiarity of the activity. Putting on my headphones was now
a reflex, something I'd done every day for the last six
months, the action never making a lasting impression. I
could, despite the content of the tapes, sleepwalk through
them. Maybe I'd become immune to people falling apart.
Maybe my heart was freezing over. The tape hissed. And
then it started. There was more static than on a lot of the
other tapes, which meant it was older, from 1965. I took
the sheet off my typewriter but I didn't press a single key.
It started with a giggle. I knew it to be Edie's. Edie and
Ondine, but he was talking less for once. She was dissatisfied. She was wasting her life. I drummed a pen against
the desk. Nothing new: the usual desperation. She wanted
to work, she liked to work, she really liked to work. She
was living in the present anyway, unlike a lot of people.
She was talking frankly, too frankly, like a madwoman
you'd turn away from on the subway. She was not living a
fantasy, she was living in the present, she had a lot to look
forward to. I thought of her in the institution now; they
said she'd lost all her fur coats. It had become a bit of a
joke. I pressed the pen into my forehead until it pinched
my skin. We're being overheard, lover, Ondine reminded
her of the tape recorder, which was always on, always in
the room with them. She told Ondine that Drella was
probably right, right to live the way he did, right to leave
people behind, dispose of them. But what if you couldn't
do it? What if you couldn't forget them? It couldn't be
the only way to live: she couldn't forget the people she
left behind. I scratched at the skin on my thighs where
my skirt had ridden up. It was her voice, her sadness was
maybe idiotic, but real. It was the voice of someone who
knew they were finished; nobody had use for them any

longer. She couldn't go on talking like this, someone had
to stop her. I didn't know how Shelley had typed this up,
but then again – I did. The sense of humiliation reminded
me of the audition. I felt mortified that this conversation was even available for me to listen to. Ondine said
there was no way of saving someone who likes to watch
people being degraded. This was a different side to him
than what I knew. He was trying to comfort her. Kinder,
patient, a friend. He wasn't performing in any way. The
tape ended abruptly and I turned it over. Moonlight came
through the window. More heavy static. Then Ondine
saying to Drella that Edie should get off the Nembutals,
get off all drugs, get some help, get more sleep. She needed
to be looked after. All the friendly chatter had tapered off.
Andy said nothing, nothing at all, noises of acknowledge-
ment that someone was speaking to him, breathing. I let
the tape play for a minute but there was nothing else. I
rewound it but didn't pick up my headphones. He was
still there behind me, in the studio. When I finally put
the headphones back on, Edie's voice was in my ear again,
saying: it's just that there are not many, they're not many
people who are special.

What would I be like when I was finished? My rages would magically vanish, horrible memories would be pushed below the surface. There would be other exciting people to introduce myself to, a climb over a bridge to witness a new and stunning vista. The tapes had hollowed me out and when they were finished, there would be nothing left of me at all. I had to abandon myself to them; it hurt less than when I thought about them. I was working straight through the day. I barely ate, their voices my only nourishment, my scrawl in my notebook, my fingers not making even the slightest error. Then, at the end of the night, I'd walk, hunched in dry, heaving heat, to an apartment to do anything as long as it didn't involve talking, The streets were wild, overrun by children making children's decisions. All reason had gone. I'll let you do anything you like, lecture at me, but please, please don't make me speak. There were other stray people hanging around, lost in their own confusion, as if looking for someone to tell them what to do, looking for their right and proper owner.

I never told Shelley I had listened to the Edie tape. I couldn't admit it. I could pretend the tape and the audition

never happened. I could pretend anything I liked. Why
not? That's what everyone else did. I wanted to be as far
away from the truth as possible, so I just rewound the
tape and placed it back on her desk.

I wasn't snooping when I found it. I was looking for
notes on an earlier tape on Shelley's desk. But the line
between what belonged to me and what belonged to
others was now permanently blurred. She should have
closed her drawer. The letter was sticking out of her black
notebook, and had an address on it which I presumed
to be her parents. I held the envelope in my hands for a
few seconds before I opened it. I felt no burning shame.
I thought I owned a part of Shelley in the same way I
thought I owned a part of Ondine. Why couldn't I have all
of them? I wanted to know how she spoke to her parents.
It was an extension of the tapes. How she described the
place where we spent our days, how it would sound read
aloud in her mother's kitchen. Didn't I have the right to
know everything? Hadn't I earned it? I briefly saw her face
as she sat on the stool, in front of the camera: demolished,
obliterated. The letter was folded into neat, vertical lines.
I unfolded it easily, as if it belonged to me. I wondered if
she believed it when she typed it. I wondered if the act of
typing made her believe it, and if that was the point.

*I'm sorry for the time in between these letters. I've been
leaving it too long, but you're not to worry when I'm slow.
Bloomingdale's has been busy. You should see the women who
come in here: they're rich and helpless. I know you'd like to see
what they're wearing. They have me do everything for them:
all they do is smile. I have to put on their gloves for them. The
manager says I'm patient (I've good genes). I get an employee
discount which I've been told is better than most places. I buy
a skirt or a blouse every month. There is a scarf I'm hesitating*

over. I try to look neat, but it's hard when the city is so dirty. If you saw me from far away, if you saw me stepping off an escalator before a shift, you could mistake me for any young woman, even one who is from here. Everything here looks like a film, and it reminds me of our Saturday afternoons together at the matinees. There is so much happening under the surface of the department store, I don't know how to start explaining it. I try to think happy thoughts. Happy, happy. I can hardly bear this heat. I wish you were here all the time. I'm sorry I left you alone and I know your days can't be easy. Don't resent me for it. I thought I'd have a lot of friends here, but there aren't many people I can talk to. I've enclosed $20. Don't think this is a burden on me. I earn good money in the store. I think about you every day. I love you and miss you, your daughter Shelley.

So she lied to her mother? That didn't bother me. It was the tone I couldn't stand. As if she wasn't here, as if she was floating away: writing this as her legs kicked desperately beneath water. Denying everything. So she was lying to her mother, so she was different than she pretended to be inside the studio. Big deal. As if there wasn't a person here who wasn't different than they pretended to be. And yet, I think I felt the same as she did when she listened to the Edie tape: the person I looked up to had never existed at all. The strangest thing in the letter was the longing in it. It wasn't for the department store or her mother. There was a longing to go back, back to the person she'd been before. I placed the notebook in the drawer and closed it. I arranged everything the way it had been arranged.

At the end of August, my choices dwindled to almost nothing. For too long I thought that being in this world, being in this city, I'd have nothing but choices – but I didn't. This realisation came later to me than it probably had to Shelley. I didn't know what her choices were, same as mine maybe. Where to sleep, where to get a drink, where to brush your teeth, where to find someone you could tolerate for an evening. The choices of everyone on the tapes were shrinking as well. Where to score, what party to go to, how to find someone that would tolerate them for an evening, how to keep going, how not to end up alone at the end of the night. Any environment could become tiny, suffocating. I'd been stupid, I knew that. A mist had cleared and now nothing looked right. After Shelley had pointed out whose name was going to be on the book, the work was transfigured. I felt foolish. It was transfigured before she even finished the sentence. I'd put myself in a position where this was all I had: no friends, no family, no one to call on the phone. The idea that I once had, the thought I was contributing – when the book appeared, there would be nothing of me or Shelley in it. It would be scrubbed clean. The knowledge of that, the knowledge of what I'd given

up, made me want to lie down, exhausted, on the silver
floor. The prospect of success, the possibility that I could
have become known through these typewritten pages: it
now seemed like an obscene, perverted dream that I could
never relay aloud. What terrified me was the thought that
there wouldn't be anything of them in the book either, just
flashes, just impressions. I didn't say this to anyone – who
was there to say it to? I still listened. My loyalty was now
only to the tapes. I was there, ready and waiting, for them
to crucify themselves. There was nothing left to do but
finish. I needed to finish.

I told Anita we wanted a raise.

Her face was sullen. 'You wanted to do this, didn't you?'

'Yeah and now I want a raise.'

She reached into her drawer and took out an envelope.
'It's not too late to go home, Mae.'

'Easy for you to say.' I took the money.

On my second-to-last tape Drella addressed us directly.
It was the first time anyone acknowledged that Shelley
and I were there. It was as if his voice came from nowhere,
it was as if it came from the sky. God himself, the great
designer. Despite everything, it was still a thrill. He knew
we were hearing every word. He was relying on it. I looked
at Shelley but she couldn't hear what I was hearing. I could
imagine him leaning into the microphone: 'I'm speaking
to the girls. This Voice is the Voice of your Mayor.' Then
the conversation turned to something else. Our Mayor. It
was a break in reality, it was a plane crashing to earth.
It didn't change a single thing.

I wanted to tell Shelley about this but, after that day, I
didn't see her for nearly a week. I couldn't believe she would
leave me at such a crucial moment. I was encountering

one practical problem: Shelley carried more than half the book with her in her briefcase. There was no amount of work I could do to replace it. Wandering around the city, carefree, with all those confessions in her hands. She could leave the briefcase in a taxi, watch the pages floating in a pond. She could just not come back. I told myself she could probably do it to them, but I didn't think she was capable of doing it to me.

One night, I was working late, reading over the chaos of my pages, when Anita gestured me over. She held out the phone receiver: a call for me. I'd never received a call there before. Before I pressed it to my ear, I asked myself, who did I really want it to be at the end of the line? Mikey murmuring into the mouthpiece, telling me to come home. Someone to have found me, confirmation that someone had been looking.

I breathed into the receiver. After a second, I said, 'Hello.'

It was Shelley.

'Come and see me,' she said. She gave me an address and hung up.

It was September and it had rained. By the time I got to her place my feet were soaked in my thin shoes. Every day, there were little reminders that my life was unsustainable, that it couldn't continue. Street light glimmered and moved in the puddles. I pressed the bell. This didn't look like a neighbourhood where girls lived with roommates. The building was ancient, uptight-seeming. The streets were full of people engaged in quiet, pleasant activity. I couldn't imagine Shelley coming back here every evening. She probably knew I'd been looking at her, thinking what a poor little girl, taking solace in the fact that she was worse off than me. She wasn't a fool. She might have found it funny. She had a puzzling sense of humour. Just as I was about to press the bell a second time, she answered. She was in one of her old-fashioned dresses, a blue thing with pleats. Her face was pale.

'Welcome,' she said.

She led me up to three flights of stairs to an apartment that was three times the size of my mother's. I let out a low whistle, but she didn't hear me. A record was playing. A long couch, a well-stocked kitchen, pristine spines of books, velvet throws, circular mirrors, high-quality furniture. Everything was spotless and cream. It was orderly, uncluttered and didn't look like a space that three women would share. I'd seen so many recognisable and stunning faces, I'd seen so many beautiful rooms. No sight awed me as much as this one. So much for the life of the runaway. I knew, without her telling me, that this was what she'd been returning to every night: safety, luxury. And here I was, with holes in my shoes and the water creeping in. I touched a candlestick on top of the fireplace. I would have liked to hurl it at her.

'Make yourself comfortable,' she said.

'How could you not?' I took off my coat. 'Are your roommates here?'

'Take off your shoes.'

'No thanks, I won't get them back on, I'm having shoe problems.'

'Shoe problems?'

'The icing on the cake of all the other problems.'

She laughed. 'Would you like a drink?'

'Just coffee. I've a lot of work to do when I get back.'

'Suit yourself,' she said. We were in her kitchen. She turned her back to me and I saw her reach for a bottle of gin, heard the clink of ice.

'Glad to see you've been keeping yourself occupied. While you've been away pretending to be Elizabeth Taylor, I told Anita we wanted a raise and we got one,' I said, triumphantly.

She didn't say anything, but she sat opposite me at the table. Shelley wasn't a great beauty, not by the standards they'd set out, but there had once been something electrifying in her gaze. Now, that had faded and she only resembled an apparition of a girl I'd once met. The room felt still and empty, as if we weren't even in it. When I leaned backwards, my chair scraped the floor.

'There's a cat around here,' she said, 'sometimes.'

'Oh, good.'

'Did you miss me?'

'You have more than half the book, Shelley.'

'I asked if you missed *me*.'

'Don't be needy,' I said. 'Of course, I missed you. Who wouldn't?'

'Plenty of people,' she said. 'Are you happy?'

'What sort of idiot question is that?' I was irritated. 'What do you mean? I'm basically homeless, my shoes are falling apart, I have to finish the book. I'm not totally jumping with joy.'

'But you have moments of happiness?'

'Sure.'

She smiled in a nasty way. 'And they're all at the typewriter.'

'Some are with you, and yeah some are at the typewriter.'

She took a long drink. 'Do you ever feel like no one is listening to you? In the studios, in those rooms. I felt like nobody could hear a word I said, as if there was some physical block between us. It all became babble. In the end, the only voices that were distinct were the ones on the tapes.'

'That's parties,' I said, coldly. 'That's parties every-where.' My hands were gripping the mug. 'I read your letter to your mother.'

'That was private, Mae.'

'Don't exaggerate, it was a letter. Like you haven't done worse. Anyway, it was sweet. Does your mother like the movies?'

A black cat strode in, its tail high, and jumped up on Shelley's lap. She rubbed behind its ears as it dopily kneaded her upper thighs. 'Yeah,' she said, 'we used to go together.'

'Watch, that thing might scratch you,' I said, 'and I hate blood.'

'He hasn't yet.'

'Anyway,' I said, 'you should have told your mother what we do.'

'Why?'

'Because it's more, you know,' I grasped for the word, 'exciting.'

Behind us, the music rose and fell. It was full of vital-ity and spoke of enlivening experiences. I could imagine Shelley listening to it in her suburban bedroom, her hair plaited, her tongue stuck in the corner of her mouth as she ripped out pictures from magazines, her real life in those pages, waiting to be found and lived. I leaned forward to pet the cat. Before I reached her, Shelley grabbed my wrist and held it tight. 'You know the work we do is nothing, right? It's a big fat nothing. I know you know it too. I'm embarrassed by it.'

I shook my wrist free. 'Where is the bathroom?' I asked.

She pointed me in the direction of an en suite. I walked into the bedroom and closed the door. The bed had a soft pink comforter. The sight of the double bed was world-altering. I knocked on the headboard. I sat for a moment, my knees pulled up to my chest. I saw a pair of man's slippers, a few shirts hanging in a half-closed wardrobe, lint rising and falling on the carpet. He was much older, I could tell by the shape of his clothes, the lines and colours. There were no photos of him but I could guess who he was: a replacement for her father, richer, and tricked by her princess act. His little pet. He hardly knew her. I wasn't too keen to find out what he looked like. I smelled a wool sweater that lay on the back of a chair, and I started laughing, like the betrayal was too huge and in its hugeness it was funny. I started laughing like a maniac. All of Shelley's talk about freedom and she'd been lying in this pink bed, staring up at this ceiling, every night: it was preposterous. I screamed into one of the pillows. The bathroom wasn't as clean as the bedroom, as if the cleaner had become annoyed at the task. Plastic shower curtain, the odd mouldy tile, anonymous, with an occasional trace of Shelley – a jar of cold cream, a large pink bar of soap. I saw a bottle of aftershave, two toothbrushes. I put the blue toothbrush in my mouth and moved it around. I looked at myself in the mirror and spat. My reflection was twitchy and terrified.

I walked out. 'Who does the cleaning in this place?'

She looked up in surprise at the question. 'I do.'

'Should have known. You're not great at finishing jobs. Have you lived here long? I mean is it someone else's apartment and you stay?'

'So what if it is?'

'Is everything you say and do a fucking lie, Shelley?'

She shrugged and bent closer to the cat, whispering in his ear. I couldn't explain what I felt let down by. The bland domesticity of it, the ugly framed photos of landscapes, the classy furniture, the drinks cabinet, the godawful bedspread. I thought Shelley's life was strange but dazzling, an experiment, more liberated than mine. She was the one who made everything seem possible. It was the force of her belief. I searched for something to say, something cruel and effective.

'The art on the walls is so boring.'

She gave me a weak smile. 'Isn't it?'

'Must be a rich guy. Is that how you were able to afford my scarf? At least I got something out of it. I'm not judging, live however you want. Did you meet him at one of the parties?'

She shook her head.

'Is he fun? Do you have a fun time together?'

She lifted the cat off her lap. 'I don't think I know how.'

'Know how to what?'

'Have fun.'

I picked up my jacket. 'Don't be so hard on yourself.'

She laughed again, and took a sip, her mouth barely touching the glass. 'You of all people must think that I deserve to be punished. Then you get to be the best typist. You get to win.'

'I don't care about that anymore.'

'Sure you don't.' Her mouth wore a horrible grin. 'I was punished though. You saw that.'

'—Shelley.'

'I mean I'd have preferred if it was less public.' She wrapped her arms around herself. 'I thought if I got a part in one of the movies, it would fix everything, fix me. They were laughing at me, Mae.'

I pulled my jacket across my body for warmth. She knew I'd been there. Her face looked waxy underneath the kitchen light.

'Well, it doesn't matter,' she said. 'I've been hurt so much it doesn't even matter anymore.'

'That's Drella,' I said quietly. 'He says that in one of the later taping sessions.'

'Such a good little typist. I think this world can turn you into a real monster. I mean you have to turn into a monster to get what you want. Did you listen to that tape I left you?'

I nodded.

'Before I came here, I didn't have a single friend. I know you had that girl, Minnie.'

'Maud,' I corrected her. 'It doesn't matter.'

'And in those first few weeks, listening, in the beginning, I thought this is what friendship is, this is what it's really about. I wanted to be a part of it. But towards the end the voices… I didn't even recognise them as human. I kept thinking if something bad happened, they wouldn't stop, they wouldn't even try and stop, they'd just keep talking.'

'That's not—'

'—Yes, it is. It's true. Why can't you admit it? I couldn't listen to them anymore. I tried to be indifferent, but I couldn't hear myself think.' She rested her forehead in her hands. 'I couldn't think, not my own thoughts. Just whatever garbage I took in day after day from them. You have to know what that's like.'

'You're being emotional,' I said, as if I was disgusted, and perhaps I was. 'So the audition was a bust. Who cares. Is this about Edie?'

She stood up abruptly and disappeared into the bedroom. When she came back, she had something in her hands. Her face was angled away from me. She put it on the kitchen table and backed away. I turned it over.

It was a broken tape, she had ripped out its insides, dug her fingernails underneath the plastic and left long black ribbons unspooling. I put my hands on the table and leant forwards. I felt, unexpectedly, sick. Already my mind was engaged in various mental calculations.

I faked calm. 'What was on it?'

'Nothing. Not much. Street sounds.'

'Why did you do it?'

She looked back at me, her face self-satisfied. 'Maybe because I wanted to.'

'Right.'

'Because I wanted to break something.'

I said nothing.

'It's better than spitting in his face,' she said.

'Not really.'

I poked at it with my finger. It was a broken cassette, it was like any piece of junk I'd seen abandoned on the sidewalk, but it swam in front of me, lost all meaning. It was the premeditation: she'd figured out exactly how to hurt him and she'd done it cleanly and without remorse. She'd attacked his work. But she'd hurt me too, whether she intended to or not. She was sitting down again, the light from the bedroom illuminating her back. I thought of the cracking noise when she hit every bowling pin. Her precise fingers on the typewriter. Her stuffy dresses, her vanity, her giggling and cowering like a little girl. It was in her the whole time. I think even she was scared of the violence she was capable of.

'You're upset,' she said, in a sing-song voice.

'No, not entirely.' I turned what remained of the tape over. I'd never listened to it and I felt a loss. I held the black ribbon between my fingers. 'What was on this, Shelley?'

'I don't know, somebody gets a cab, someone else says something hilarious, hahaha. It's all filthy and candid, the usual, a good time is had by all, nothing we haven't heard before.'

'What was on it?' I insisted.

'I already told you – street sounds.' She reached for the bottle of gin and poured herself another large dollop. She sat up straighter.

'I've reason not to believe you,' I said.

'He won't remember you, Mae, if this is what it's all about. He won't remember me either for what it's worth. We won't leave a legacy, either of us. We'll grow up and no one will remember we were there.' There was a real viciousness to her now. 'Drag any little girl up from Queens, watch her become a typist. How could you be so naïve?'

The record had stopped without either of us noticing. I could hear her breathing now, the shuffle of her feet on the linoleum. She turned the glass several times in her hands, as if examining it. 'You probably think I'm pathetic,' she said. 'Coming here, wanting to be on screen, not getting anything I wanted. And now I can't go home. I won't go home, Shelley. Even here in this apartment is better than that. I won't ever go back.'

I was still clutching my jacket. 'A lot of people don't get anything they want,' I said.

'What do you think will happen to me now?' she asked. 'Will I get fired? Will they put me in a movie and throw insults at me? Will I turn into a psychotic bag lady who attacks people in the park? Do you think he'll ruin my life?' She was smiling but I could sense a genuine fear.

I finally put my jacket on and wiped my clammy hands on the front of my blouse. 'I can't say what will happen to anyone. You know, I gave up stuff to be there too. You're not the only one. We all made sacrifices.'

'Of course you did,' she said, 'that's the whole point.'

'It's raining,' I pointed out the window. There was nothing else left to say.

'It doesn't rain in California. When are you going?'

I was staring at the entrails of the tape on the table, its guts spread and rearranged.

'Take it,' she said, 'I know you want to.'

I swept it into my bag, without looking at her.

'It's just if it's not fully complete, I won't get paid. And I don't know about you,' I said, pointedly, 'but I need the money.'

'You think it's about money,' she said, sadly. I thought she might cry, and I wasn't going to comfort her. I wasn't going to walk across the kitchen floor. I wouldn't bridge that gulf between us. 'And maybe it is, but the man I live with here, he looks at me like I'm not real, like I'm a fantasy. He's the only person who's ever done that. That's what it's about.'

'You could have tried to live your own life.'

'I did try,' she said.

I closed my eyes. 'Bye, Shelley.'

I ran down the three flights of stairs. Outside, the rain was coming down in sheets. She knew I'd do this. It was as much a test of me as it was of him. I kept running, my feet hitting puddles, water streaming down my face. She'd knew I'd leave and try and fix it, go back to the studio, get down on my hands and knees, bend myself into all sorts of positions, stay there for hours, days if necessary, debase myself for reasons I couldn't explain, for people who wouldn't remember my name, emerge into the morning light, defeated, made incoherent by my own obsession.

I was back at that familiar door. I took off my shoes. It was open; it was always open then. My feet hurt and my hair dripped water all over the desk. I emptied out my bag. The tape was dead, inert. There was no reviving it. I wondered if, by some miracle, I got it working, if I placed it into the player and I put my headphones over my ears, what would I hear? A part of me envied Shelley her moment of destruction. It must have been so satisfying to do it. The silence, at last, must have been astonishing. I sat there for several hours. People came and went. Dolores shouted at me across the room at one point, asked me how I was, what was keeping me in so late.

'Nothing,' I replied, 'the weather.'

I didn't expect to see her again. In my mind, she lived permanently in that kitchen and what happened there would be the end of us. I told myself I didn't give a damn, but our friendship played like a film reel in my mind. I began to listen to her tapes, began to type them up, as if the book could still be saved. Then, one Monday, she was back, marking up her pages, putting them in order. She moved leisurely, in no particular hurry. The sound of her briefcase clicking open was ominous. I'd already begun to grieve for her, so seeing her was like the dead reappearing. The dead walking in and beginning to type. The dead with a silly ribbon in her hair. The dead choosing an unhappy life in order to escape another unhappy life: that was no choice at all. I couldn't dislike her; I just felt sorry for her. We nodded at each other as if we were strangers, as if were just two people gliding by each other on the street. I wasn't, by then, capable of deeper conversation. Our typing was finished. My life had no particular destination. The city itself seemed rotten, blasted open, as if the summer had been an earthquake that had left only devastation. The bleached-out light in the boys' bedrooms had begun to make me feel very far away from myself. The people in the cafés wore evil looks as if they knew something I didn't. Men loomed over me on the subway. Without the book, I was alone and growing paranoid. Without the buffer of the tapes between me and the world, I despised myself. In truth, I wanted to know what was on that tape but I resigned myself to the fact that I never would. The thing that was meant to save me hadn't saved me at all. But that happened every day. That was nothing mysterious.

Every morning, Shelley came in and sat at her desk for the full eight hours. Her old ambition had returned; I could sense her steeliness. She was impervious, she was a wall. She made a special effort, as if that could deflect her pain. Her teeth and eyes were bright, her hair back to its natural brunette, her lipstick neatly applied. All of this seemed calculated. She was getting ready for her unmasking. I wondered, when confronted about the missing tape, if she would cry or confess. I didn't want to see her humiliated. My instinct for that had gone. If anything, I wanted to find out who she was.

I handed back the box of tapes. Shelley and I put together the book, my half and her half, amiably, as if we had never done anything else. We were just two colleagues: she was unrepentant and I was unavailable, only the surface of myself in the studio, the rest hidden, tucked away. When we handed it in, Anita congratulated us and expressed surprise that we had actually done it. If Anita knew anything about Shelley's audition, what she went through, she never showed it. I wondered how she maintained the strength for everyone's duplicity, for these power grabs. I made my face pleasant, as if I was receiving a medal at school.

'I knew we would,' I said. 'Eventually.' Shelley was standing so close to me, I could feel the wool of her sweater rubbing against my arm.

I think we would have possibly gotten away with it if Shelley hadn't been the person she was.

'Hey,' Anita said, stopping both of us before we stepped into the elevator one evening, 'Can I have your help with something?' It was night-time and the place was nearly deserted, except for us three and him. Plans were in motion to move, but to where they weren't particularly sure. They weren't sure; there was this option, there was that option. Uptown, to reflect the new clientele. On Anita's desk there were some cigarette butts, a novel open to a page with markings on it, notebooks with names and numbers written down: all of it reminded me of my first day. I don't think things had gotten better for Anita, her own private disaster playing quietly alongside ours. She had upended the box.

'There's one missing,' she said.

Shelley beside me was practising her surprise, a thoughtful creasing of the forehead. She was being so obvious. This was her only revenge, and she was shaking. If she was afraid of being excommunicated I no longer was. What good was any of it to me now? I'd reached the limits of myself, my desire. The book would come out, that was all that mattered. That was all I wanted. And I wanted Shelley to leave with some dignity. Whenever I doubted my decision, I thought of her sitting on the stool in her underwear, the camera fixed on her disbelieving face as she talked about her mother, her father, the life she couldn't possibly go on living. I hadn't saved her before, so I tried again: I knew the lie was the only one that would work, the only one he might allow.

'My mother,' I said to Anita, 'before I moved out, I mean this was part of the reason I moved out, she found one of the tapes, she's really crazy. Anyway she listened and she destroyed it.'

'Destroyed it?'

'Yeah, she couldn't take the obscenities.' I gritted my teeth. The lie hurt more when I spoke it aloud. 'The language, she had a problem with people speaking so freely. But she just does things, insane things, when she's drinking without really knowing why she does them.'

Shelley turned and looked at me.

'I've stopped longing for a loving mother,' I said. 'Hey, there's no point. You get what you get in this life.' I put my hands in my jeans pockets. 'I'm sorry but it wasn't a good tape anyway, all the good stuff is on the pages we've given you.'

Anita stared at me a for a long time. 'OK.'

'Don't hate her for it.' I meant it.

I watched when Anita told him. He was across the room in black pants and a crumpled t-shirt. During the conversation, he stepped back, his palms up as if he were being threatened. I tried to summon the contempt Shelley had for him, but found I couldn't. Anita moved closer, as if to cover him, protect him, stand between me and him. I couldn't hear what she said. His jaw did all his feeling for him. He looked so ordinary. All the energy expended to try and figure him out, all the conversations in cabs, all the language, the tangled-up tape – and for what? I watched him listen. I watched him turn his back.

It was understood that I wouldn't be back. We weren't given any final payment. When I started packing up so did Shelley, as if my dismissal was all she'd been waiting for. I covered the typewriter with the sheet. I took a long last look, knowing there was no reason: it would all be rearranged in my memory. The tapes were left in their box, their voices rewound and undisturbed, waiting to be played, waiting to be unspooled. When we were in the elevator, Shelley said, 'Thank you, Mae.' It was dark so I couldn't see her face. And that was it. There was no narrative to live inside anymore, no lives to pretend to be a part of.

On the street, we walked for a while. Outside a store-front, she stopped and said, 'Do you want to know something? I'm not even that good of a typist. I'm pretty slow. I make a lot of mistakes.'

I laughed. 'Is that right?'

She pulled my jacket up on my shoulders. It was the one Mikey had given me. 'I think you're really strong, Mae. You're not like me.' She pressed one hand to my face. 'You act like you want to please people but I don't think you want to at all. It makes me very proud that I knew someone like you, even for a little while.'

We stood together for a moment, waiting. It couldn't end like this. I wouldn't let it. I looked from the grey of her eyes to the whites, I really looked, until she turned and became a hunched figure in a green coat, navigating the traffic, joining the crowd.

I got another job. I tried to do secretarial work, but I couldn't wear the skirt and blouse combo. The music in the department stores where I went to buy these plain outfits was unbearable. I couldn't pretend to be interested in what the other girls were saying. I couldn't type up the banalities. I was afraid then – afraid of my new desk, afraid of the typewriter. I was afraid of what my life was going to become. I started to see the same fear on every stranger's face.

I lasted one week and then I got a job at a movie theatre instead, taking money, handing out tickets. When the owner told me they showed a certain type of movie at night, I enquired about what happened in these movies. He said that if it made me uncomfortable, I didn't have to take the job, if I thought it was sleazy, a lot of girls didn't like that.

'No,' I said. 'What happens in these pictures? Tell me exactly.'

I started on a Saturday night. My customers were mostly male. They smiled at me hopefully, and then emerged from the theatre several hours later, performatively shaking their heads, gazing at me as if I could reform them. I can't say any of it bothered me. I got to watch all the shows for free, day and night, the lights lowering, the breeze cool, like I was sitting in front of the sea. I let the images wash over me. I moved into a building with other girls. I finally had roommates. I didn't go out much. I liked to watch the light move across the living-room floor. Winter, spring, summer again. I kept expecting Shelley to turn up, press her face to the glass of the ticket booth. In the dark, I thought I felt Mikey's elbow beside mine. It was the summer of 1968 and I was the loneliest I'd ever been. Those hours in the dark of a movie theatre were my only reward.

They were in the movies too. If not physically present, they were in every sex scene, in every second of furtive excitement, every dark and seedy backroom. In the most powerful moments, they were there. Everyone was copying them and hoping they wouldn't notice. It was hard for me to believe their lives hadn't stopped when I stopped listening. It was exceptionally hard for me to believe that. I'd heard some things. The machine was accelerating,

more European exhibitions, endless work and still: parties,
travelling in packs, diagnosing their sicknesses and neuro-
sis, waiting for him to cure them. Still shaping the city.
I wondered when the web that connected me to them
would disintegrate. I wondered if it ever would.

When I heard, I was getting ready for a night working alone, a prospect that made me slightly nervous. It
was summer and we were busy. I'd started wearing short
t-shirts, cut-offs, clothes that I'd paid for. A regular – a
man who usually seemed reasonable but who occasionally had weird, dissatisfied energy – told me. A lot of the
city had dissatisfied energy then. The decade was coming
to a close and nothing had turned out like we thought
it would. He leant against the glass and announced it. I
was counting money. It was all over the news, had I not
heard? He could die, he probably would, Andy Warhol,
two shots, the regular said, before asking for a ticket for
whatever was showing.

'How can you go to the movies at a time like this?' I
asked.

A pause. 'Something to do.'

I monitored the aftermath. The next day, I bought
every paper. My first instinct made me realise the extent of
my devotion – I needed to know if the tape recorder had
captured it. The gunshot, the crack, bullet piercing skin.
And then him, all cut up, being moved to a place where
nobody understood him, the astringent smell, the lights
being turned out in the hospital at night, the long road
back to the studio. I felt closer to him than in any of the
rooms we'd been in together. The pitch of our terror must
have been deafening. I imagine it could be heard all over
the city, in every moving crowd, on every street corner. I
was sentimental the day after it happened. I cried at all

the sad movies. I wanted to stop mothers in the street, I wanted to call my own mother. I finally had some feeling for him and all he had to do was get shot. That struck me as amazingly funny, and I laughed to myself alone in the ticket booth. I laughed so much I shook.

When I saw a picture of the woman who did it, I expected to recognise her, a face from a party, but I didn't. I know she wouldn't have recognised me either. I might have seen her once but she didn't register with me in those rooms. You had to be special to register in those rooms. I searched every paper for Ondine's name, but didn't find it. They lined up to condemn her, to distance themselves from her. What they didn't say was that they understood it too. They understood it when she said he had too much control over my life. Everything they said about her. Well, they had to. They had to make her strange, because it could have been any one of them. Shelley could have done it, but she wouldn't have missed, those typing fingers nimble and sure. Still, this unpleasantness must have been better. It must have been better because what would have been left otherwise? Ten years later, they'd meet on the street, all that talk, and then nothing, how are you, fine, how are you, weather is good, weather is bad, nothing to say. Nothing to say after all that talk. They must have been grateful to her, grateful that she ended that period of their lives with a big, big bang. Wasn't she an ugly woman? Wasn't she dangerous? Imagine how unhappy you'd have to be to do something like that? That was what you heard everywhere that summer. That was what you heard if you weren't listening closely.

After it happened, I got worse. I had thoughts like – I should jump off the Brooklyn Bridge. My face was harsh

and regulars shied away from me. Films became delu-
sional. I thought about smashing the theatre's projector
with a hammer. I didn't want these ideas transmitted to
anyone else. They were troubling ideas, ideas that made
people like Shelley hope. I imagined my mother seeing
me holding a hammer over my head and thinking yes,
that's right, that's how I expected things to go for her.

Anita found me. She was waiting outside the ticket
booth in the middle of a cloudless August day. It didn't
ease my sense of paranoia. They'd been watching me
the whole time. They'd been destroying my life from the
inside. If I allowed my mind to run away with itself it
was always Ondine who found me. He would bring me
on an adventure through the city, into the parts I could
never know, reward me for being the only person who saw
him, who knew him deep down. It was inconceivable the
stuff I came up with. It was quite embarrassing. Anita was
probably the person I wanted to see least and she carried
herself like she knew. She was in a short red dress and
looked hollowed out. She no longer had her professional
sheen. I knew she had thought about what to wear to see
me, and it reminded me how I'd once, painfully, done the
same for her.

'Welcome to my home,' I said, opening my arms wide in
front of the ticket booth. 'It's small and has no furniture.'

She asked me to go for a drink with her when my shift
ended, and I had no reason to say no. I finished early
that day.

We went to a bar with closed, dirty windows and men
whose long moustaches trailed into their drinks. The place
was silent. We took a booth down the back.

I was calm and faintly amused. I was a mechanical
version of my old self. Nothing I did would have betrayed

the fact that I was constantly close to crying, that nothing good in life seemed reachable or attainable anymore. She slid a folder towards me. I didn't open it. I took a sip of my beer.

'This tastes like mop water,' I said, turning the label to face her. 'Don't ever get this.'

'There's a few corrections to make,' she said, assuming her usual, instructive tone. 'You probably know more than me. There's places you can't identify who's speaking. Maybe change some names too.' She picked at the label on her bottle. 'Obviously, we'll pay you double. He's working on it from hospital. We have a publisher now, which is exciting. If you must know, we need someone who knows the material well.'

'Stop trying to appeal to my ego,' I said. 'It's boring.'

She looked away, examined a customer as if she might know him.

'Did your boyfriend go back to his wife?' I asked.

'You're the one selling popcorn, honey.'

'The machine breaks a lot, so I'm not always selling it,' I said. 'He did then, I'm sorry to hear it.'

'You can't go back if you never left in the first place,' she said. 'You look so different. I remember when I first met you. I kept you away from that creep, if nothing else.' She brightened. 'Now you look mature, really grown up, Mae.'

I gave a quick nod. I didn't want to fumble down memory lane. I ran my fingers over the folder and then I pulled it towards myself. 'How is he doing?' I asked.

'Good.' She looked uncertain. 'He can read now. He's looking forward to this project, and a few other projects.'

'Projects,' I rolled my eyes. 'Projects? What an answer. You know I don't work for a newspaper.'

'I can't give many details anymore,' she said, 'besides I don't have much experience with these things. I don't have much experience with people getting shot. Never learnt that in college.'

'Why are you still doing this?' I asked.

'The same reason you lied for Shelley,' she answered. 'Because they're my friends.'

I didn't say anything. I just finished my beer and took the folder. Before I left, I asked if she gave Shelley her half. 'No,' she said, 'I couldn't find her.'

On the journey home, I felt a happy hum. I couldn't deny it was the most excited I'd been in a long time. I spread the pages out on the kitchen table. I had no typewriter so I made notes. It felt totally right living in those words. It was an equation only I could solve. I was surprised at what I remembered, how fluidly I could work. I changed all of the names, as I'd been instructed. It was all so easy. It was everything else that was complicated. I knew if I had to go back to the start to work on the book, I'd do it. I'd give up everything. I'd suffer all over again. Maybe they felt the same way, maybe they always had. All their misery laid bare in the service of art. Out of the garbage and into the book.

When Anita came back to collect the pages, I was watching a movie. The boy who worked on weekends told me she was at the door. He was trustworthy, a kind face, strong enough to withstand the blow of Anita's hostility. He reminded me of Mikey in a way that made me feel safe. I handed him the folder and told him to give it to her. I whispered in his ear: 'Tell her I said, "With compliments to The Mayor."' When he returned he gave me a long envelope full of cash, more than I'd been promised. On screen, a famous man in a long white nightgown

brushed his teeth rigorously, up and down, around and
around.

Initially, I resisted buying a copy. I walked everywhere
slowly because of the snow that gathered in wet sludges
on the sidewalk. I didn't want to fall. I no longer wanted
to do any damage to myself. I celebrated Christmas with
my roommates. We had a small tree that worked more as
a symbol than a decoration. A week later, I relented and
got a copy. I dressed up for the occasion, but passed over
the cash without looking at the girl behind the counter.
When the weekend boy in the theatre caught me reading
it, he asked me shyly – of course, he asked everything
shyly – if I liked it.

'Yeah,' I said, 'I wrote it.'

It was my last secret. I expected to be hit by a full force
of feeling when I read it. But a lot of it didn't land, all
these voices, manic and needy and hungry, drowning each
other out, like a mad chorus. It was packaged all wrong –
shocking, lewd, look at their obscene lives. They put a
picture of a beautiful woman on the back cover. I guess
Ondine wasn't pretty enough. If you didn't know there
was a tape missing, you never would have been able to
tell. I was surprised by one thing: Shelley's half was better
than mine. I transcribed them but she understood them.
She added feeling, energy, spirit. She'd found a way in.
How could she not see it? Everything she couldn't bring
to her audition, she brought to the book. When I read
those pages, it was like I was alone with her again, pulled
in by her personality. I knew she was reading it too, probably in that kitchen, while he was at work: diligent, pen
in her mouth, searching for traces of me. Irrefutable proof
we had been there. One of my roommates borrowed my

copy and I freaked out. I went really berserk, and then felt
bad about it. She couldn't have known what it meant to
me. How could she? My name wasn't on the cover.

I don't think it sold well, despite the publicity of the
shooting. I thought the whole city would want to eaves-
drop on the people they were fascinated by. I was wrong.
They wanted the movies, the parties, the pictures. The city
wanted the fantasy. In the newspapers and magazines, the
people in the photos were so attractive now, and he stood
beside them like a fan. I heard everything had moved and
I guessed it was to a place with a lot of locks on the doors. I
could hear the double bolt sliding across like Anita's face
shutting-down when I asked how he was.

Just after New Year's Eve, I handed in my notice at the
movie theatre. I wanted to be somewhere else for a year.
The publication of the book had filled me with resolve.
If I stayed, I wouldn't have been capable of any new intimacy. On my last night, the boy I worked with took me
ice-skating. I had fun for the first time in over a year. I was
startled by how much fun I had: a freedom and release I
hadn't known since the first days at the typewriter.

'You're more graceful than I expected you to be,' he
said.

'I'm a good dancer too,' I told him. 'I had lots of
practice.'

I was no longer waiting for something to happen, waiting for some idea I had about myself to be confirmed. I
packed a small amount of stuff. Before I left, I found a
phone booth. My voice was high and tense as if I was at
a job interview, as if I was speaking to someone I didn't
know. I was making a tape of my own. What was there
to say? I pressed my mouth close to the receiver. 'Mikey, I

asked, 'have you ever been ice-skating? I think you'd really like it. We'll see each other again. You'll probably see me next week.'

And then I was gone.

the queen of freedom.
1985

In my new life, I regarded myself as a hard-headed prag-
matist. I drove down the steep little hill down to the
supermarket twice a week. I was in bed before midnight
when I wasn't working. I had no desires I couldn't name
or place. I'd worked a number of different jobs, but over
the last few years had been working consistently in a bar.
Nothing in particular had attracted me to this town. In
fact, it was the lack of particularity that had attracted me.
I spent my night overhearing the community gossip while
trying to stay separate, apart. My boss at the bar played
the same rotation of songs so often that my serving technique felt tied up with them. T. Rex was blasted almost
every night, my boss's shirt billowing up to expose his
belly as he mouthed along with the lyrics, wanting to be
in a better bar, a better time, glitter cascading from the
ceiling. I was older than most of the girls who worked
there: girls whose primary motivation was getting out.
I know something about me terrified them. I could tell
by how they smiled at me, their worried eyes. I looked
normal, but I was here, working the same shifts, avoiding
the same customers, wiping the same tables. If I could fail,
could they fail too? They didn't know that was the life I'd

made and I was proud of it; a life where I didn't need to be looked at, admired. Whenever I felt a hatred towards these girls who judged me in a way that felt uncomfortable and familiar, I thought about their bedrooms: the little sparks of individuality, the postcards from whatever exhibitions they attended, discarded perfume bottles, fashionable but cheap dresses, all the ways they tried to make themselves invincible. I couldn't hate them at all then. In a way, I still gravitated towards their small and fantastic dramas. We all did karaoke together one night and I sang 'Bennie and the Jets'. I don't know if I was any good. I was maybe more rigid than I should have been. It's harder than it looks to be a generous and electric performer. Still, perhaps because of my verve, or song choice, the girls cooed over me afterwards, asked if I missed my friends in New York.

'One or two,' I said.

I'd gone through a drinking phase. Like all desperate people, I had gone through a reading phase – my pen poised to underline sections that pertained to me, that offered brief glimmers of understanding. The two phases weren't dissimilar. I hung around the big Barnes & Noble in the self-improvement section. The self-mythologising of the 1960s and 1970s was over and now there were just people in bookstores looking back on their lives and asking: why did that happen to me? What sort of pathology did I possess that allowed it? We hurtled through those two decades like falling from a high window. The gruelling part was over, we were told, and now we were moving into a family-oriented time, a time of security and confidence. I thought the people on the television looked ridiculous. I pointed this out at the Bible study meeting I sometimes went to. I said: I think a large chunk of society is starting to look ridiculous and not in a way I enjoy.

The other attendees nodded in agreement at this observation. The leader said it was a singular observation. They were an accepting sort. We were divided into two distinct sections: people who wanted to hold on to their innocence and people who'd lost it and wanted to regain it. We pored over sections in the book, trying to find meaning, in a way that felt familiar and natural to me. I often sat down the back, squinted my eyes whenever someone mentioned Jesus, as if I was trying to identify someone in the room. That was my own joke. The meeting led to nothing except people I didn't really want to acknowledge saying hello to me in the supermarket. In truth, I felt more shame about these hour-long meetings than I had about any actual shameful event in my life. My mind rotated through any number of excuses I could use if I was caught: these were AA meetings, grief counselling. At one of these it was suggested, as a fun exercise, we should turn to the person next to us and ask them whatever we liked. I'd never really lost my appetite for other people's secrets. What the purpose of this exercise was I didn't know. Perhaps we were trying to uncover the devil. Perhaps he'd reveal himself if we just asked. That was his trick all along. I couldn't think of a single question and then I did. I turned to the middle-aged woman next to me and I asked: are you a pushover?

I was out the back when I got the call, on a break. I still smoked even though we were learning nicotine was bad for us. We were learning a lot of stuff was bad for us. I was surprised by these new facts, and I felt an affinity with people who, like me, had to muddle through this deluge of information. It was beginning to get warm again. On

my answering machine at home, I gave the bar's number.
I always acted like I didn't care who found me, but I went
to the effort of leaving that number. I figured it was only a
matter of time before someone found me, but nobody had
yet. I took the receiver from the girl I worked with. I pressed
it to my ear. Nobody said a word, but I stayed on the line.
Light breathing, my lips on the grimy mouthpiece. A fan was
turning and I could hear the hum of the fridge beside me.
I leaned in closer. The bar appeared to change shape, bend
and recede. Then a click, a whirr, a dial tone. Nothing. Who
had asked for me, I asked the girl later. Whose voice was it? I
don't know, she said. It was muffled, a woman maybe.

There were no photos of us, and the photos were what
endured. I thought there might be one of Shelley, the one
who had something, even if what she had was strange.
She was, at least, memorable. Her charming, slightly
askew smile, and me, looking furious, ignored, in the
murky background. I looked at photos from that time,
and I had the same thoughts as anyone else – the parties
looked like fun. I was as disconnected and estranged
from these images as someone who hadn't been there.
It must have been a good time. All those people trying
to make each other laugh. I couldn't remember what it
had really been like. I wasn't allowed to remember. The
pictures from the last few years were glamorous, but
something wasn't quite right. The good humour seemed
self-conscious, try-hard. The clothes were conspicuously
wealthy: the brand was the statement. The parties were
showy, unconvincing with a heavy mood, as if people
had come from a funeral. Probably because they had.
The atmosphere, the gestures, the language. None of
these things were quite right now. Or maybe I was just
older, harder to impress.

But I knew if it had been Shelley on that call, calling from the same apartment, or perhaps somewhere more rural, a sleepy house nestled in a suburb, if it had been Shelley and she worked up the courage to speak, we would have arranged to meet, now that we were more civilised, free of all our sensational impulses. We would have said: now there's time, let's get to know each other again, let's have a drink. We would meet, and laugh and laugh, about how crazy we were then, and how dull we were now. Wasn't the world bigger and more varied than we expected it to be? We'd drain our drinks. We'd be endlessly polite to the waitstaff. I wouldn't withhold; I'd really get to know our server. But as the night went on, as it moved to 2 a.m., and we got drunker, more ponderous and nostalgic, I knew I'd lean across the table, grasp Shelley's arm, grip tightly and ask the only question that could be asked. The decision to ask would be no decision at all. I'd try to force a confession, the trick he pulled off every night. I'd lean forward with my eyes lit up like a fanatic's and say: Shelley, tell me what was on that tape.

I thought of my mother often in those years. Her in her waitress uniform, nightmares where she had a white sheet pulled over her head. As the years passed, I expected to feel indifference towards her and Mikey, but it never happened. I thought I'd be happier being away from them, but I wasn't really. In the end, I never had to call her. She called me. It was like that one phone call in the bar had opened the gates of my life, and now anyone could wander back in. I was standing in my kitchen, looking at my withered plant in the corner, and there she was on the phone, talking like usual, like no time

had passed at all. She didn't say how she found me. She
didn't say why she hadn't looked before. She was sober
now and hated the meetings with a passion. 'They expect
you to tell them *everything*,' she complained, 'as if I need
their permission not to drink.' At the end of the call
she told me, as casually as she could, that Mikey was
ill. He was in hospital, and he might not have a whole
lot of time. But who knows? Doctors had been wrong
before. You just couldn't trust doctors: many of them
were wrong about how much time people had left, or
even how ill they were. I felt a fleeting second of inner
conflict. Then I watered my plants, already shrivelling,
already neglected, and made flight arrangements. My
boss had made a pass at me earlier in the week, rubbed
my neck as if we were both young and open-minded,
as if we were similar creatures. The gesture, disarmingly
intimate, like I was his wife, made me feel like I'd just
exchanged one type of captivity for another. I have to
go, I told him, it's late, my plants are dying. The experience rattled me. What did I want to say? Never mind
my dull exterior, ignore the fact that I work here – don't
you know who I am?

I called my boss from the airport, my rucksack on
my back, my jacket tied around my waist. More than
anything, I resembled a runaway. A runaway at thirty-five.
I said I'd made a mistake. I meant to say my parents, *my
parents* are dying. I asked for a few days off, fully paid, and
he gave them to me, possibly imagining a long, drawn-
out lawsuit. A power-grab. Women were mobilising,
becoming ambitious. All this time, it turned out we were
as blindingly obvious as men, and men were astonished
by it. I had caught sight of him looking at himself in the
mirror while he was trying to seduce me. That took me

back. That was his one endearing gesture. People are rarely so nakedly self-involved.

I didn't sleep on the flight: my mind wired, moving at high speed. I read magazines, stared at the empty seat beside me, kept trying to get the attention of the air hostess and when I did, had nothing to say to her, nothing to ask for. I was the only one attempting talk; headphones were plugged into every other passenger. I kept thinking the plane wouldn't land, I'd stay circling up there forever. I'd grow old and die up there. Mikey would take the empty seat beside me. The sun would be shining. When I entered the city in semi-darkness, it put me in a good mood. I couldn't help it. It took me several seconds to remember why I was there. It was Halloween, and the streets were filled with happy, vicious strangers. The girls were frantically sexy, dressed in stockings, hair swept back, winged eyeliner, no discernible costumes, respectable girls enjoying their night of trash. On the subway, there was an Andy and a sullen Edie. His costume was the familiar one – a striped t-shirt, jeans, cheap frames. There was something puzzling about his expression underneath the wig. He was easily dismissed but there was a touch of the real Edie about the girl. They were turned away from each other, their body language – something I knew from the self-help stacks in Barnes & Noble – was all wrong. They were probably fighting, already regretting wearing costumes that tethered them to each other for the evening. Even if they tried to separate, someone at the party would announce, 'Andy, there's an Edie here, you have to meet her.' I'd watched Edie's screen test. It was perfect, it was unforgettable. Her face filled your imagination. It was so beautiful to be filmed by someone who had loved you. When I was getting off the train, I half-smiled at the couple. Maybe I envied the night ahead of them, all the indignity and heartbreak. When I hit the fresh air, I realised I could have conjured the whole scene.

On the phone, my mother told me Mikey had been beaten up a few years previously. Two black eyes, damage to his internal organs, loss of confidence. He wasn't the same afterwards. She'd bought him a camera, a VCR to put between him and the world. The last few years he'd been confused, disoriented, cancer eating away at him. She didn't ask me to come, her pride would never allow her, but I knew anyway. Like a child imploring an adult to lead them. I wanted to see him too, I wanted to speak to him. I wanted to say so much I'd embarrass myself.

I walked most of the way to the hospital. The city still offered cheap and dirty thrills, even as it moved closer to safety. It was like an amusement park of desires now, it was all accessible if you had the cash. In the hospital, every-thing was distressingly white, the sort of white that made you feel like you were already dead. Every hallway led somewhere horrible. The television in the waiting room played obligatory laughter. I sat for a while. A reception-ist called my name and I said: 'I'm here.' I stood outside Mikey's room for a few minutes, watching him through the small window. I stood outside for so long that I forgot what I was looking at. Then I went in.

A NOTE ON THE SOURCES

Writing this book would have been impossible without the wealth of remarkable writing that exists on Warhol: Bob Colacello's *Holy Terror*, *Andy Warhol* by Wayne Koestenbaum, *Warhol* by Blake Gopnik, *Popism: the Warhol '60's* by Andy Warhol and Pat Hackett, Arthur C. Danto's *Andy Warhol*, Lynne Tillman's writing on *a: A Novel*, amongst others. For a different perspective, *Andy Warhol and the Can That Sold the World* by Gary Indiana and *Scum Manifesto* by Valerie Solanas. There is no other book on earth quite like *Edie, American Girl* by Jean Stein. And, most of all, to *a: A Novel*, a fascinating, stubborn, enduring work. I'm indebted, like so many others, to the film *Chelsea Girls*. Looking through the endless photographs, reading, watching, visiting exhibitions – all of this was nothing but a pleasure to me. My last words are Andy Warhol.

ACKNOWLEDGEMENTS

Many thanks to Cliodhna and everyone at Temple Bar Gallery Dublin, where a large amount of this book was written. As always, I'm indebted to the Arts Council of Ireland. A special thanks to Beatrice and all at Santa Maddalena, Italy. I'm grateful to Declan Meade and the *Stinging Fly* for their continued support.

Thank you to Tom Morris and Ian Maleney, first and best readers, whose insight and kindness I value so highly. Thank you to Tracy Bohan whose generosity and belief in me has shaped this book, and all of my writing. Thank you to Alexis for her vision, wisdom and patience. Many thanks to Daniel Loedel and everyone in Bloomsbury for their faith in my work.

For my sister and her family. For my friends, who make it so easy to write about friendship. I love you and I'm so grateful you love me in return. And, finally, for Sean, a book about staying out late for someone who was going to go home early. Thank God you didn't.

A NOTE ON THE AUTHOR

Nicole Flattery's short story collection *Show Them a Good Time* was published by Bloomsbury in 2019. Her work has appeared in the *White Review*, the *Stinging Fly* and the *London Review of Books*. She lives in Dublin.

A NOTE ON THE TYPE

The text of this book is set Adobe Garamond. It is one of several versions of Garamond based on the designs of Claude Garamond. It is thought that Garamond based his font on Bembo, cut in 1495 by Francesco Griffo in collaboration with the Italian printer Aldus Manutius. Garamond types were first used in books printed in Paris around 1532. Many of the present-day versions of this type are based on the *Typi Academiae* of Jean Jannon cut in Sedan in 1615.

Claude Garamond was born in Paris in 1480. He learned how to cut type from his father and by the age of fifteen he was able to fashion steel punches the size of a pica with great precision. At the age of sixty he was commissioned by King Francis I to design a Greek alphabet, and for this he was given the honourable title of royal type founder. He died in 1561.